SHADOWFAE

SHADOWFAE

ERICA HAYES

St. Martin's Griffin
New York

SHADOWFAE. Copyright © 2009 by Erica Hayes. All rights reserved.
Printed in the United States of America.
For information, address St. Martin's Press,
175 Fifth Avenue, New York, N.Y. 10010.

www.stmartins.com

Library of Congress Cataloging-in-Publication Data

Hayes, Erica.
  Shadowfae / Erica Hayes.—1st ed.
      p. cm.
  ISBN 978-0-312-57800-8
  1. Fairies—Fiction.   2. Incubi—Fiction.   3. Melbourne (Vic.)—Fiction.
I. Title.
  PR9619.4.H394S53 2009
  823'.92—dc22   2009017005

First Edition: October 2009

10 9 8 7 6 5 4 3 2 1

For Sherrill and Robert,
the best parents ever,
who believed me
when I said I could be a writer.

Acknowledgments

I would like to thank the following: My agent, Marlene Stringer; Rose Hilliard and everyone at St. Martin's Press, for taking a chance on a new author; the magnificent Valerie Parv, for her mentorship, inspiration, and humor over the past year, and for wanting so hard for it not to win, that it did; my writing group, the marvelous and formidable Go-Go Girls, for laughs and hot chocolates and insisting the story wasn't dreadful, over and over again, until I suspected they could be right; and Sean, for helping me chase my dream.

SHADOWFAE

1

The dark shape in the bed didn't stir. I trailed tingling fingers over silken sheets, carpet soft and luxurious beneath my feet. I inhaled crisp male cologne and sweat, and it made me drunk with excitement. The French window lay open, city lights glittering beyond, citrus summer breeze teasing the pale lace curtains. They drifted over me like a lover's sweet touch, and I burned. If I didn't have this man soon, I'd spend the night sick and sorry. And I didn't even know who he was.

Sometimes I feel so cheap.

My demon lord, Kane, calls it *rapture*. Our victims, if they live long enough, call it the sexiest thing they've ever seen, which of course, is the point. It's easier to suck out someone's soul if their attention is elsewhere. Only problem is, it's the succubus equivalent of a raging hard-on, and frankly, it's humiliating to slaver like a sex-starved ghoul over some fat chauvinist gangster or unwashed backroom drug dealer just because they were foolish enough to cross Kane and his charming minions, the Valenti crime family.

But it's my job. I'm in thrall to Kane for a thousand years. I was just glad no one could see me this time.

I crawled toward him, arousing my scent so it drifted over him like a sweet cloud. The sheet slid off his massive shoulder, baring his chest, and I bent to sniff his stubbled throat, my hair brushing his face.

He didn't stir.

The dark smell of his skin made me moan, and I slid my tongue along his warm collarbone, desperate to taste him. My breasts ached as I pressed into him, only my thin tank top separating us.

He didn't even twitch.

I dragged my fingers through his lank fair hair, and his head fell sideways, limp, no breath forcing from his slack mouth.

My racing heart missed a beat. I fumbled on the bedside table, switching on the dim lamp. His hard features lay softened in death, his tanned skin already pale.

I stared. I knew that blond ponytail, that unforgiving mouth, those rigid gym-built muscles. I'd danced with him, dined with him on amatriciana and red wine at Valentino's, peeled his big hands off my ass more than once. Nino Valenti. Gangster, extortionist, multiple murderer. Ange Valenti's right-hand man.

Kane had sent me to kill one of his own minions. And Nino was already dead. His glazed eyes shone vacant, colorless, their once-steady blue drained. No blood, no vomit, or marks on his body. It wasn't a typical mob murder. He wasn't drugged, shot, strangled, fae-poisoned. Someone had sucked out his soul. They'd beaten me to it.

What the hell?

I sat up on my knees, my chest heaving, frustrated desire radiating off me like sultry summer heat. Dead. But still fragrant, still warm. Which meant . . .

My back thudded into the soft mattress, the weight of a hard male body between my legs pressing me down. Strong hands grasped my wrists, trapping them above my head, strands of my hair pulling in their grip.

"Wrong place, wrong time, sweetheart." The voice was low, breathless, a hint of exotic Hindi accent. I glimpsed dark tangled hair, a flash of golden-brown eyes, fragrant brown skin. Fresh desire burned over me, my urgent breath searing my throat, my entire body straining, yearning for sex.

Sweat trickled on my skin, running into my hair and dampening my hands. I couldn't believe this. Of all that could possibly happen to me this evening, I'd never imagined I'd end up panting with lust under Rajahni Seth.

Not that Rajah wasn't worthy of some serious panting, along with a scream and an *oh, god* or two. He was the kind of incubus who didn't need the rapture to get his victims begging for him. I'd never even spoken to him before. The words *out of my league* didn't even approximate.

The words *you killed Nino Valenti*, however, did.

"Get off me!" I kicked, wriggling, but succeeded only in pressing him tighter between my legs, my thin skirt rucking up to the tops of my thighs. He wore no shirt, and in the lamplight, his taut brown skin glistened, sweat running on curving muscles.

He twisted his dark head back a little so he could see me, wet dark strands falling in his face. Sexual energy glimmered off him in waves like a heat haze, his eyes glowing with desire, his ripe lips parted and slick. His magic didn't affect me, of course. An incubus's rapture doesn't work on succubi—or vice versa, for that matter. But I was worked up enough already, and likewise I couldn't imagine the smoldering need in his eyes and the deliciously hard bulge pressing into my crotch had anything to do with me.

"Jade?" His sinful lips formed my name, caressing it like a kiss. "Kane's Jade?"

He recognized me. My mouth watered. God, I hoped I had underwear on, or I'd make a mess of his jeans. Then again, if I wasn't wearing any, I could unzip him, squeeze myself onto him, and do something about this wasted rapture that made me ache.

Of its own accord, my leg wrapped itself around his thighs, straining, pleasure flowering at the pressure. "Well spotted, genius. You gonna get off me?"

His fingers tightened on my wrists and he ground against me with a helpless little groan, but his eyes glinted with amusement as well as lust. "Are you sure you want me to? I could get off in you, if you like."

Anger boiled my desire, though the thought of him thrusting into me, exploding deep within me with his lips on mine, made me faint with longing. No way would he use me for his twisted little games, even if he was a secret fantasy fuck of mine from way back. "Give it a rest, Seth. That's a dead body, in case you hadn't noticed."

His lips hovered over mine for a heart-stopping instant, but before I could slide my tongue out to taste him, he rolled off me and rose, pacing, scraping tense hands through his hair.

I sat up, fury searing away my regret. "What are you playing at, using a Valenti for sustenance? Kane'll have your ass."

But I couldn't help watching as he found his shirt and slipped it on. They sure built them beautiful in seventeenth-century Lahore, or wherever the hell he was from. Dark locks tangling on his collar, sensual mouth quivering, perfect nose, strong chin, upswept cheekbones. Legs long and muscular in soft black jeans, tight ass begging to be squeezed with both hands while he fucked me. Broad golden thrall bangles, thicker than mine, glinting tight on his forearms. He moved with raw grace, his movements swift and tense as he struggled to contain his rapture-soaked lust.

He retrieved his etched brass soultrap bottle from the carpet and dangled it in front of my eyes, wiggling it so I could see from the weight that it was full. "Kane's orders. I don't ask; I just fuck."

Which explained the state he was in. He hadn't consumed Nino's energy, but trapped it, and he'd obviously ignored soultrapping rule number one: Don't let your victim come first. I'd never pictured Rajah as going both ways. Maybe he hadn't either, but Kane's word was law. I sympathized. All the same, my sex ached just thinking about a threesome.

I scrambled up from the bed, jerking my damp skirt down over my exposed thighs. "Yeah, I've heard that about you."

He gave a wicked smile and hissed like a cat, miming striking claws. "No need to be nasty. I offered." His smile turned sultry. "Sure you're not tempted?"

My heart pounded. Oh, I was tempted, all right.

I struggled to keep my mind on the issues. What would Kane want with his own minion's soul? He'd get it soon enough anyway. And why had he sent both of us to do the same thing?

But Rajah's dark, spicy scent wrapped me like a sweet mist, my rapture blinding me to everything but him, his eyes, his wicked black lashes, the pulse throbbing at his throat, that slutty mouth made for pleasure. . . .

I stepped closer. He stepped closer. He dropped the soultrap bottle with a soft thud and ran his fingers into my hair, twisting, sliding in deeper. My breasts brushed his chest, my nipples so hard, the pleasure hurt. I slid my hands over his hips to his gorgeous firm ass and pulled him against me. He was hard, pulsing, so ready, and wetness slid from me, staining my skirt, painting the insides of my thighs with hot need.

We both groaned, the air around us shimmering. Already his burning fingers sought my skirt hem, dragging it upward. He nuzzled my throat, his lips firm and insistent, his clever tongue making me shiver. "Jade," he breathed, his voice thick with lust, "I never knew you were so damn beautiful."

Cold humiliation washed over me, spoiling his glorious caress. He'd never noticed me before. What was I thinking? He was Rajahni Seth, the hottest incubus in Melbourne; who had any woman he wanted with a single sultry glance from those bedroom eyes. And I was me.

Stick-thin, mousy-haired, tongue-tied me. Certainly not beautiful or engaging. It wasn't like we could have a relationship, not in our line of work, even if I wasn't the world's most boring woman and so far below his standards that even a glance from him was charity. So we'd have sex in a cloud of drunken rapture, it'd be magnificent, and I'd be miserable for the next six hundred years, pining for him. And he'd forget about me, we'd meet in the street or a bar and smile uneasily and look away, and he'd laugh with his friends about how he was once so desperate, he had to fuck me.

"This is a bad idea," I whispered, trying to push him away though my body still ached for him to give me release, my treacherous hands still wanting to explore him, pleasure him. "I don't even know you."

He stilled, his lips wet on my throat. "Are you serious? Most girls don't want to."

Now I did shove him away, my hands trembling more with fury than with desire. "Am I supposed to feel sorry for you? Just get out of here before—"

Fists thudded on the apartment door. "Police, open up!"

Before anyone finds us here.

Too late.

For a few pulse-rippling seconds, Rajah's lips bruised mine, shocking, arousing, our teeth clashing in a feral kiss. "Some other time, princess," he breathed, and vanished.

I stumbled into the space where he'd been, the spicy taste of cardamom still stinging my mouth.

Jesus. He'd disappeared. I couldn't do that. How did he do that?

I cursed, and scrabbled on the carpet, but his soultrap bottle was gone. He'd taken it with him. Leaving me with the cops and a dead Valenti body in a room that reeked of sex, and a most unflattering wet patch on my skirt.

On the rooftop, Rajahni Seth leans over, hooking his elbow into the wrought-iron trimming, and watches the uniforms bundle Jade into the back of the blue-and-white Holden double-parked in the street below. Other drivers slow down as they pass, rubbernecking, and a gleaming silver tram rattles up the middle of the street, wires sparking, bright lights pouring from square windows advertising broadband Internet.

Warm summer breeze whispers through Rajah's dark hair, drenched with the smell of thunder, tracing teasing fingers over his hot skin. A million city lights from skyscrapers and neon signs block out the stars, their reflection glowing orange in scudding storm clouds. The brass bottle burns his hand, the fresh soul energy within bubbling angrily in its new confinement, and Rajah's cock tightens even more as he thinks about what it means. One down, three to go, and Rajah will be free of Kane's thrall forever. The legend is true. He knows it. He can taste it. He senses it in the soul's mad struggles in his bottle. He feels it searing through his blood.

It was sickeningly easy to get. He'd seen the burning green aura that identified Nino as his target days ago, and he'd bided his time, contained his excitement, weighed up his chances. Nino wanted so desperately to be straight, it was painful, and to have another man get his cock hard made him glow with shame and sick hatred. Once they'd made it to the apartment tonight after a few solid hours of watching Nino drink and eye him off, Rajah made the moves, and Nino's face darkened, he pulled his .45, yelled that he wasn't fucking gay, that Seth could get the fuck away from him or he'd blow his girly faggot ass to hell.

But a fragrant shimmer of rapture changed all that, dragging the poor kid kicking and cursing exactly where he wanted to go. Nino had beautiful, grabbable hair and a professionally sculpted body, even if he was a self-hating homophobe and Neanderthal dumb, and Rajah relished the thought of claiming that rock-hard far-from-virgin ass, working inside into the heat, and stroking Nino into orgasm that way. But Nino couldn't wait; he'd started to come before Rajah had more than a finger inside him and then it was too late.

But it didn't matter. Rajah had figured aching balls were a small price to pay for this first special soul. Perhaps he'd head down to Unseelie Court on King Street and tease a blow job from one of those willowy blue-haired banshees who were forever giving him the eye, just to silence his rampant rapture.

And then Jade showed up. Slender, slate-eyed Jade, with her sexy mouth, gorgeous little breasts, and narrow, perfect ass. No makeup, short plain nails, simple clothes, gently brushed dark hair falling in her face like she couldn't be bothered with it.

He's seen her before, she's Ange Valenti's trophy girl, but she'd always dropped her gaze or scowled or pretended not to see him. Suspicious of his good looks, wary of his reputation. A woman of class like that probably thought him a slut and a pickup artist. He'd never imagined he'd be lucky enough to have her lithe body straining beneath him, her wet little cleft hot and tempting against his bursting cock even through his jeans. Yeah, baby. It made him want to fill her, stretch her, hear her scream his name.

He watches the cop car drive away down the tree-lined street toward the river and St. Kilda Road, still staring long after it's gone. She didn't want him. Not really. It was just the rapture, right? No way she'd ever want a party boy.

Sure, he gets his share of women who aren't business, men too. Most are easy airheads looking for a good time or a dark taste of danger. Not like her.

I don't even know you, she said. Like she might one day want to.

He wonders what that would be like, and something diamond-cold in his heart softens.

But he can't let anything distract him, not now. He's waited centuries for this chance, and he won't throw it away because a sexy little waif gets his cock hard. Really hard. Can't-walk-properly hard. Maybe he'll find that banshee after all. But first, to hide this soul away where not even he can get at it, just in case.

Rajah turns away with a stretch and a sigh, his fingers tightening around the quivering soultrap. Just the rapture. Just a sweet little succubus, embarrassed by her lust.

Imagine that.

2

This is bullshit." I glanced at the photographs again, dragging on my cigarette. Minty smoke burned my throat, and I coughed. I don't smoke, not anymore, but something about the St. Kilda Road cop shop makes me nervous.

My reflection in the one-way glass along one side of the interview room showed me hunched over on the steel chair, my hair tousled, dark sweat patches staining my tight gray tank top, my flimsy white skirt smeared. My skin gleamed sickly, my lips dry, the hand holding the cigarette shaking. The circles under my eyes stood out like stage makeup, making my eyes look darker blue than they were. I'd calmed down an hour ago, but all that unrequited rapture was taking its toll. I needed energy, and I looked like a junkie denied a fix. Not a class act.

Fluorescent lights glared too bright, and the air-conditioning hummed like a pissed-off insect, maddening. I shivered. It was too cold in here, and my clammy skin wore goose bumps, the stink of rapture-suppressant spray stinging my eyes.

"Look at the damn pictures, Jade." The man sitting opposite me across the aluminum table drew on his own cigarette, golden links shining amid dark hair on his heavy wrist. He flicked ash onto the floor, brushing an imaginary fleck off the sleeve of his expensive gray suit. Detective Sergeant Killian Quinn, Melbourne Homicide's paranormal expert. Black shirt, no tie, sweat gleaming in brown curls, golden chains tangled around his thick throat. Pale brown eyes, blank and hard like an animal's. Cunning, handsome, madder than a cut snake.

He's also the crookedest crooked cop in town. Unfortunately, he's on DiLuca's payroll, not Valenti's, and he looks at me with the leering, sexual hatred of a man who never goes out with the same girl twice. If one thing in particular makes my nerves seethe about St. Kilda Road, it's being alone in a cold white room with Quinn.

"This has nothing to do with me," I said again, shoving the pictures away, my stomach turning. I didn't know why he showed them to me, other than to weird me out. A dead fire sprite in close-up, gnarled limbs awry on some back-alley floor, his delicate crimson wings limp and trampled, dirty ice crystals in his flowing white hair. A banshee, lifeless, her lissome head thrown back, skin drained pale, blue blood trickling from the corner of her dead mouth. No one I knew . . . hang on. That pale green hair and sharp nose did look familiar. Maybe I'd seen her at Kane's house parties once or twice, one of those demon groupies who flirt and flutter their rainbow lashes at him, and learn too late what they're letting themselves in for.

I knew the fire sprite, too, now that I thought about it. The other night, at the pub across from Valentino's. Sylvain, Silver, something like that, one of Ange's couriers. He'd slipped golden fairy sparkle into my drink for a sly joke, and I'd spent the next few hours giggling and blowing bubbles in my champagne.

Harmless enough. I didn't know why anyone would want to kill him.

There were more pictures, but discomfort twinged my pulse, and I didn't want to look. Detective Quinn was just poking me to see if I'd squeal. I finished the cigarette and tossed the butt away. "You're wasting my time, Quinn. Ask me about Nino Valenti. That's what you pulled me in for. Not to look at your porn collection."

The blue-uniformed constable standing at ease by the door—presumably to make sure Quinn didn't beat the tripe out of me, or maybe to help him—hid a grin. Most other cops think Quinn's delusional, with his tales of fairy drug dealers and bloodsucking gangsters and soul-stealing succubi. Lucky for us, they don't take him seriously.

Quinn leaned forward, his elbows on the table, and I smelled tobacco and metallic sweat. He offered another photo, this one of dead Nino naked on the bed. "Let's look at yours, then. Does that one get you off?" A twang of Irish accent stretched his vowels.

Second rule of soultrapping: Don't tell the cops anything. If Kane wanted Nino dead, that was Kane's business. And embarrassment still burned me when I thought about Rajahni Seth. No way was I mentioning him. "I told you, he was dead when I got there. I didn't see anyone. I didn't even touch him. What are you going to book me for, attempted fuckup?"

"No wounds, no drugs except alcohol. Evidence of intercourse. Eyes drained of color. Ringing any bells?" Quinn sniffed, dragged on his cigarette, and blew the smoke upward, tense. His shiny gaze flickered, his tight fingers drumming on the table's edge.

He was a speed-addicted fruitcake, but he wasn't dumb. He

knew how the rapture worked. "It wasn't me. I told you. Jesus, do I look like I've had much hot action tonight?" I pointed to my wan face and peeling lips.

"Don't look like you've ever had any to me, you cold skanky whore." He said it with studied insolence, relishing it.

I didn't know why Quinn hated me. Right now, I didn't care. He'd hit on me once, months ago, and I'd laughed at him. Maybe he just wasn't getting enough. "Hear that, Constable? Detective Quinn just propositioned me. Isn't that illegal?"

Quinn didn't turn around, didn't shift his hungry gaze from mine. "Leave us."

The constable shifted. "Boss, perhaps you should—"

"I said piss off." Quinn's thick fingers crunched around the cigarette pack, crumpling it. Longing and disgust swirled together in his eyes. A tiny smear of blood escaped from his nose. Sweat trickled on his temple, his jaw quivering. The constable made a hasty exit, and the steel door banged shut.

Fuck.

Was it too much to hope anyone watched from behind that one-way glass? "Look, Detective, I'm sorry I can't help you. I really don't know anything—"

"Shut up." He jerked to his feet and moved swiftly behind me. I tried to turn, to follow him, but he clamped his huge hand on my shoulder and shoved me down in my seat, the metal edge digging into my back.

"Get your grubby hand off me." I tried to skid away, my heels slipping on the smooth floor.

He held on, bruising my collarbone. "You're disgusting. You and your whole weird-ass crew. How long did he stay hard after you drank him up? Enough for you to get off?"

"You're a fucking psycho." I wriggled, but he gripped my neck with both hands, pressing his thumbs hard into my spine. A thin wire of fear pierced cold.

He leaned over me, his breath hot and damp on my shoulder, his sugary amphet sweat reeking. "How does it feel to fuck a dead man? I guess you know that already, since you're screwing Ange Valenti, too. You doing the whole family now?"

My stomach churned, and a horrid heat crept up over my skin. Humiliation shook me. I wanted another cigarette. I wanted away from Quinn, his hot breath, lustful eyes, and hateful grin. Away from all men who assumed a succubus was no better than a cheap whore, men who knew nothing of thrall or rapture or the sweet slither of a demon lord's command in your blood.

I rammed the chair leg back into his shin, and he howled and let me go. I sprang up to face him, anger burning in my heart, brandishing the chair between us to ward him off. "Yeah," I invented to taunt him. "All of them. I spread my legs on the kitchen table at Valentino's and the whole lot of them do me one by one. Two or three at a time, if they feel like it. I take it everywhere."

"Dirty slut." A sickly spark kindled in his eyes, and he swallowed, his face twisted in fury. His fingers writhed, as if he longed to grab me, and a dirty dark green shell glimmered and brightened around him, translucent like an aura.

I faltered. What the hell was that?

But I didn't have space to worry about it. I plonked the chair down and leaned over it, daring him. "Hell, I'll screw anyone— the deader, the better. But I'll never screw you, Killian. I won't sink that low."

Bright blood trickled onto his upper lip. He sniffed, gritting his teeth, that strange green aura writhing. He pulled his .38

from beneath his jacket and cocked it, his thumb sliding lovingly over the hammer. "That so? Maybe you should screw this, you horny bitch."

My heart stopped, cold slivers of dread piercing my veins. I imagined what he'd like to do with that gun, and backed away, my nerves screaming at me to run. I'm deathless—more or less— but I'm not indestructible. "Jesus, Quinn, don't."

The door snicked ajar, and before it opened fully, Quinn hid his weapon away.

Relief flooded me like alcohol, and I detested Quinn more than ever. I turned, shaking. "I'm done with him, Constable. He never lasts long—"

Red lips, curled into a vacant smile. Hard black eyes rimmed with golden lashes, crisp choirboy hair the same metallic color falling around a gentle jaw and soft, rounded cheekbones. A black suit with a garish blue tie, like he'd stepped in from the office.

My thrall bangles tingled, and heat prickled up my arms, sickly sweet. Inside my belly, my drug-sleepy rapture coiled content- edly, lazy like a deadly snake in the sun. Thrall always knows its own, no matter how I squirm and evade.

Kane stared at me, green sparks of amusement dancing in his hair. My heart sank, but at the same time, an unfamiliar, unwel- come warmth shivered through my blood. For once, I was pleased to see him.

Quinn backed off, wiping a red smear from his nose, and the constable bundled in behind Kane with anxious eyes. "Sorry, boss, I couldn't—"

"Killian Quinn." Kane's soft voice crackled with chill, and behind him a fluorescent tube shattered, raining glass shards. "I believe I'll take this from here."

"Sure." Quinn swallowed, the strange green aura flaring. "Whatever you say. Just the job, no hard feelings, okay?"

Kane just looked at him, fingernails blackening.

Blood erupted from Quinn's nose, painting his shirtfront crimson. He choked and stumbled backwards, cursing in bloody bubbles. Uselessly he bent over, trying to stop the flood with his hand. A dark puddle spread on the floor, fat drips plinking, and the warm coppery stink rose, fresh and tasty.

The constable blanched, darting a glance at Kane. "Jesus. I'll get some ice. Umm . . . wait here." He raced out, glad of the excuse to leave us alone.

Petty satisfaction toasted my heart, and I resisted an impulse to run up and kick Quinn in the balls while he was down. Sometimes Kane's justice is cruel, but it's always deserved.

Kane strolled up to the table and riffled through the photos. He paused at the dead fire sprite, trailing his fingertip over the limp white hair. "I like this one," he remarked, and held it out to me like a child sharing an ice cream.

I took it, and he slid his icy hand into mine and walked me out.

3

If I were a demon lord, I'd want at least a palace, if not a castle, with a moat and a slimy rat-infested dungeon in which I could incarcerate misogynist bastards like Killian Quinn. I'd have candlelit banquet halls, ballrooms, dusty libraries full of spellbooks and lost novels by the greats. My bedroom would be festooned with a luxurious four-poster and a massive claw-foot bath, and I'd have cooks, cleaners, manicurists and masseurs, people to furnish my wardrobe from the finest boutiques.

Kane lives in a town house in Toorak. Alone, with a sixty-inch LCD TV, a microwave, and a designer futon.

Sure, it's a nice town house, and Toorak is one of the ritziest suburbs in Melbourne. But Kane just doesn't get it. Maybe he's bored with immortality and having whatever he wants. Or maybe it's just that if there's ever a point, Kane will miss it.

He didn't speak the whole way home, just twisted his rings on his slender fingers and stared out the darkened car window, the occasional spark zinging from his hair. Passing headlights glared over his face and glinted in his ink-black eyes.

The driver's hulking body blocked the windshield, fat green

troll fingers gripping the wheel. I shifted around, trying to unstick the fragrant leather seat from my thighs. Exhaustion racked my limbs, but I'd no hope of sleeping. My head ached from hunger and the rapture suppressants, and my neck still hurt where Quinn dug his apelike fingers. It didn't help that I couldn't read Kane's expression, and I didn't know if he was filthy with me or not.

The troll pulled up in front of the wrought-iron gate and held Kane's door open with a massive green fist. I scrambled out after Kane, my skirt gluing to my legs. The night air plastered warm and thick on my skin with the imminent storm. Bats flapped in the trees out in the street, and eucalyptus stung fresh in my nose, waking me up and stinging my nerves with trepidation.

My heels clattered on the slippery slate tiles of the courtyard path, and the heavy front door swung open at Kane's approach. I followed him into the sandstone entry hall, where downlights already shone, the polished mahogany floorboards glaring in my eyes. He draped himself over the low white couch in his candlelit lounge, elegant, arranging his suit so it wouldn't crease. Flames reflected off the dark TV screen as brightly as they did from his shiny eyes.

"Sit down," he ordered softly, tiny red flames licking his fingertips.

Cold compulsion gripped my soul, and I sat opposite him in a rush, my heart constricting. He was filthy with me, all right. He's normally careful with his imperatives. A careless order can be disastrous when you're in thrall. We don't have to obey his every whim, and can even do stuff on purpose to annoy him if we dare. He can't stop us. But a direct order we can't ignore.

Kane stared at me, cocking his head to one side and then the other. "Tell me what happened at the apartment."

"Nino was already dead when I got there. Someone . . . someone else trapped his soul before I could. I saw him . . . he grabbed me, we—"

"Who was it? Tell me."

I swallowed. "Rajah. Rajahni Seth, I mean . . ."

Kane's eyes narrowed, a swirl of violet light disappearing into their depths, and it dawned on me. Kane had no clue what this was about.

My throat stung with indignation. Rajah lied to me. Kane hadn't made him trap Nino's soul. He'd done it for his own sneaky purposes and dropped me in it with the cops just for fun.

Humiliation scorched me for the hundredth time that night as I remembered pressing his body onto mine, drinking in his spicy scent, enjoying his hard cock grinding between my legs, wanting it. Bastard.

Kane's mouth twisted ruefully, ice crystals glittering on his lashes. "Rajah," he murmured, thoughtful, before returning his attention to me. "What were you doing in Nino's apartment, Jade? You cheating on Angelo behind his back?" He hugged his knees to his chest and leaned forward, eyes bright and fascinated. Kane loves infidelity and gossip, so long as he's not the one being cheated on. He reads *New Idea* and *Famous* from cover to cover every week.

"No, of course not. I was . . ." Confusion wrinkled my forehead. "What do you mean? You sent me there."

"Empire Tower Two, LaTrobe Street?"

"That's r— Oh, shit." My heart sank. The Empire apartments were brand new, boasting identical twin towers. The cops picked me up in Empire One.

What a shitfight. I'd blundered into the wrong apartment.

Which made my romantic evening out with Quinn—not to mention my almost-wild almost-night of sizzling almost-sex with Rajah—even more irritating. I shouldn't even have been there. "I'm sorry, Kane. I'll get it done, I promise—"

"No matter. Forget it. Perhaps you'd like to show me that picture?"

I'd forgotten I still held it, and I offered it to him smeared with my sweat. "This? What's this all about?"

He studied it, tracing the fairy's soft jawline. "So pretty," he murmured, smoke wisping from his fingertip. "Naughty, pretty fairy. Dead. Have you noticed a lot of dead pretties lately, Jade?"

I shrugged, glad to have the subject changed. Melbourne cafés and nightclubs were littered with fairies, banshees, spriggans, and other assorted fae, if you knew where to look. The fae were into pick-me-ups and psychedelic substances. Fairy drugs were magical, reckless, darkly edgy, an experience like no other. Their shit was so fine, you could barely give away chemical drugs anymore. Fairy dealers had practically run the Valenti family out of the party-drug business, so naturally the Valentis put the hard word on them and now they worked for us.

Or they had, until DiLuca started seducing them away, and the whisper in Carlton was that a war was brewing, a clash of brass and blood to rival anything we'd seen in the nineties. But by nature, the fae lived on the edge of chaos, and it was to be expected that one or two would turn up dead every so often. Now Kane mentioned it, I recalled we'd had to hose quite a few off the street out the back of Valentino's lately. "Not really. A few."

"Detective Quinn has. He's asking questions. I don't like Quinn's questions." The photo's surface bubbled under Kane's touch, scarlet flame flickering up to his wrist and disappearing

into his sleeve. "This child worked for Angelo, the fair blue banshee in Quinn's picture, too. Someone is poisoning my fae."

I frowned. "Poisoning?"

"Do you see the ice in this child's hair? Ice on a fire sprite,
Jade. Not normal."

Disquiet coiled in my stomach. If he was right, it was bad news.
Melbourne belonged to Kane, and the demon court usually re-
spected territorial boundaries. Which meant the DiLuca gangsters were using their imagination. Not good. "Maybe it's just a
bad batch. Too much fluoride in the water or something."

"I think not."

"You think it's DiLuca."

Kane shrugged, elegant.

I'd heard Angelo curse the DiLuca family often enough, but
lately they'd thrown a whole new clove of garlic onto Ange's
pizza. Salvatore DiLuca, the patriarch, had turned up drained of
blood in a Dumpster—a savage business that Ange claimed
he had nothing to do with, though if anyone asked me, I know
where I'd be pointing my finger. It took vicious strength to suck
the life from such ancient stock, and whatever else Ange was,
he had strong and vicious in spades. Anyway, Sal was dead, and
the new guy had come out from the old world supposedly to
settle things down. No one knew much about Dante DiLuca,
except that he was young, powerful, and passionate, which in
some people's books were three perfectly good reasons not to
like him already.

I realized what Kane wanted, and icy discomfort crept up my
spine. "No. No way. They'll find me out in five seconds—"

"Not if you do it properly." Kane's black gaze was innocuous,
but it bored into mine like a power drill, ineluctable. "News gets

around. You could stage a fight with Angelo, make Dante think you're avoiding me. I must know what his game is, Jade, and you will find out for me."

And there it was. My heart sank, but already the itching need to obey tingled in my weakened muscles and churned sickly in my blood. The narrow thrall bangles stung my wrists, cold and hard. I'd have no rest until I did as he asked. Men. Always more men for whom to humiliate myself. It never ended. And my thrall to Kane had barely begun.

Warm breeze whistled from nowhere, ruffling Kane's golden hair, guttering the candles. The photo slipped forgotten from his fingers onto the floor. "Come here."

I didn't want to. I crawled over, my limbs aching with fatigue, and sat next to him, sinking into the soft white couch, close enough for him to touch me. I just wanted to curl up and pass out, but sleeping wouldn't help me. My body cried out for sustenance, the kind I couldn't get from food or alcohol or drugs.

"You look tired." Kane stroked a gentle thumb through my hair, whispering lank strands over my forehead. His gaze locked on mine. "My poor Jade. So hungry."

Kane isn't a subtle man, and my breath quickened, the shattering need for energy making my pulse race at his touch even as my stomach sank. I recalled the spicy taste of cardamom, the burning pleasure of Rajah's kisses, his willing body on top of mine, and my head swam with regret. If I'd just swallowed my pride and taken him, I wouldn't have to endure this.

But Kane's ageless scent of wind and thunder and midnight heat dizzied me. It isn't thrall that makes Kane smell good, but sheer power. Emerald fire kindled inside his irises, and my lips parted of their own accord, my throat dry. "It's been a long night."

"Let me help you." He cupped my cheek in his hard palm, pressing my mouth open with his thumb, leaning into me so agonizingly slowly that I whimpered. He brushed his crimson lips across mine, not icy but hot, slick and alluring, promising, and I'm not sure I'd have backed off even if I wasn't enthralled.

He tasted of charcoal, fire, ash. His mouth demanded my surrender, his smooth tongue wrapping around mine, but at the same time, he gave himself freely, and his energy flowed through me at last, alien and unpleasant but also delightful.

Warmth and vigor surged into my mouth, down my throat, through my veins, penetrating my deepest insides, feeding my exhaustion, sating it. My skin relaxed and thickened, my pulse thudding stronger. My hair stretched, springing with new luster, sparks rippling over my scalp. I felt strong, energetic, alive, my flesh tingling.

Deep satisfaction flooded me, not sexual but invigorating, and I slipped my fingers into his crisp sparking hair and held him, caressing his hot, willing lips with mine, taking as much as he'd let me have. He's a demon, after all. It's not like I can suck out his soul or anything.

At last he pulled away, licking a remnant of wetness from my lips. "Jade," he murmured, and smiled, guileless like a child. "I like it when you kiss me." He licked his bottom lip, tasting it, and for a moment it trembled, his hard black eyes softening to clear liquid gray, betraying loneliness he didn't have the words for.

Compassion pierced my heart, spiking the unease already squirming there. Why shouldn't I use him? He used me. I didn't owe him anything.

But it wasn't as if he could date like an ordinary guy. Sooner or later, they all ask what you do for a living, and I knew what it was like to dread that question.

Unwelcome sympathy warmed me. Kane's not such a bad guy, really, for a demon lord, and he's a talented lover as far as the physical stuff goes. He just has no clue about the emotional side.

I don't mean that he's cruel, or means to hurt you, though he often does without intending to because he's so strong. You just don't lose yourself in Kane. There's no substance to him, no matter the centuries he's lived or the countless lives he's known. You come quick and hard, gasping, and then a few minutes later once your legs stop shaking, you wonder why you bothered. And then he asks if he pleased you, and you truly don't know what to say.

I couldn't cope with Kane tonight. Not after Quinn and Nino and Rajah. I squeezed his hand, dreading that he'd order me to stay even as I wished he had someone other than me who ever did.

He brushed a stray strand of my newly lustrous hair from my shoulder, his fingernails gleaming a hesitant magenta. "Maybe . . . that is, if you'd—"

"No." I angled away slightly. Guilt stung me, maddening. I didn't owe him this. "I can't."

"No." He traced his knuckles over my jaw, reluctant. "You're right. You can go now. Do you need a lift home?"

"I'll get a tram." I stood awkwardly, not wanting to seem in a rush, but I just wanted away, before I could change my mind. In the entranceway, hot breath dampened my shoulder, and I spun around, startled. But Kane remained sitting on his sofa, tranquil. I swallowed, shivering. "Kane?"

He quirked one elegant golden eyebrow, a lick of flame curling around his earlobe.

"Who was I supposed to trap tonight?"

Kane gave a wistful little smile. "Doesn't matter," he said softly. "I believe it's no longer his lucky night."

Invisible, Rajahni Seth watches Jade stalk by in the entranceway, inches away. Compelled, he lifts his hand to touch her shining hair, making her jump. She's even more beautiful now she's fed, her skin glowing, her eyes alive like a stormy ocean. Watching Kane kiss her, the demon's eager sensual tongue stroking her lips, sent spasms of fury through him, but it was worth it to see her like this. Glorious.

The rampant itch attacking his skin has subsided now he's answered Kane's silent summons, but he waits, and only when the door clicks shut and Jade is gone does Rajah shed his cloak and reappear.

Burning fingers squeeze his throat, crashing him into the wall. Sandstone ridges jam into his spine, pain flaring, and hot demon breath caresses his lips, the ashy taste searing his mouth dry. "Rajahni Seth," hisses Kane, an inch from Rajah's face. Sharp fingernails sink into Rajah's throat, warm blood trickling. "Give me Nino's soul."

Kane's body is burning hot, unyielding, his fingers crushing Rajah's neck, immensely strong. Rajah's thrall bangles burn, but to no avail. Rajah can't swallow, and saliva spills from his mouth, but dark amusement makes him laugh.

"Give it to me." Kane's teeth sharpen, glinting, and he bangs Rajah's head into the stone for emphasis.

Rajah's vision doubles briefly, dizzy pain sheeting through his skull, but he grins, satisfaction bubbling black inside. "I can't," he chokes.

"What?" Shock flushes Kane's face red, and his grip loosens.

"It's in a very safe place. Safe even from me. Command all you want, it isn't happening. And soon I'll have the other three."

Kane laughs, and scarlet flames lick his hair, steam hissing. He shoves Rajah away, watching him fall. "Do you really think you can escape me?"

Rajah stumbles to his knees, choking, ashy residue still harsh on his tongue. He touches his warm bangle, where the engraving still shines clear after nearly four centuries. He doesn't need to read it to know the words: *odium, primordium, terminus, animus.*

Four words, four souls. Drink them down, the bangles will shatter and he'll be free. Free to go where he pleases, love as he chooses and not at a demon's behest. Free to live a mortal life.

For four hundred years, he's searched, and fate has finally brought him here, to the new world and Melbourne, where the streets and bridges drip with fell magical energy and dark fae auras glow bright and unfettered under fat southern stars. If freedom lurks anywhere, it's here.

He struggles up from the floor, but Kane's hand descends on his shoulder, unyielding. "No. Stay on your knees. You look good there."

Hatred radiates off Rajah's skin like sunburn, and he glares up at Kane, the floorboards hard beneath his knees. Kane traces a finger along Rajah's jaw, and Rajah has to grit his teeth to stop from snapping.

Kane laughs. "Do you like the word *minion*, Rajah? I've always preferred *slave* myself. Tell me what you are."

Rajah bites his tongue, blood spurting, but the thrall bangles sear and itch. Compulsion swells the words to bursting in his larynx and he must speak or suffocate. "I am . . . your slave."

"Again." Kane's fingertips trace Rajah's lips, hot, tingling arcs of blue static crackling.

"I am your slave." Niter stings Rajah's tongue, and he swallows it along with his humiliation, thick, black, festering.

"Yes, you are. Defy me, and every grotesque agony I can dream up will become your best friend. And I assure you, when it comes to torment, I have a vast imagination."

Rajah swallows again, licking stinging lips. "You can't stop me."

"No." Kane twists his fingers in Rajah's dark locks, hungry, and his voice roughens like sandpaper screeching on glass, smoke hissing between his teeth. "But I can make sure you spend the next six hundred years invisible so people won't run screaming from how hideous you are. I can make you vomit blood every time you smell a woman's juices. I can make your cock sting with the fire of a thousand scorpions every time you fuck. That's a tough call when you need to fuck to live. How would you like that?"

Rajah stares up at him, inches from rubbing his face in Kane's lap. Kane is breathless and hard, his cock straining against his pants, his fingers clenched in Rajah's hair, forcing him closer. The smell of his arousal is strong and smoky, like a bushfire, and Rajah's cock awakens in memory. He can already feel smooth naked muscle in his hands, the velvety hardness in his mouth, the hot charcoal taste of pale demon flesh pressing against his palate, the gush of seed that burns his throat like acid.

But defiance sears away any inkling of desire. "Say it," he suggests coldly. "Make me suck you off, if it'll give you a laugh.

You can fuck me, too, if you like, since you didn't have the guts with Jade. It won't stop me leaving you."

Kane screeches in fury like a vulture, green lightning crackling between his fingertips, and his palm smacks into Rajah's cheek like a thunderclap. Blood splashes, and Rajah tumbles to the polished floor, laughing in salty scarlet bubbles.

4

I leaned my head against the warm window, orange street-lights looming and fading as the number eight tram rattled and thumped along its tracks. Tall brick university buildings blotted out the stormy sky and cast gloomy shadows on the wet black asphalt.

It was the last service for the night, and the carriage was almost empty, the lights flickering on and off as the current spiked. The tart stink of pot stung in the overconditioned air, and in the corner, a skinny banshee in tight leather pants and a lacy corset made out with some guy. Smoke drifted from the joint she held loosely between two fingers, bluish-white hair sliding over her bare shoulders. She straddled his lap on the vinyl seat, crooning an eerie song deep in her throat as they kissed, her purple lips plastered to his. Sweat trickled down his temple from his shaven head, his eyelids flickering to show bloodshot whites, his grimy gold-ringed hands planted firmly on her ass.

Two in the morning had come and gone, and the air thickened with the smell of distant thunder when I got off the tram at the corner of Lygon Street and walked the couple of blocks to my flat. Warm breeze lifted my hair, sultry and pleasant on my skin after the chilly tram. Voices and music from a few pubs still drifted, and I passed a gang of drunken students, a dreadlocked Jamaican who sidled past and offered me a twist of shiny foil, a teenage girl in thigh-high boots and red hot pants arguing into her phone.

Against the wooden fence at the corner of my street crouched a spiky-haired spriggan, giggling, poking at a hunched figure with her yellow claws, her narrow black eyes shining with glee.

"Leave him be." I kicked at her. The vile pest hissed and scuttled away, leathery black skin gleaming, pointed knees and elbows flailing like a crab's legs. The homeless guy groaned and rolled over into the bluestone gutter, his greasy coat flapping open to waft out his beery stink. Even if he wasn't paralytic, he probably couldn't see through her glamour, and would have thought he was being dissed by some insolent foul-mouthed teenager.

Most mortals are easy prey to fae glamour, and never see what's right in front of them. Some aren't, and they wander the world with a glazed look in their eyes, constantly slipping over the edge from one reality to another. Not every whacked-out fidgeter or hollow-eyed nutcase is just a junkie.

I stepped over the drunk and into my shabby little enclave. Kane probably didn't know or care where I lived, but I knew Angelo didn't like me renting such a tiny beaten-up place. It's only a cheap student flat, just a couple of rooms, a kitchenette and a shower. But I liked it here. I liked the smell of old floorboards and furniture polish, the creaking peppercorn tree above the tin roof. I liked that it was away from the traffic so the stray cats that darted in the street didn't get run over. I liked that my neighbors were students, waitresses, musicians, bad artists, and petty criminals. People who didn't look down on me.

The hours I kept, they probably thought I was a prostitute, or some wannabe drug dealer's or gangster's girlfriend, and it was close enough to the truth that I didn't bother to correct them. I'd tried real jobs, in bars, cafés, secondhand bookshops, whatever I could get, but they never lasted long. Employers didn't like it when you tore off in the middle of a shift because your bangles started itching, and now Ange won't let me work. He says it's undignified. For him, maybe. There's not much dignity for me in taking his money.

My front door hid at the end of a concrete path, squeezed under a rickety iron fire escape. I reached it to find a green fairy swinging by his knees from the heater pipe, his knotted yellow hair dragging in dust eddies. His wings fluttered lazily, pearlescent colors glittering, and he sang to himself as he swung back and forth, beautiful and breathy like a siren.

He heard me coming and flipped to his feet, wild sunflower tangles springing up like a bird's nest. His narrow green face split into a toothy smile, and his ruby eyes glinted with delight. "Jade-Jade, come see! The river's full of gold!"

I sighed, though a smile tugged at the corner of my mouth. "Babe, it's three in the morning—"

"But the river's golden like the sun. Come see!" He tugged my hand and twirled me around, fluttering a few inches off the ground, raindrops glittering on his green-veined skin.

I chuckled, stumbling, hair falling in my face. Nyx was my best mate, if I had one. I'd known him only a few months, but it seemed like more. We hung out in cafés, caught movies, shared a drink or two. When he didn't disappear for weeks on end, flitting after some eldritch fae whim, that is—but that's what fairies do, and you don't ask or berate.

I hadn't seen him since we'd sunk a few too many shots together at a kinky dance party a week ago, but he had a knack for showing up when I felt out of sorts. Once when I was working as a coffee girl at Starbucks on Swanston Walk, he ran in, jumped over the counter, and dragged me out, insisting that the city was on fire and I should come see. He flew me to the base of the blue neon spire on the arts center roof, and we watched the scarlet sunset flashing on glass skyscrapers, cool wind dragging our hair back in glowing blue warmth. I lost that job, too, but somehow it didn't matter.

Now, he tickled my cheek with a knobbly green finger, his glassy claws shining. He wore bright magenta tights, a red silk sash and a short tank top made of tight green nylon that left the bottom half of his torso bare, and he looked totally fabulous, as only a fairy could. "Jade-Jade? Come see? Hurry, hurry or it'll be poof! Gone like the moon."

I tried a proper smile, and weight eased from my heart. "Just for a bit, okay?"

Nyx grinned and swung my hand in his as we walked down the lane, his sharp green feet skipping bare on the gutter stones. His pointed ears twitched. "Just a bit. Bit, bit, bit. Tequila?" he added, hope shining in his eyes.

I winced, my stomach curling in rueful memory. "Not this time. No way. Not a chance."

Pale pre-dawn faded the jagged city horizon, and I swayed on the concrete riverbank, dangling my legs over the edge. Sultry heat shimmered, a warm watery smell rising from the river. Nyx lay beside me on his tummy with his feet kicked up, warbling softly and wafting salty breeze over us with his wings. Behind us, decorative gaslights flared one by one atop square metal obelisks, heat bursts searing my back, and the brown river water reflected burning pillars of flame. Golden, like the sun. Just like he said.

Warm gritty concrete rasped my thighs through my thin skirt, and I watched with glassy chemical delight as a little black ant labored over the mountain of my knee.

Nyx laid another glittering line of banshee blue on my thigh and snorted it, his breath tickling. He pressed his warm green-veined cheek on my skin, water brightening his eyes. "Peaches," he stated, and licked soft lime lips.

The ant disappeared into Nyx's hair, and I followed it with my finger, laughing.

He poked his sharp nose into my palm. "Like you smiling, Jade-Jade." He spread the last of the crystals on the back of his bony hand and held it under my nose.

I cringed inwardly, though my dry mouth stung and the four margaritas and three salty shots and who knew what else running around in my head did happy somersaults. So much for not wrecking myself. I bent and inhaled, the sharp citrus taste of blue swirling with Nyx's sweet apple sweat.

Thudding pulse rushed in my ears. The river's surface glared, and I squinted watery eyes. I felt bright and shiny, like a cool and distant star, and vaguely I recalled I had something to be unhappy about, but it wouldn't focus and I let it drift away.

I laughed, licking blue dust remnants from his knuckles. He tasted nice, sugary and comforting, his skin smooth on my tongue.

He giggled, wriggling slender pink-clad legs, and cartwheeled into the river with a splash.

More laughter bubbled inside me, and I hugged my aching ribs and let it take me. It felt good to laugh, and when he surfaced with a spray of brown water and a happy whoop, I laughed still more. Sweet, silly Nyx. He didn't have to be here, cheering up the most determinedly miserable woman in Melbourne. Didn't have to spend time with me or buy me drinks or share his manic sense of fun. He just did it, and even safe inside my glittering high, I was damned if I knew why.

He fluttered free, rainbow wings shining, and wobbled onto the bank like a drunken butterfly. He shook himself, doglike, showering me with smelly river water from his flying yellow hair. I shoved him, laughing, and together we stumbled away, leaning on each other lest we fall.

The riverbank was almost deserted, just a few drunks throwing empty cans at each other, and a lone banshee curled up atop a concrete pillar asleep, her bright blue mane swaying in the breeze. As we staggered into the dark concrete breezeway beneath the spire, a wailing brown spriggan wearing nothing but a paper party hat hurtled by on a skateboard, black toenails digging into the concrete to push her along. Nyx pointed at her with a shiny claw and laughed like he'd crack his wings off, water spraying from his hair to saturate me again.

I wiped my face, only to get wetter as he dropped his slender green arm around my shoulder, giggling and hoping to stay upright. Instead we staggered against the pebbled wall, limbs tangling in a sprinkle of water from his wings.

"You fucking idiot, you're drenched." Already his rough silky hair was trying to spring back to its normal wild vertical tangle. I dragged clumsy fists through it, and warm water tumbled out, spilling down my arms to soak my tank top. I tried the same with his shirt, and my fingers slipped down his slender green midriff to where he was bare, his starved fairy muscles tight and wet.

He felt nice, smooth, safe. I wanted to slide my hand inside his shirt, caress him, soak up his warmth. Heat kindled inside me as my rapture murmured and stretched, awakening. . . .

God, what was I thinking? My face heated, even though the light was dim and he wouldn't see. The banshee drug sloshed about in my head, elevating my senses, befuddling me. Awkwardness twisted my guts, and I pulled my hand away. "Sorry."

But Nyx grabbed it and pressed it against his chest, his long lime fingers folding over mine. His breathing pulsed against my palm, slow and definite, and my treacherous heartbeat quickened. He leaned his damp forearm against the wall above me, sheltering me in a bower of glowing blue-green wings, and his ruby gaze shimmied shyly onto mine. "Jade-Jade?"

The catch in his musical voice tore my heart, so akin to my own lonely ache that it stripped me bare. His green lips quivered, shining, moving closer to mine, and I tried not to look at them, not to think of kissing them, of pulling him close and losing myself in his sweet body. He was my best friend, not just some guy. I'd never dared to think of him like this before, but I didn't want to ruin what we had. He deserved more than I could give, more than I could ever be.

His hot breath brushed my lips, teasing my tongue, and need shivered down my neck, dangerous. Wet desire licked my nerves. I swallowed. This was a rotten idea. "Nyx—"

Too late.

He kissed me delicately, sliding his lips hesitantly on mine like he wasn't sure I wanted him, and it felt so right, I choked back a sob. Poor shy fairy. Of course I wanted him. Who wouldn't want him, with his devilish green smile and naïve imagination and beautiful bleeding heart?

I'd just never dreamed someone like him would ever want me.

Tears swelled my lids, aching, and I opened my mouth and kissed him back.

He tasted of oranges and cherry brandy, his jagged teeth stinging my tongue. He explored my hair, curling it around his fingers, sliding a tantalizing claw down behind my ear to make me quiver. My rapture slithered in my belly, murmuring dark promises, and I stamped it out firmly. Not this time. Not him.

I slid my hands around that tempting midriff, his skin so slick and warm, and he cooed into our kiss in pleasure, fluttering closer so our bodies pressed together, shifting. Our drenched clothes crushed between us, the friction burning me all over. I could feel his sex swelling against me, another big twist of hardness laid over all that tight fairy muscle, and longing prickled my skin, sending a gentle, welcome ache between my legs. For once, a man with no Kane-baggage attached who desired me, no rapture or thrall involved, even if we were staggering drunk and high and so lonely, it hurt.

He pulled back, wings quivering. His ruby eyes shimmered in the dark, blond lashes jeweled with shiny blue tears. "More, Jade-Jade. Hold me."

I'll hold you all you want, babe, I wanted to say, but nothing came out. My thrall bangles tingled, a gentle warning, but I ignored them. I brushed the blue smears from his cheekbones with my thumb, and he leaned in and kissed me again, only this time it was urgent, deep, hard, his sharp teeth pricking the insides of my lips.

Need burned over me, muddling with drug-addled sadness. My nipples tweaked hard against wet fabric, longing for his caress. I hopped, impatient. He caught me with both hands on my ass, pressing our hips together, and lifted us both off the ground with a strong beat of his wings. We drifted upward, his translucent wing membranes twitching, and swiftly I wrapped my legs around his slender hips, inhaling his tempting toffee scent. I wanted to feel his cock hard against my sex and know he wanted me, not just a fuck but me, Jade-Jade, however many times he wanted to say it. I wanted to slide him into me and bring him off, make him feel good so I could pretend everything was okay.

I held on, clutching my arms around his neck, wrapping my tongue around his, and he let go for long enough to pull his clothes out of the way. He slid bony green fingers beneath my skirt to support me, caress me, open me for him.

I wasn't totally ready—I could feel a sliver of hot wetness inside me, not enough—but I didn't care. He slipped a finger deep into me and out, spreading the smoothness. Nerves sparked inside, and a lot more moisture seeped. When he did the same with two fingers, my muscles clenched tight with desire, pressing his claws into my flesh. I wanted all of him. "Nyx, please, it's okay."

He fluttered his wings, his pleasure scintillating the membranes with color, and a hot violet breeze wafted over us as we floated in the dark. "Jade-Jade," he whispered with a breathless laugh, his clever tongue curling over my ear. "Hot like chocolate.

I love chocolate." And he slowly curled his fingers from me and replaced them with his cock, spreading me so he could push inside.

He was big, and it hurt. Burning ripped my skin like acid, and before he was halfway in, I winced, my teeth gritting.

"Oh, not good? Sorry." Nyx bit his lip, the green veins in his cheeks flushing blue, and he started to withdraw.

"No, it's fine." I halted him with my hand on his slim green hip, bearing the sting as best I could. I just wasn't wet enough, I guess, and he was too big. We'd be good in a moment.

I reached under and adjusted with my fingertips, sliding my flesh free. This time when he pushed he went all the way, and I swallowed a scream, my thighs quivering. God, he was massive, I could barely cover him, but that was nothing compared to the caustic agony chewing at my flesh, burning like he'd shoved molten iron up there. And I was wet, I knew. It wasn't that. Maybe some weird fairy chemistry.

Shaky, I lifted myself and settled on him again, harder. Nyx's wings jerked, and he sucked in a sharp breath. I squeezed my eyes shut. God, it was worse. I sat up and slid my fingers over him to make sure there was nothing in the way, but I found only smooth fairy skin over firm tissue.

Something was wrong with us.

I tried again, but the more I moved, the more it hurt, and finally I couldn't help but cry out. "Ow. No, I can't."

Nyx's pretty cheeks dulled with moisture, his gemlike eyes glazed. "Jade-Jade, sweet, I think—"

"I'm sorry, babe. I can't." I pulled him out of me, fluid sticky on my fingers, and the burning eased a little. He set me gently down, and I staggered, not wanting to move my thighs until the stinging stopped. Tension clawed me, my nerves alight with embarrassment.

He stared at me, yellow hair still dripping, his fingers still slick and shiny with my juices. His wings twitched, awkward. "I'm so sorry. I didn't mean it. I wanted to make you smile." Indigo tears flooded his eyes, and he bit his wobbling lip and flitted away into the dark with a whoosh of warm toffee breeze.

I stumbled a few steps after him, acid agony still fresh inside me. "Nyx, please, it isn't . . ."

It isn't your fault. It's not you, it's me.

But he was already gone.

When I got home, white early-morning sun pressed against my blinds, heat already leaking in, and the place stank of the oily takeaway egg linguine I'd eaten for dinner about a hundred hours ago. I stole past the dirty dishes lurking in ravenous hordes on the sink and dropped onto the bed in my river-stained clothes, too exhausted and wasted and tearful to shower or brush my furry teeth.

I lay there, restless, long minutes ticking over on my neon alarm clock, my mind too worked up to sleep. Distant pain still burned inside me, and my flesh felt raw and ripped. Nausea crawled around in my guts like a mutant snake, and the ache in my heart wouldn't ease, no matter how I rolled on the sweaty sheets or tugged my hair in frustration.

What a fuckup. I hadn't merely screwed my best friend and regretted it, a few days of awkward tension and then we'd laugh it off. Nothing harmless like that. I'd spectacularly not screwed him, and chances were I'd broken his heart and he'd never speak to me again.

I wriggled, the air sticky and sick like a soaked blanket on my skin. What was I thinking? Why did I have to bring sex into everything? Sure, I wanted a lover who cared for me. But I wanted a friend more, someone who didn't care about Kane or Angelo or how I had to spend my time, who liked me for myself and not my glamour. Who didn't expect anything from me. Nyx did all that, actually treated me like a person and not a sex doll, and I had to throw it back in his face by trying to fuck him.

Maybe what they all said was true, and I'm not good for anything else. Or maybe it's just been so long since I had a relationship that didn't involve screwing, that I didn't know what else to do.

Something wet and heavy thumped into my door like a bag of mud, and I groaned. If that cheeky red spriggan pissed through my letterbox again, I'd rip his pointy nose off. I dragged myself up, stomped to the door, and yanked it open. "Bugger off, you manky little shit—"

The dead bolt snapped from my fingers, and my breath caught. It wasn't the red spriggan. It was Nyx, insensible, sprawled twitching on my doorstep in a wet blue puddle.

"Babe?" I scrambled to my knees to cradle his fine-boned head. His moist cheek slid on my fingers, cool blue tears spilling over my hands. Moths flickered and crawled in his hair, their brown dust smeared on his green-veined cheek. His beautiful wings lay crushed beneath him, limp and wet. Their color bled, iridescent streaks of viridian and cobalt puddling like diluted watercolors onto the cracked concrete step.

My heart constricted, Quinn's dead fairy photos flashing in my memory. "Nyx, wake up."

He murmured something unintelligible, his lips pale and slick with blue phlegm. I slung his limp arm over my shoulder and half dragged, half carried him inside. Hue leeched from his wings to soak my clothes and streak the lino with wet rainbows.

I helped him into my bedroom and laid him on his side on the crumpled bed, bright moisture soaking the creamy sheets blue and green. I popped the lamp on and peeled his sticky clothes off, arranging his damaged wings behind him. Yellow light glistened on his paling skin, glowing veins pulsing dimly in his slender apple-green throat. A faint sour smell rose, like something turned slowly rotten, and his breath stained my pillow where his soft lime lips pressed into it.

I swallowed. I'd wondered what he'd look like in my bed, but this wasn't what I'd had in mind. Swiftly I examined him where he'd touched me, fingers, mouth, groin. Nothing was burned or torn. It wasn't me.

He stirred, groaning, and I stroked his hair back gently. Instead of tangling in wild yellow springs above his head, it hung limp and slick, soft gray moths darting. His clammy skin shocked me, cold. He should have been warm. I didn't know what was wrong with him. I'd never seen a drug like this before. "Nyx? What happened? Did you take something?"

His eyes flickered open, shimmering red, his curly blond lashes clotted. He coughed, thick. "Jade-Jade?"

"I'm here, babe. Take it easy." I clasped his damp hand, his glassy claws flexing weakly. I dragged the feather quilt up to cover him, heedless of the dripping mess. I knew Nyx was some kind of air sprite. Maybe he was just starving. I visualized the contents of my refrigerator: milk, yogurt, sliced sandwich bread, bananas, Tim Tams . . . What did I have with bubbles? "I'll get you some mineral water or something—"

"No . . . not hungry . . ." His beautiful voice scratched like he had a rotten case of bronchitis. He swallowed, sickly blue liquid spilling from his lips, his fine pointed ears twitching wet as he tried to smile. "Just sick . . . I'll be okay. Nowhere else to go. Thanks . . ."

I nodded, stroking his hair, heat swelling in my throat. "Sure. No worries, babe. You just rest now." But we both knew fairies didn't get sick.

I tucked the quilt under his pointed chin, and my hand came away stained green. "Kane said there was poison. Did someone attack you? Was it the DiLucas?"

Nyx laughed, and choked, coughing sea-blue ichor, his broken wings jerking feebly. "Stay away from him, Jade-Jade. Promise me." His eyelids slipped shut, only his quivering wing membranes and the breath wheezing sticky on the pillow betraying any life.

Tears burned my eyes even as my thrall bangles itched and hummed. That was one thing I couldn't promise, and frustration and sorrow squeezed my heart.

I leaned over to flip the old bar heater on, oil gurgling in the painted pipe lining the wall, and climbed into bed. I heaped the quilt up over us, pulling the edges in around him, and clasped his poor shivering body to mine. Sour, cold moisture soaked through my skirt and tank top, plastering the fabric to my skin. I tucked the top of his head under my chin and held him to me, rocking gently, his wings pulsing feebly, ever weaker. Despair soaked into my heart, burning. If I could feed him, give up my energy to help him, I would. But I couldn't. All I could do was kill.

I didn't mean to sleep, but I must have dropped off, my arms still wrapped around him, his dripping head on my breast.

When I woke, he'd melted.

Just a mass of watery blue gel, cold and sticky on my skin, the mattress beneath me drenched with indigo liquid like blood and the sour stink of decay.

Gone. Precious, giddy, lonesome Nyx, who laughed and chased butterflies through the air in Carlton Gardens, who cartwheeled into the river for fun and did handstands in the street at midnight when it rained. Who had no one better to come to when he knew he was dying than me.

I hadn't said I loved him, like a best friend should, or that I was sorry it never worked out between us. I hadn't said thank you. I couldn't even stay awake while he died.

I lay alone soaked in sticky blue mess and cried, bright heat bleeding between the dusty venetians.

5

Valentino's is your typical Lygon Street Italian restaurant. Red leather seats, soft white tablecloths, a tiny vase of flowers and a fat white candle in a shining glass bowl on each table, painted walls draped with curtains, tassels, silent movie stills, and sepia photographs of olive orchards in old Sicily. Vito, the maître d', wears a black suit and drapes a napkin over his arm. And the smell is glorious, like something out of heaven's kitchen, roasting lamb, simmering meat sauce dripping with oregano, onions frying in butter and tomatoes, always tomatoes, grilled, sautéed, fried, stewed, any form you can imagine. The scent wafts out onto the street like a warm mouthwatering cloud, mingling with the same from a dozen places on that block.

I got there about nine, having spent the afternoon washing sheets and scrubbing up the mess. Blue fragments of Nyx still stained my fingernails, though I'd scratched at them with the brush until my cuticles ripped and bled, and the decaying stink still soaked my nostrils, sour like guilt. The burning inside me was gone, not even an itch remaining, but injustice seared worse than any chemical scald. Whatever it was, he hadn't deserved it.

The last breath of sunset faded from the sky, stars peeping through, and restaurant signs buzzed in red and green neon, flashing over the crowded black pavement where café tables spilled out to the street. The Valentino's blackboard leaned against the wooden rail by the gutter, specials tonight braised lamb shanks and fettuccini pescatore. Customers chattered, white plates and dark wine bottles gleaming.

I checked my reflection in the window before I went in, wiping my nose one last time with a wilting tissue. I looked awful, despite my fresh terra-cotta shift dress and strappy heels. I'd left my hair down for some semblance of dignity, but you could still see my puffy cheeks, and despite me larding on mascara and dark gray shadow like some trashy emo chick, my eyes still glowed swollen and red.

I didn't care. Let Ange think I was upset about Nino. Hell, he probably wouldn't even notice.

Tingling discomfort whispered up my arms, raising the hairs, my thrall bangles stinging, and tension coiled in my intestines. Kane's words echoed in my heart, a persistent, baleful imperative I couldn't ignore: *You will find out for me. You will . . . you will . . .*

"Yeah, yeah," I muttered, stuffing the crumpled tissue back in my black satin handbag.

The restaurant was busy tonight, only a few small tables at the back unfilled, and Vito made me a little bow as he hurried past, turning sideways to fit between the chairs. As usual, Ange and whichever corrupt judge or greedy politician he entertained that evening took the round table by the side window. I excused myself around tables and chair backs to approach him, an oily feather of unease sliding in the back of my throat.

Angelo Valenti looks like some of what he is, a hard-ass gangster with loads of cash and no regrets. His eyes are gray and hard, his broad forehead uncreased, his blunt fingernails always clean. In his pockets there'll be the keys to his Monaro, a thick roll of fifties, a Ziploc bag of white crystal powder, and a silver-flashed .38. Tonight he wore a dark red shirt under a black leather jacket, black curls cropped short at the base of his neck, a golden crucifix on a chain falling over his collar.

He doesn't look all that smart. He also doesn't look 350 years old, so go figure.

His companions wore dark suits, no ties, guns lumpy under their jackets. A fat plate of marinara sat half-eaten in the middle of the table, split shellfish still steaming in mounds of pink-sauce-smothered spaghetti. I walked toward them, pasting on a smile, but it froze when I saw who sat there, and I halted, my guts warm and tight.

Fabian and Santino Valenti, two hulks with the trademark heavy Valenti build, hard men whom Ange drags out from under the stairs when there's killing to be done. Worse, Tony LaFaro, Ange's fae-born cousin from the old country, sadistic and half-mad from his fairy blood, his yellow eyes double-lidded like a reptile's. No wives. No girlfriends. This was a war council, and if the five empty merlot bottles on the table were any guide, it was already well under way.

I clasped my bag in my lap, suddenly wishing I hadn't come, no matter the itching thrall. Just because Ange doesn't need to eat regular food doesn't mean he isn't a bastard when he's drinking.

He saw me and smiled, genial, beckoning to me with one thick hand and signaling to the wine waiter with the other. "Another one, Paolo. Jade, darlin', have a seat."

I didn't. "Just saying hello, Ange. Hi, Tony, Sonny, Fabe. I heard about Nino. I'm sorry."

Tony flickered his forked tongue at me, grinning. The Valenti boys nodded, but didn't get up. They were old-school Sicilian, and I wasn't anyone's wife.

Ange dipped his head, solemn. "May he rest in peace. Listen, love, can I have a word? Just a minute, boys." He glided up from his seat, swift and elegant for such a bulky body, and ushered me out into the little corridor where the toilets are, wooden walls lit by a single white bulb.

I swallowed, my nerves jumping. This might be difficult.

Ange leaned against the wall, trapping me in his broad shadow. "Where you been? You look like hell, girl." His accent is Italian-Australian, comical. No one ever laughs.

"Nowhere. I just—"

The hard heel of his palm smacked into my temple, and colored sparks danced in my vision for the half second it takes the signal to reach your brain.

Jesus. I never see it coming.

Pain lanced through my skull, my skin burning, and my vision wobbled dimly as I staggered. Maybe convincing him I was leaving would be easier than I thought. "You asshole."

"You were with Nino, Jade. Kane told me. What happened?"

"Nothing. I don't know, okay? It's nothing to do with me." A fierce ache throbbed in my head, threatening to blind me, and I blinked, a tear or two soaking onto my painted lashes. Already I could feel a lump growing.

Ange sighed, like I'd offended him and he was genuinely sorry to hear it. "You screwed him. Say it."

Was that all he cared about? "Not that it's any of your god-damn business, Ange, but I didn't, okay?" I tried to push past him, wobbling.

He grabbed my shoulder to stop me, anger showing in his tense mouth, the way his teeth pressed against his lip, straining. "You little whore. You screwed my cousin to death, and now you lie about it?"

Like that was the worst sin of all. Ange's corrupted morals always stung sourly in my mouth, and disgust seared my throat like rising bile. He's callous, violent, a lousy shag. I would have left him months ago, if the whole thing hadn't been on Kane's orders.

I shook him off, trembling, my head still throbbing. "Don't you ever hit me again. Get your filthy hands off me."

"The Lord have mercy on your soul. You gotta repent, or you'll go to hell." He clamped his fingers around my wrist, gray irises spiraling blue.

I backed away, hot shame stinging my face at the fear that speared into my heart. Sick loathing writhed inside me. "Don't, Ange, not tonight. Please."

But the wooden wall thudded into my back and I had nowhere to go. He pulled my straining forearm toward him. I struggled, yanking back, my biceps bulging, but he was strong, effortlessly strong, and horror crunched icy teeth into my bones as he bent and fastened his lips onto the soft skin inside my elbow. My skin crawled in horrible anticipation, and I couldn't help but cry out.

I have no clue where romantics get the idea that being bitten by a vampire is sexy.

It fucking hurts. The horrible metallic slide of his teeth under my skin, the vile pop as the vein broke, the burning agony of my blood forcing out, faster than the hole wanted to let it because he was sucking, drinking, tearing the hole bigger. Pain skewered my arm, my fingers clawing. Sick heat spreading in my abdomen, and I gritted my teeth so hard, my jaw ached. I wanted to vomit, or piss myself.

I scrabbled in his hair, trying to drag him off, stiff black curls scratching my fingers, but he didn't let go until he was finished.

He straightened, sucking crimson remnants from his lips, catching his breath. A healthy flush warmed his skin, like he'd exercised or spent time in the sun. "You're filthy with sin, Jade. Get to confession, be absolved."

"Go to hell." I clutched the crease of my elbow, bending my arm up, blood already dripping. He hadn't taken that much. I didn't feel faint or anything. I just wanted to kick his head in for pushing me around.

"I will. Why you think I wanna live forever?" He licked his pointed teeth clean and wiped his mouth with the back of his heavy hand. Not a drop stained his clothes. "Get out of my place, whore. Don't come back till you're clean."

I laughed, incredulous. "Are you listening to yourself? Ever hear of throw the first stone, and all that?"

"Jesus was a nice man. I'm not. Get the fuck out." His lips tightened, mean and hard, and the pulse in his jaw quickened.

For Ange to curse in front of a woman, even one he despised like me, he must be dead furious. Time to burn my bridges. I raised my voice so the whole restaurant would hear. It wasn't like they weren't all straining their ears already. "You know what? Fuck you, Ange. I'm sorry I had to kill Nino. He was a better screw than you. At least I could feel it when he stuck his cock in me."

And I walked out, shoving awkwardly past customers with my hand still clamped on my bleeding elbow, my heels clicking on the tiles. The Valenti boys studiously kept their gazes down, but Tony's graveyard chuckle followed me, and as I reached the street, I heard the crack of smashing timber.

Across the street, Kane sits on the sidewalk in a shimmer of overwarm air, tapping listless black nails on the white plastic café table. Streetlights burn golden haloes onto the pavement, traffic cruises by in whiffs of carbon and warm metal, bats flicker and flap on fragrant currents dark with kinetic mystery.

A glorious summer night, brief and frantic like a chemical mood, ripe for mischief and power games. But Kane shifts, discontent itching his skin. He sighs, restless, and a car swerves, the driver spooked by some cosmic fluctuation.

The waitress approaches, a blond child with bony hips and tendons standing out in her swanlike neck. She places a tall frothing drink before him on a saucer. "One lime soda. That's five fifty."

Kane dips the straw in, mixing the scoop of ice cream into the creamy green fizz. "You're not too fat."

She blinks, froglike. "Excuse me?"

"To be a dancer. The directors don't ignore you because you're too fat. You're just not good enough." He digs a banknote from his pocket and hands it to her, a yellow fifty. "Keep the change."

She gulps, and snatches it.

But Kane's lost interest. His nails gouge the table's edge, his knuckles popping sparks. Because there's his pretty Jade across the street, walking out of Valentino's in her lovely red dress, black makeup chalked like tears on her cheeks. Bleeding, that hot steely smell he loves, but beneath it her real smell, delicate and fresh like flowers. He inhales deeper, compelled, and his nails glimmer blue with longing.

He forces himself to relax, and swallows a lime-flavored mouthful, his throat aching. All he need do is whisper her name, and she'll come to him, talk to him, maybe even smile for him. That seems important. Kane isn't sure why. Such a brittle thing, a smile. Such a lie.

He smiles himself, just to prove it, and green froth bubbles over his hand, the sour smell of turned milk stinging his nose. At the next table, a woman wrinkles her nose and puts down her latte, licking at the inside of her mouth in distaste.

His blood-splashed Jade stalks between restaurant tables and scuttling waiters, her jaw clamped so tight that little wrinkles line her pretty chin. Kane stares, golden flames darting between his fingers, and his clotted heart warms, demon blood flowing. So fragile. So broken. Only he can fix her. No one understands her like he does. She should come to him.

Her name burns on the tip of his tongue like an ember, flickering. But an idea shocks frost into his hair, and on the table his soured green drink crackles and freezes solid, the straw crushing upright. What if . . .

He frowns, his lashes crusted with ice. What if instead, he went to her? *Surprise, Jade, don't cry.* Maybe then she'd smile, and he'd feel better.

He hops up, but pauses, a splash of nervous magenta bleeding into his nails. What if she doesn't see him? Sometimes he's invisible to her. He isn't sure why, but sometimes she doesn't notice the things he says to her. Usually it's when he feels like this, itchy and uncomfortable and pink, and he stammers out something crazy and gentle and she goes quiet and stops seeing him for a while.

He watches her walk around the corner, out of sight, and slowly he sits, snow melting to trail icy water on his scalp. He doesn't want to be invisible. Better if he leaves her alone.

"You cold, sweetie?"

Kane blinks, his mouth tingling with ashen sorrow. The curdled latte woman is gone, and a slender white fae girl smiles at him, scarlet flame licking in spirals through her long pale hair. A sultry, grasping smile. Not like Jade's. His claws spring, flushing an angry sea green. "Not that kind of cold, child."

The fire sprite twists her spine, her flimsy dress slipping up on her thighs, glassy wings fluttering as she squirms her chair closer. Sparks jump from her lips, fresh and fragrant with carbon. Her body heat twinkles the air, inviting, but sour desperation taints her zeal. "You got somewhere to go? I can warm you up."

Ice flakes from his lashes like snow, and his skin twitches, tempted. But they never really want it, not when he's in this kind of mood. They just think they do. "You wouldn't like me warm."

"Think I would. Think I really, really would. Taste?" She stretches a golden-veined white arm, flames ribboning, and reaches out with her index finger to touch her claw to his frozen drink. It melts, hissing off a puff of green steam.

The fairy winces and snatches her hand back, yellow eyes brightening with pain. "Bee, bee! Nasty green bee."

Kane sniffs the steam, curious. Nothing, just rotten cream and water. "Did that hurt?"

She stuffs her wounded finger in her mouth, sparks gushing, and her nail cracks off like glass, splinters sticking to her lips. Fear glazes her eyes. "Nope. Nope, nope. Gotta go." She scrambles from her chair and weaves out, wings jerking.

Kane carefully pushes the ruined drink away with one finger. He'd thought she smelled ill. But sick fairies only remind him of Jade, and Jade's gone, off to work her own poison on Dante DiLuca. Cruel envy writhes in his blood, uncomfortable.

The skinny dancing waitress sidles up to him again. "You done with that?"

He glances up at her hard, tired eyes and her tight mouth, and despite his discontent, the animal scent of soul prey sparks demonic hunger in his heart. He gives her his human smile and flicks his lashes at her with a gentle waft of hellish compulsion. "Yes, child. Sorry about the mess."

She scoops up the sloppy saucer and hesitates, her gaze slipping. "Did you really mean . . . shit. Never mind. Forget it."

Kane grabs her wrist to keep her, and inhales to taste her name. "I haven't forgotten, Claire. I won't forget you. Ever." A lie. But so is her effort, her desperation. So is her life.

She gasps, her pulse bubbling warm against his palm. The dirty glass slides on the saucer, and milky green froth splashes her black apron. "How did you know?"

"I know. Do you want to be better?"

"I train and train. Six hours a day. But—"

He digs his fingers in, growing them until his claws cut her soft skin, and lets his voice deepen to a growl. "Do you want to be better?"

The girl gulps, her eyes wide, the shiny sweat of fear coating her face. She sees. She knows. But she can't stop. Her body quivers with longing, and her whisper floats out on warm soul-drenched breath. "Yes. Oh, yes. Please."

Kane lets go, satisfied, the ashen taste of hellfire already crisp and arousing in his mouth. "When's your next audition, child?"

She licks her lips, greedy now. "Sunday. At the Palladium."

"I believe you'll get the job." He beckons, and when she leans over, he whispers a date, flames from his lips licking her ear.

Realization flushes her, and she backs away, her eyes wide and wet. "No. I'll only be . . . That's not long enough. Please."

Kane smiles, faint. "Enjoy it while it lasts. I'll see you soon."

I stalked out onto the footpath, clutching my aching elbow, and the diners sitting under the canvas canopy politely looked away as I passed, or quickly found something particularly interesting to talk about with their partners. A girl coming out of Valentino's covered in blood isn't something you want to stare at. You never know who might come out behind her.

Stupid tears stung my eyes, and I walked blindly away under strings of yellow and white lights, my temple still aching where Ange had hit me. He wasn't following. He was too busy with his brutish war to bother with me for now, beyond breaking a bit of furniture and getting filthy drunk. But my skin burned with shame, hotter than the blood already growing sticky on my arm, and I seethed inside with rage and disgust. At Ange for treating me like shit, at Kane for making me put up with Ange's crap, but most of all at myself.

I turned the corner—any corner, to put Valentino's out of sight—and threw myself against the whitewashed wall. I wiped my face, heedless of smeared mascara, and clotting blood squelched as my elbow unfolded. "Fuck," I muttered, and scrabbled in my bag for more tissues.

When had I turned into such a pushover? Thrall didn't mean I shouldn't stand up for myself. Sure, I had to hang around Ange, doll myself up, look pretty on his arm. In his bed, too, or wherever else he wanted it. Sex is always a given with Kane's little assignments, and since I started needing sex to live, I'm not so much a princess that I can't close my eyes and bear it when I have to. Ange's energy is cold and bristly with rage and gives me the creeps, but it's food.

That didn't mean I had to let him beat me up and drink my fucking blood in public.

Red streaks smeared on the inside of my arm as I tried to clean it up, fragments of bloody tissue sticking. The hole was ragged, the soft skin torn between two fat puncture marks. Already a scab formed, and by morning it'd be healed. A swift-healing vampire bite, the original and best domestic violence. It's gone before you have to say you walked into a door.

I tossed the sodden tissues into the gutter and gingerly fingered the egg-shaped lump on my forehead. This one wouldn't fade so soon. Okay, so physically he was stronger than me. He's a vampire; I can't help that. Maybe I was being a bit hard on myself.

Or maybe I'd heard *whore* and *slut* and *useless bitch* so often, I'd started to believe it.

A lump swelled in my throat, too, and I swallowed, sniffing, my eyes stinging again. At least I didn't have to endure Ange anymore. But there'd be another one, and another. All the same. All violent, angry, mean. Nice guys don't do deals with Kane. And if one finally beat me to death, or killed me during their nasty little sex games—even if I jumped in front of a train or swallowed a bottle of pills—there'd be Kane, breathing my life back, making me go on. And on. Nothing could make it stop.

I let my hair fall to hide my burning cheeks. I didn't want to go to a café, where well-meaning people would lean back and widen their eyes and ask if I was okay. I wanted to go home, stand under the shower alone in the dark and scald off the stink, but the place still smelled of Nyx, bitter and sad.

Poor Nyx would have tried to cheer me up. He'd sing to me in that beautiful breathy voice, bring me a bird's nest or a seashell, roll in fresh-cut grass in the park so he could shake it over me from his crazy yellow hair. Sweet, clueless fairy. Dead.

I smacked my palms against the wall, the rough concrete stinging my skin the way anger stung my heart. My eyes filled with burning mist, and this time I let the tears come.

"Jade?"

I wiped my face uselessly, trying to swallow a sob, my throat aching.

"Jade." A gentle hand on my bare shoulder, warm, hesitant. Not a Valenti.

I forced my eyes open, wiping them again until I could see, and my stomach tightened even further.

Dark concern shadowed gold-flecked chocolate eyes, the streetlight gleaming softly on brown skin and shedding an elusive autumn shimmer into midnight hair. He wore a black T-shirt over faded jeans, casual but elegant. With a body like that, he'd be elegant wearing a garbage bag. Even in my state, I couldn't help checking him out. Damn. He looked just as hot without the rapture.

No doubt he knew it, too. Nice guys don't get in thrall to Kane either. I pushed his hand away. "Go away, Rajah."

"Funny. Not until you stop crying, or bleeding. Both would be nice."

"I don't need your help, okay?"

"Okay. How about my sympathy, then? You can have that for nothing." Hurt glimmered on his tone. He licked his lush bottom lip, and for the first time I noticed it swelled a little out of shape, bruised.

I wiped my nose, contrition chewing at me. "What happened to your face?"

"Kane. It doesn't matter. What happened to yours?"

Maybe Rajah knew a bit more about my kind of thrall than I'd thought. Kane has never hit me in the 140 years I've known him. Then again, I've never soultrapped one of his minions just to piss him off. I sniffed and swallowed, my voice indistinct through my blocked nose. "Angelo. Doesn't matter either. What do you want? Were you looking for me?"

He glanced at the swelling on my forehead, my red dress, the blood clots streaking my arm. "No, but you're not exactly inconspicuous." He fiddled with the turned edge of a thrall bangle, indecisive, and then he stuck out his narrow hand to me. "Come on. I know what you need."

I laughed, bitter. Sure. So did Ange. So did Kane. So did everyone, and none of them had a clue. "The world's full of men who know what I need, Rajahni Seth. Don't think you can astonish me."

His eyebrows lifted, and he stuck his hand back in his pocket, awkward. "I was thinking of rogan josh and a mango lassi. Is that what they all say?"

I blushed, warm. Him, awkward. With me. Imagine that.

The thought of spicy food made my mouth water, and I had

to admit the thought of the company did, too. Absently I rubbed my wrists, where the thrall bangles already itched and moaned. I should have been thinking about how I was going to fool Di-Luca. "Don't you have somewhere to be?"

He shrugged. "Angelo's finding someone for me. It can wait."

I wondered what he was doing for Ange in return, and decided I didn't want to know. "But—"

"But they itch?" He grinned, cheeky, stunning. "Sure. So does a mosquito bite. Doesn't mean you have to scratch it right away."

Pleasure glimmered in my heart at the prospect of defiance, even for an hour or two. I mustered a grin in return. "Okay, then. Your shout."

6

I stretched out on tasseled white floor cushions, my stomach pleasantly full, the wonderful aroma of Indian food still drenching my taste buds. Oil wicks burned in copper lamps by the ceiling, the flames flickering gently in the breeze that fluttered through the open doors, and our low linen-covered table was littered with empty copper rice bowls and a ceramic handi smeared with the remnants of our glorious rogan josh. We'd eaten with our fingers, scooping up yellow saffron-stained rice mixed with toasted cumin seeds and chunks of spiced lamb so tender, they melted in my mouth, flavor exploding.

It was late. We were the last ones here, and the place was closed, the rest of the cushions tidied away and the tables wiped. The fat little owner seemed to know Rajah, who chattered away with him in Hindi or Urdu or whatever it was and convinced him to let us stay.

I'd been to the ladies' and washed my face, so at least I didn't have ruined makeup caked to my lashes and black streaks down my cheeks, even if my face was still puffed up like . . . well, like my best mate had just died.

I flexed my bare feet, aware of Rajah watching me, dark and inscrutable, his long legs relaxed as he stretched out next to me like a big lean cat. He hadn't tried to hit on me, or touch me. We'd had an ordinary, funny, charming conversation about the food, the cricket season, this never-ending summer, the places we'd lived, and the times we'd seen.

He'd talked with glittering animation about Lahore before the Raj, when the Mughal Empire ruled the world from the gleaming marble court of Shah Jahan and the demon lords fought spectral battles in warm lamplit corridors. His dark eyes danced as he described intrigues with poison-fanged efrits and black-hearted djinn, and he laughed with me as I reminisced about Havana in the fifties, watching Sinatra in the ballroom at the Hotel Nacional with Meyer Lansky and Charlie Luciano, back when hellbound gangsters still had manners and knew how to show a girl a good time.

I hadn't mentioned Nyx, and Rajah hadn't asked, content to let me say what I wanted to say. He didn't ask why I'd been crying. He didn't even mention last night, but he didn't seem embarrassed or avoidant. It was like he'd forgotten about it. But I hadn't. I still felt him on me, the delicious heat of his body, his fingers clenched in my hair, his lips hungry on my throat. And I still saw that brass soultrap bubbling with angry Valenti energy, and Kane's clueless expression when I told him about it.

I drained the last of my lassi, the milky liquid cool and sweet in my throat. "Do you mind if I ask you a personal question?"

Rajah shrugged, easy, licking icy kulfi remnants from his spoon. I liked watching his mouth, the way his lips moved, sensual, deliberate. Even the split and the swelling bruise just made them more riveting.

I cleared my throat. "What are you really doing with Nino's soul?"

He paused for a moment and put down his bowl, considering, averting his eyes. "If I were to say '*odium, primordium, terminus, animus,*' would it mean anything to you?"

My heart skipped, and I laughed, nervous. I knew the story, had read the words carved into my bangles a thousand times. I'd never let myself think about it too much. "That's a myth."

"Is it?" He looked up, capturing my gaze with his, and such longing burned there that rapture awakened moaning in my soul. My skin flushed and tingled, and surely the air around me shimmered, but he didn't seem to notice or care. "Have you explored this city, Jade? You're so young, I wish you could taste this air like I do. It's fresh, clean, new, there's power brewing in the sky like a storm. Even the water stinks of magic. Haven't you noticed the fae glow brighter here? The banshees' song is sweeter? Vampires go longer without blood? And the rapture . . ." He licked his lips, shifting on his cushions, and laughed, a handsome flush staining his skin. "The rapture is like it used to be, when I was young. It takes me places I barely remember. Surely you've noticed everything's different here. That's the taste of freedom. If it's anywhere, it's here."

Sweat burned my forehead, slick, my pulse swelling. Freedom. To cast off this thrall, to leave Kane and his never-ending power games and go anywhere in the world I wanted, do what I wanted, be with whom I wanted. To die in peace, without hell's coarse whispers in my soul. Surely the magic words were a myth, and freedom an impossible dream.

I swallowed, my voice hoarse. "How? How do you do it? Tell me."

He leaned close to me, tempting, but calculation glinted in his eyes. "Why?" he murmured. "Why should I? Why should you even want to be free? You're glorious, smart, captivating. Why not live for a thousand years?"

"To end it." The words rushed out, thoughtless, and I caught my breath, mesmerized by the potential and the sight of his precious lips, only a few inches away. No matter that I'd been wondering exactly the same thing about him. "To be rid of it all. Why else?"

"Why else?" He laughed again, lost, and took my hand, pressing it to his warm chest where his heart beat, rapid and strong. Brightness animated his face. "To live, the way I was meant to. A mortal life, a family. Not to spend ten centuries dead at another's whim, my heart not my own. I'm sick of watching people die around me."

"But . . ." I couldn't concentrate, not with my hand there, his flesh hard and tense beneath my fingers. "But without the thrall, you'll die soon enough. Why not just wait it out, if you're so desperate for mortality?"

He tightened his grip, sliding deft fingers between mine. "The year 1615, Kane cast these bangles on. Do you see any tarnish? Any cracks? What do you think happens after those thousand years?"

I swallowed. "Kane said I'd be free to die."

"And you believed him."

Horror twisted my guts. Kane always seemed so matter-of-fact, too ingenuous to carry off such a big lie. Truth is, sometimes I forget he's a demon, and on that one I had believed him.

My hand started shaking, and Rajah gripped it tighter. "I won't take that chance," he insisted. "I've nothing to lose by trying. Four words, four souls. It can't be worse than this."

Longing swelled my throat. It sounded so easy, the way he said it. But nothing was that simple. "You'd damn four innocent people to be free?"

He brushed his lips over my knuckles, leaving a hot, damp trail. "Wouldn't you?"

I thought of all the people I'd already sent to hell. Men and women, old and young. All willing, all seduced by the rapture, their souls bleeding out in their final deadly ecstasy. Most of them on Kane's shit list through every fault of their own. Liars, murderers, greedy parasites with no care for those they crushed to make their way and no kind thought for anyone but them-selves.

Four more seemed insignificant.

My blood burned, and I pulled my hand away, letting my head fall forward to hide the hunger surely apparent on my face. My hair brushed his arm, tangling over the thrall bangle, and I swear I heard him catch his breath. "Tell me. What must I do? Those words, they're nonsense to me. How did you know it was Nino you needed?"

"*Odium.*" Rajah's hot whisper tingled my scalp alive. "That one was easy."

"*Odium,*" I repeated softly, closing my eyes. "Hatred. I don't understand."

"Neither did I until a few weeks ago. It's the moment, get it? Not just the person. You have to pick the moment when they truly hate you. I've probably missed a thousand chances in four hundred years. But in this city, you can see it. It shines around them like—"

"Like an aura." I could barely hear my own words for the thudding pulse in my head. In my mind I saw Killian Quinn, face twisted, pistol cocked in his thick hand, his body glimmering with swirling gray light. If anyone truly hated me with every straining fiber of his body, it was Quinn. *Odium.* The first key to my freedom, within my reach.

Rapture burst within me, flooding my nerve endings with hot sensation. I gasped, my muscles rippling, tension wrenching deep inside, like an imminent orgasm that just wouldn't break.

"Jade? Are you okay?"

I didn't dare look at his face, his swelling lips. My hair touching his arm was bad enough, his spicy scent thick and delicious on my tongue, every slight movement of his body so close to me an agony. But it was Quinn I burned for, vile Quinn I longed to subdue, crush, devour with every seductive wisp of glamour I could muster. I didn't care that I loathed the thought of touching Quinn, of letting him touch me. I wanted his soul, and my mouth watered.

Rajah's warm fingers brushed my chin, the briefest of caresses. "I'm sorry. I didn't mean for that to happen. Come on, I'll walk you home."

Sensation shot through me where he touched me, along the skin of my throat and down to my breasts, a promise of pleasure and release. I jerked away and scrambled to my feet, my face hot. "I can find it, thanks. I'm not lost."

"I know that. But you're not going alone, not after what Angelo did to you. He might be watching for you."

That was kind of sweet. I felt sorry I'd snapped at him. But I didn't want Rajah at my place, not tonight, not while I shuddered and yearned. Too easy to embarrass myself. I tried to step around him. "I'll be okay."

He blocked my path, stuffing his hands in his pockets with a disobedient smile. "I can argue until the sun comes up. If you want any sleep tonight, you'll have to submit." Still I hung back, and he grimaced. "Believe it or not, I understand what you're going through. Look, no hands. Three feet away at all times. I'll walk you to the door and disappear. I won't even kiss you good night. Good enough?"

Like he would have wanted to kiss me good night, if I let him? I scraped a hand through my hair and sighed. "I'm sorry, okay? It's just—"

"I know. You don't have to explain, remember?" And he stood back and held the door to let me out ahead of him.

This part of Brunswick Street was closing up this late on a Sunday night, the restaurateurs and café owners switching their lights out and locking steel grilles closed over their windows. The pub on the corner was still open, the smell of beer drifting, the band's thudding bass vibrating onto the footpath. A drunken troll hunkered in the gutter at the traffic lights, snoring, his horned head lolling on one leather-clad shoulder, his curled black toes twitching.

Heat haze shimmered the air above the road, the concrete tram tracks sparking as a tram clunked past toward the city. I walked along, sweating and silent, my arms crossed, my blood cooling only slowly. My hair stuck to my neck in strands, itchy, and my fingertips stung with the need to touch someone, anyone. Another shower for me when I got home, this time a cold one.

A pair of seagulls pecked squashed chips and fallen figs off the concrete on the corner of Carlton Gardens. Huge Moreton Bay trees loomed in the dimness above sun-browned lawn, fruit bats circling in the streetlight's halo. A sunflower-hued water sprite hung from the streetlight, swinging lazily from one translucent long-fingered hand, dripping sweet-smelling silver droplets from her rippling wings onto the footpath. Her soft song floated on the still air like dust, lonely. I thought of Nyx, and my heart ached.

I glanced across at Rajah, who was keeping his word, walking on the footpath's outer edge, not looking at me. I realized I didn't know where he lived, and I wondered how far he was going out of his way for me. The least I could do was say something. "How do you do that, anyway?"

"How do I do what?"

"Disappear."

He shrugged, sweat gleaming on his arms. "Barely. It's a mortal trick I learned from a *jaduwala* in Kabul. A magician."

"You learned magic?" I was intrigued in spite of myself, dread tightening my stomach. I'd dabbled in a bit of witchcraft once, when I was young and stupid.

"It's what got me into this mess. I was irresponsible. I lusted for more power than I could handle, and I got careless. A student of mine . . ." Rajah's eyes stormed briefly, dark. "He watched me, I let him get too close. He stole everything I had, my power, my reason, my dignity. He traded me to Kane in return for some tricks." He shook his head, damp black hair sticking to his cheek. "I never wanted immortality. It's funny how things work out. How about you?"

Nervousness tingled, and I pretended I didn't know what he meant. "How about me what?"

"You know. Those." He gestured to my bangles, careful not to touch me.

My cheeks burned as I reflected on the hellish convent

where I'd grown up. The stink of piss-starched linen, shutters pulled forever over the windows. Days of prayers, lessons, more prayers, starvation rations, and a thrashing the penalty for a mistake. Biting my split lips when the bruises stung under the rough white cloth that hid my face. Sleepless nights waiting in terror for cold, grasping hands. The night I finally escaped, I was limping as I crawled out into the stinking dung heap, squinting through one eye at magnificent, sprawling, shit-streaked London, the other eye swollen like a pea stuffed in its pod.

Fifteen endless years old, with neither love nor pity in my heart. I sank into rebellious days of picking pockets and robbing graves, confidence tricks with my hair stuffed under a boy's cap or curled in ringlets like a lady's. Nights of mad absinthe-soaked reveling, ripped satin gowns dyed verdant with arsenic, paste diamonds in my ears, all the men I wanted and some I didn't but took anyway because I could. I got diseases, and I sloughed them away with vinegar or whiskey or some other poison. I never got pregnant; the nuns and their gnarled beating stick had seen to that. I cursed the Church like it cursed me, and crawled laughing into the fringes of a shadow world, where the altars were dark, the crosses upside down, the rituals blended with blood and orgasm. The Continent, Paris, Amsterdam, Constantinople, wherever the black word spread me.

And then Vorenus Luna, the most beautiful man I'd ever seen. The face of an angel, the body of a god, and not the slender weeping god nailed to those crosses but a glorious, virile idol of the weird who fairly glowed with power. *Come with me, Jade, kiss me once more and I'll show you real magic, not just fucking on an altar to spite some foolish absent lord. Take me the way I want it and I'll make you immortal.*

Now I had real diamonds, silk gowns embroidered with golden thread, a carriage with horses, and all the man I wanted, for I only wanted one. He trained me in his every pleasure, molding me in his sensual image, and I wallowed in it. We played every game, twisted every kink, left no vice untried. Our library was hidden in a locked room, ancient books with human skin for covering, grimoires, poison recipes, the devil's handwriting in blood on singed black paper. Luna's power proved elusive, difficult, always just beyond my reach.

And one day he tired of me and left me chained to a wall underground, visiting me every so often to make me eat and to humiliate me with things I no longer wanted to do, at least not with him. My silk gown wore thin and greased up with grime, the curls falling from my hair. I cursed Luna as I'd cursed god, but a liar doesn't need belief to thrive, and I'd learned no power that could ever hurt him. He'd made sure of that.

Two months later he lost me to Kane in a faro game. End of story.

I hadn't thought about Luna in a long time, and I didn't like talking about it. I'd wanted immortality once, to spite that skinny god who insisted I must die as he had. I've changed since then.

Now I looked across at Rajah, this oddly animated, disturbingly attractive stranger who longed to escape Kane's thrall so he could live, not so he could die, and an empty place deep in my heart yearned. I wanted him to understand me, and not just because an incubus was probably the only man who could, but because for some deluded reason I thought Rajah might actually care. I wanted him to care. I wanted him to know me for myself, not just as some desperate rapture-drenched screwup or a scared little princess who gets beaten up by her jealous vampire boy-friend.

I took a deep breath and told him the whole thing.

He walked in silence for a minute after I finished, his hands still stuffed into his pockets. "Our stories are similar," he said at last, and looked up at me with a dark hint of smile. "We searched in the wrong places. There's no shame in that."

We turned the corner into my street, and I couldn't help but smile back, his gaze steady and warm on mine, until after a while his candor made me uncomfortable and I looked away.

He surveyed my door, squashed in under the stairs like a rabbit hole, and laughed. "You'll go a long way to make your point, I'll give you that. You know Kane would put you in a South Yarra mansion if you asked him to."

"I'll never ask him to." I shifted, awkward, and held out my hand. "Thanks."

After a moment he took it. "No worries. If Ange bothers you, call me."

I flushed to remember that he'd walked me home so Ange wouldn't beat me up again. Not because he actually wanted to talk to me or anything. "I didn't mean that. I meant thanks for dinner. And . . . and for wasting your night on me, I guess."

"It wasn't a waste. I . . . umm . . . had a good time."

He didn't drop my hand, and my skin burned even hotter. He was teasing my wrist with his fingertip, wearing a tragically innocent look on his face. A shiver whispered up my arm, delicate, genuine, not a contrived shimmer of rapture but honest desire. I thought of my flat, humid and dark, sour with that blue-drenched smell. I didn't want it to smell of Nyx. I kept Nyx in my heart, where he belonged, not smeared on my floor like excrement.

I wanted it to smell of rogan josh, the sweet smoothness of lassi and the dark, fresh aroma of Rajah's sweat.

I swallowed. "Rajah?"

"Yeah." He slid his fingers over mine, tracing them one by one, watching, transfixed.

I didn't pull away. "You're still here."

"So I am." He brought my hand to his beautiful lips, and his clever tongue flickered tingles over my fingertip.

I couldn't help but gasp at the rush of desire that flooded me, burning, all the way to my hardening nipples, my trembling thighs, the desperate ache starting between my legs. I wanted to slip my finger into his hot mouth so he could suck it. "Didn't you say something about disappearing?"

He gave a sultry half smile and nibbled my fingertip again, this time grazing it with his teeth. Damn, his wicked mouth turned me on. "Do you want me to disappear?"

God no. I wanted him to undress me, trail his mouth over me, worship me, plunge his tongue between my legs and drink me until I screamed. I shifted closer, and I could feel the beginning of slick wetness down there, where that ache was getting worse, my flesh swelling for him, blood pounding. "You mentioned kissing me good night, too."

He guided my hand into his satiny black hair, gentle but insistent. "I think I mentioned not kissing you good night, actually."

"So how's that looking?" I grabbed a handful, dark locks caressing my wrist, my nails grazing his skin.

"Not good. Keep doing that and I'd say hopeless." He tossed his head back, sighing in pleasure.

The action brought me even closer, and my tight nipples scraped his chest through my rough linen dress. Pleasure zinged straight to my sex, so immediate that I moaned. He must have felt it, too, because he crushed me against his hard body, his hand leaving mine to cup my waist, strong fingers holding me, supporting me.

I dragged his head down to mine, my fingers clenched in his hair, and his eyes gleamed with anticipation. I was mesmerized. I inhaled, my lips parting, tasting him in advance, that cardamom flavor doing wild things to my pulse. He groaned and bent his tempting lips to mine.

The kiss seared my lips, shocking. Blood throbbed in my clit, and I staggered, faint. Rajah pressed me close, keeping me upright, his lips caressing mine so beautifully, sliding hot over my mouth, taking me exactly where I yearned to go. My mouth sparkled, alive with his energy, not edible and nourishing like Kane's but pure sex, spearing through me, filling my womb, making my flesh weep with longing.

He danced his tongue lightly over mine, playing, teasing me until I whimpered, begging for more of him. Then his tongue plunged into me, taking me like he might with his cock, long smooth strokes that had me gasping and locking my arms around his neck, pressing against him to feel his straining erection.

The taste of him made me drunk and reckless. God, I wanted him filling me. A man who cared what I thought, who actually gave a damn what I wanted. And it wasn't like it could ruin our friendship. Nothing to ruin. Just because I told him my most humiliating secret, and he not only sympathized but actually understood, didn't mean I cared, right? And it certainly didn't mean he did.

But I knew from the way we kissed, the way his body responded, that he craved me, too, wanted to take me hard, with his cock, his tongue, his deft fingers, everything. My breasts ached against him, burning for him to suck them, and my swollen clit demanded the same. I hadn't wanted like this in an age. My eyelids swelled, treacherous tears cool on my hot cheeks.

He gentled the kiss, his mouth leaving mine to brush the tears away, his lips tender and soft on my face. "Good night, Jade."

Urgency speared through my veins. He probably didn't like me, not really. Just liked turning me on, liked my body and the idea of fucking me, another way he could get one up on Kane. But I didn't care. I twisted my fingers in his hair, yearning for him.

"Stay." Hell, that sounded desperate. I was desperate. For him.

He caught his breath, closing his eyes for a moment. "Don't. Please. You're upset, you don't really . . . I can't." He sighed, reluctant, and gently but firmly set me away from him.

"I'm okay. Really. I just . . ." But I couldn't stop the tears falling. It was that easy for him to take it or leave it. He didn't really care what I wanted. Just some mortal remnant of his conscience, stopping him from screwing a woman in tears.

He bit his lip and lifted his hand to my face, but checked it before he touched me. Instead he reached over to trace his fingertip in the dusty glass on my door. Digits. His phone number. "Just call me if you need anything, okay?"

And before I could say anything, he'd vanished, only his delicious scent lingering.

7

Rajahni Seth stalks down the dark street, his shadow long and black like a hellish shade. He's seething, his palms burning and lust trembling in his roaring blood. That Jade. Like her. Want her. Damn her.

So delicate, almost translucent in her beauty, yet wild and passionate, sighing into him like she meant it, the acid scent of her wet sex—wet for him—seeping over her to drown him. His cock aches to fill her, bring her off, make her scream. His mouth waters at the thought of tonguing her hard little nipples, her smooth flat belly, the fragrant creases at the tops of her thighs. Wrapping his lips around her secret flesh, feeling her blossom and come in his mouth, with no thought for soultrap or nourishment or thrall, only her pleasure and his, over and over . . .

He kicks at a pebble, sending it skipping into the gutter. He wants her, so hot and hard, his desire almost blots out the torrid shock of her words from a few minutes ago.

But not quite.

Vorenus Luna. Hearing the name on Jade's lips nearly floored

him. The face floats in his mind, the memory nearly four hundred years gone but still fresh, bleeding.

Rash hatred fills him, mixing seductively with his lust. Luna. Trickster, thief, confidence artist, oozing latent aptitude like he oozed sex appeal. A magnificent predator. They'd been enemies, fierce competitors, reluctant but compelled colleagues, attracted by some fell magnetism of mischief. They'd whispered in dark ocean grottoes with demons, made love to soul-stealing fae in candlelit stone halls, dragged ghosts screaming from their rest to demand the answers to death itself, just for the sheer hell of it all.

Until Luna decided he wanted the power more than he wanted the fun, and betrayed Rajah to Kane in return for immortality.

Luna is here. In Melbourne. The lost echoes of Rajah's power call to him, in the whisper of the wind at midnight and the electric buzz of neon. But he can feel Luna in his blood, too, in the same cells that sparkle in delight at the sweet potential whetting this infant city's pristine air. Luna will have sensed that also, with whisper-sharp perception both stolen and innate, and if there's one thing our Luna will never miss, it's a party.

Sweat curls around the rolled edges of Rajah's bangles, running over the magic words inscribed there. *Odium*—hatred—he's done with. Next comes *primordium*—the origin—and *primordium* has Vorenus Luna written all over it. The origin of his thrall. He just knows that when he finds Luna—which was what he intended to see Angelo Valenti about tonight, before he got distracted by a stunning handful of intoxicating, sexy woman—when he finds Luna, that aura will leap out like wicked sunshine.

He wonders how long before Jade realizes the same thing.

He doesn't know what *odium* means to her. It could be anyone. But from the heart-wrenching story she told tonight, Luna and *primordium* are one and the same.

They can't both drink Luna's soul. And if they don't drink Luna's soul, they can't be free. Frustration claws at his heart, and he almost wishes he'd left her bleeding on the footpath by Valentino's. Why did it have to be her? Why now?

For four hundred years, Rajah would have sent any soul on earth to hell in order to be free. But Jade engages him like no other in all those centuries. Never mind that tonight he couldn't take his eyes off the smooth inviting shape of her hips, her kissable breasts, that tiny bud of a mouth he wanted to claim over and over. Her heartfelt misery calls to him, makes him forget thrall and freedom and centuries of servitude. He wants to shield her from her sorrow, thrill her, prove to her with wits and humor and the sheer joy of living that death isn't the only answer to thrall.

The hottest night of wild pounding sex she ever had might help, too.

He grits his teeth, painful, and in his turmoil he flickers in and out of sight like a misbegotten shade, the air shimmering and drifting around him. He's thinking with his hard-on, and he knows it. His heart is his own. Not to be owned or shackled, no matter how enticing the chains. If he has to use all his wiles to steal Luna away from under Jade's cute little nose, he'll do it. Let her hate him forever. He'll be free. That's all that matters.

But for some reason his heart aches, and his thoughts seethe so dark and bitter that he doesn't notice where he's going, not until the yellow lightglobes of the theater glare in his eyes and

crowds jostle around him. Tonight's show of Lloyd Webber at the Princess is letting out, and chattering music theater fans mill on the footpath beneath the shining cantilever. He pushes through, fingers tensing at his sides, and slips down the side street into the dark.

A scrape behind him—a footstep?—makes him pause, glancing over his shoulder to listen. Nothing. A shadow. But even shadows follow, sometimes. He listens for a moment longer, sniffing the air like a fox, and walks on.

Icy tentacles wrap around the back of his neck.

He leaps against the dark brick wall, his heart thudding, syllables of warding stinging on his tongue.

Frigid fairy fingers trace his collarbone, yellow eyes glittering in reflected streetlight. "A moment, incubus. Please."

He swallows an angry retort when he sees her face, pale and drawn, ice crystals clogging her lashes. "Watch who you surprise like that, sweetheart. You don't know me."

The fire sprite smiles, but the skin around her ample mouth cracks, flaking off to shatter on the ground like glass. Ice forms in the scar, stained with sluggish amber blood, crystals rapidly multiplying. "I'd like to know you," she husks, but no pretty sparks fly on her breath, no flame curls in her crisp white hair or leaps from her cold broken fingernails as she touches his lips. "You're so warm. Kiss me."

"You don't want that." But Rajah's skin burns, his fingers stinging. The body yearning into his is slender, delicate, girlish, reminding him of Jade. His cock hardens, too fast, painful. Rapture writhes hot in his blood even as he registers that she's sick, disintegrating with unnatural cold, her flame dying. Maybe what he's heard about fae poison doing the rounds is true.

She slips one narrow hand between his legs, sexy despite the chill radiating from deep beneath her marble skin. Her glassy wings jerk, amber shards splintering over him like cold petals, and she wraps her spindly leg around him, impossibly flexible, the joint cracking sickly. Compelled, he slips a hand beneath her, pressing her tighter. His cock strains against her failing warmth, where there should be searing heat, and he gasps as rapture increases the pressure to compensate, hardening him to bursting.

"It hurts," she gasps, her voice weary and rough with pain. "So cold, so deep inside. They say you can suck out a girl's soul. Do a girl a favor?"

Ice crackles on his lips from her breath, and he licks them, anger and misplaced Jade-lust heating his skin. There's something perverse about this, he shouldn't be dying to fuck this poor girl, but he is, see if he can't make her overflow with his heat before the life drains out of her.

She strains closer, and he tries to pull away, sickened, sympathy butting hard against his callous lust. "No, don't—" But her icy mouth clamps over his, her phosphorous taste tainted with salt.

Defeated, he thrusts his tongue into her mouth, kissing her hard, closing his eyes to the sudden urgent shimmer of rapture in the air. A whisper of her poisoned chill soaks into him along with her energy, and she moans brokenly, her lips cracking under the pressure. Urgent now, he squirms his hand under her dress, searching for the last remnants of heat. She's wet, but it's cool and his fingers are burning. He finds her knotted little clit and presses, making tiny circles. She gasps into his mouth, moving against him, her brittle skin crumbling against his wrist, and after only a few seconds she cries out, shuddering. A dark mass of sour liquid flows into Rajah's mouth, running cold down his throat, and she slumps against him, still.

The rapture sizzles in triumph, and Rajah chokes, his pulse throbbing. He pushes her aside, trying to lift her gently to the ground, but her bones crack, her skin ruptures like thin ice on a pond. Her broken body sags to the ground, her head lolling, her amber wings splintering to dust.

A fist of pain thrusts into his guts. He doubles over, and black acid spews forth, searing his throat. He coughs and spits, his mouth burning. The poisoned soul puddle writhes on the dusty pavement, shrinking, hardening to a crisp black crust.

Rajah reaches blindly for the wall, the rough brick skinning his palm, and cool male laughter grates in his ears. Panting, he looks up into empty blue eyes.

"So it's true what they say. There really is a fae-murderer at large. I do believe I'm aroused." Sweat glistens on a pale brow, drops sparkling in dark curly hair. Crisp blue jeans, silver belt buckle, white shirt splashed with a few drops of blood.

Rajah spits, deliberately close to the man's shoes. Got a fucking nerve, slinging around the word *murderer* like he gives a shit. "She was already sick, DiLuca. Fuck off."

Dante leans his shoulder against the wall, casual, his cool smile revealing nothing. "I heard you were asking about me. No, I said, it can't be true. He hasn't finally come to his senses."

"Don't get your hopes up. I'm just looking for a guy you might know." Rajah straightens, catching his breath. Luna will surround himself with a false, glittering crowd of liars, con artists, and vacuous beauties to prove how superior he is. The kind of people Dante delights in baiting. He'd thought it worth a try.

Slim dark eyebrows lift. "I believe your last words to me

were an obscenity involving my mother and something about a cold day in hell." Dante leans closer, and Rajah can smell him, salty and strong with blood. "Well, it's warm in hell, Rajahni. Warm and excruciating. I've been there. I'm not going back. If you want my help, you'll earn it."

Sour guilt gnaws at Rajah's guts, alongside fear that Dante's been following him, has seen him with Jade. He's always thought he'll do anything, give anything. Any soul on earth. Any blood-stained bargain. Anything but thrall. But imagining his sweet Jade in Dante's hands has him twitching with rage and sorrow.

His Jade. It sounds good. "I told you before, I won't play your games."

"Even to spare your luscious little whore of a girlfriend?" Dante shows his teeth at last, sharp and gleaming in the street-light. "Fuck or feed, that's always the question."

Fury ignites, flickering like static along Rajah's already taut nerves. Worms of irritation wriggle in his skin that Dante always knows exactly how to taunt him, but Rajah can't let it lie. He steps closer, their shadows mingling like ink on broken concrete. "Listen to me, you sick prick. I don't want your blood, I don't want your screwed-up life, I sure as hell don't want you. And if you ever threaten her again—"

"You'll what?" Dante sniffs, testing the air, inhaling Rajah's scent, and licks fine scarlet lips. "Finger-fuck another fairy to death?"

Rajah's temper explodes, melting his common sense, and he slams Dante back into the wall with a vicious swipe of his gold-wrapped forearm. Dante hisses, reddish spit running on his teeth. His dark shape blurs like a spiteful shadow, and the next thing

Rajah knows, he's retching on all fours, his guts cramping and sharp grit digging into his palms.

Iron fingers yank his hair, dragging his head down, and wet vampire breath burns the back of his neck. Bloodstink sears, sickening. "Don't provoke me, slut-boy. I'll tear you in half and bathe in the mess you make."

Rajah chokes, kicking, but Dante's grip is fast. "Fine," he gasps, slick phlegm coating his lips. "I'll find him myself. Just leave her alone."

"We'll see." Dante's wet tongue flicks down along Rajah's throat, tasting, and in a rush of warm breeze he's gone, an empty space where his shadow lay.

Rajah spits and hauls himself up, twisting his neck with a crack. Dante's spit slides on his skin, and he rubs it off, wincing. He'll just have to find Luna himself. Stupid, to imagine DiLuca would soften at a decent request. And the thought of Dante stalking Jade with his warped and vengeful appetite churns sick disgust into Rajah's aching stomach. He wants to seek her out, warn her, protect her, keep her for himself.

But she's a big girl. She can take care of herself, and she never asked for his help. For all he knows, she's into that kind of thing. It's none of his business. Right?

He shakes his head, bile bright and sour in his mouth, and walks stiffly away into the dark.

8

The queue outside the club stretched down the street inside a black velvet rope, blue neon glowing overhead. Bats flapped in the streetlights. Cars cruised past, drivers hanging out the window to check out the scenery, and there was plenty to check out. Unseelie Court attracts the finest and freakiest Melbourne has to offer, and the line was a flashbulb forest of Lycra-bursting breasts, tanned female legs in fishnets, buffed boy muscles in rainbow colors, and the glitter, glass, and glamour of gorgeous fae. The hottest action, the coolest drugs, the most expensive drinks in town—the Court had it all.

The other thing about Unseelie Court is that on paper it was neutral territory. Owned by neither DiLuca nor Valenti, it wasn't off-limits to anyone, so either everyone was safe or everyone was fair game, depending on which way you looked at it.

I ducked under the rope, attracting some envious glares and a sneer or two. It wasn't actually true that you couldn't get in unless the bouncers thought you were hot. But it was a useful myth for management to foster, and in any case, I had a certain advantage when it came to first impressions.

I stalked up and smiled at the big black-shirted troll on the door, igniting my glamour with a crackle of static. "I'm expected."

He flushed darker green, his beady gaze fixed on my chest, the vein in his biceps pulsing. "Sure, honey. Go on in."

I winked. "Thanks, big guy."

He pushed the metal door open, releasing a warm breath of smoke-stained air from inside, and I hopped up the stairs and into the Court.

Music throbbed, dark art rock, the off-rhythmic beat vibrating in my lungs. The dim air flashed with colored lasers and sweet white smoke. Brilliant strobes stabbed at the shining floor, snapping shots of sinuous bodies moving to the rhythm, glittering off oiled muscles, piercings, lissome limbs, iridescent fairy wings. Along one side, the bar glowed, girls in tight black T-shirts serving colored spirits and sparkling fae-drenched wine.

Fragrant remnants of my rapture turned heads as I sidled through, and I didn't stop or look. I thought I looked okay, in a tight black halter dress that reached only halfway down my thighs and a pair of low heels—that is, if you liked skinny, no breasts, bony hips—but I knew they weren't really looking at me.

I could do with a fix, after once again so nearly screwing Rajah's brains out last night—didn't look like I'd learn the no-Rajah lesson any time soon, not the way he made me ache and burn and moisten—but my golden bangles buzzed, Kane's slick insistent whisper creeping in my heart. I wanted to scratch myself all over, the pestilent itch of thrall maddening me. It would only get worse until I found Dante DiLuca and did as Kane ordered me. I hankered to hunt down Detective Quinn, too, suck his hate-filled soul into my trap and begin this horrid freedom ritual, but as always, thrall overrode my own wants. My black lust for Quinn's soul would have to wait.

I shouldered through to the glowing glass-topped bar, impatient, and ordered a tequila shot, leaning my elbows on the warm surface. The place was pumping tonight, and as usual no one cared much what anyone did or who saw. On a couch in the dim corner, a peach-skinned water sprite with long tapered wings like a dragonfly's was going down on some moaning mortal girl, her leather skirt twisted around her waist. Her ankles were locked around his slender neck, his long pointed tongue lapping at her glistening sex, feeding. I wondered if she could see through his glamour to what he really looked like, like I could, or whether she just thought she was getting it from some hot mortal guy with an acrobatic tongue.

My drink came, and I tossed it back, the strong alcohol searing my throat. How should I approach this? How smart was this Dante anyway? Rapture didn't work too well on vampires. Perhaps a direct come-on was too overt. Then again, notorious vampire gangsters are still just men in the end: when it comes to thinking, it's dick first, fangs second, brain a distant third.

I ordered another drink, relaxing the curve of my back on the bar while I waited. Against the wall at the end, a half-naked shaven-headed guy with the body of an athlete took a panting blood fairy from behind, pumping into him with fingers clenched on his narrow hips. Sanguine sweat trickled on the fairy's naked back, his wings glowing crimson, wet dark hair falling in his face.

"Let me get that."

I watched them, fanning myself with my hand. Damn, it was hot in here. I realized someone had spoken. "Huh?"

"I said, let me get us a few drinks so I can work up the courage to hit on you." The voice was amused, unruffled, a touch of sexy continental Italian.

I turned, and a short rebuff died on my lips. He was cute. Sweet smile, neat dark curly hair just right for crushing, the most amazing indigo eyes. Expensive clothes, dark shirt and trousers on a tight, fit body. Great ass. A hint of fresh scent that warmed my belly. No, he was more than cute. Sexy, in a nonchalant *I might not be Rajah, but that doesn't mean I'm not hot* kind of way.

Guess my rapture must still be showing. I sighed, regret stinging. "Look, you don't understand. I'm not really . . . This isn't really me, okay? You'd be disappointed."

The bar girl delivered my shot. I gulped it, fire flowing into my blood, and he gestured for another. "I don't think so. I have a pretty good idea what to expect, and I still really want to hit on you, Jade."

I suddenly realized my bangles no longer clamored quite so loud, and I flushed, my nerves twisting. Jesus. Did I have to screw everything up?

He just held out his hand, rings glinting. "Dante."

I took it, hoping I could repair my mistake. He kissed my hand, just the briefest brush of warm lips before he released it, and faint warmth flooded my cheeks. From any other guy, the hand-kissing thing was trying way too hard. This Dante did it like he wasn't thinking, like I just deserved it. Smooth.

Sharp teeth glistened at the corners of his mouth, and I smiled in return, uneasy. At least he had manners. "I've heard of you."

"Really? What did you hear?" He leaned toward me, his forearm on the glass bar, and then he grinned, bashful, and dropped his gaze for a moment. "No, scratch that. Let's talk about you. What brings a girl like you to me?"

I laughed. They were all the fucking same, even charming ones like this. "Yeah, I bet you know a lot of 'girls like me,' right?"

"You mean touched with sorrow? Wasted? Unfulfilled?" His blue gaze didn't waver, and for an instant my insides lurched like I was falling, drowning in warm indigo bliss.

I shivered, pleasured, and tossed my head with a nonchalant laugh. "Wow. You work fast, Dante DiLuca."

"Only when there's no time to waste."

"Really. So what's your hurry this time?"

The bar girl brought the drinks, only it wasn't tequila but golden fairy wine, fragrant mist wisping from the tall-stemmed glasses. Dante slipped one into my hand, drawing closer to clink his glass against mine. "To get to know you before you get all dutiful on me and go back to Angelo."

His closeness warmed me, made me feel good. Not challenging, or frightening, or sexually threatening. Pleasant. Alluring. Moreish. The icy glass stung my lips as I sipped, giddy fae essence leaching from the wine onto my tongue, melting like snow. I vaguely recalled I was supposed to be pretending rebellion. "What makes you think duty means anything to me?"

He gave a tiny shrug, awareness of his movement washing over me in a rash of goose bumps. "Why else your sorrow?"

My heart swelled. Jesus. He knew all the right things to say. I'd felt more genuine interest from him in two minutes than I'd had from Ange in a month. And he smelled fantastic, something I couldn't place, berries or fruit or . . . something.

Concentrate, Jade. This guy's dangerous. You're supposed to be getting information out of him, not gazing into his pretty vampire eyes. Make him try harder, uncover himself, let something slip.

I shrugged, light and heady. "Maybe I had a lousy day, and I'm just looking for some fun."

Dante laughed, a glint of fascination brightening those wonderful eyes. "Five people dead last night in a street fight your idea of fun, Jade? Such charming chaos. I knew I'd like you."

The war had started, then. I hadn't heard about any fight last night, but Ange sure wasn't in a good mood when I left him. I shook my head and laughed, like it was all too complicated for little old me. "Don't blame me for your gang bullshit."

Dante leaned closer, confidential. "Why not? It wasn't me who accused Angelo of having a small dick. Nice play, by the way. Is it true?"

So he'd heard about my quiet conversation with Ange. Great. I drank again, trying to look uninterested, and obligingly my mind swayed and drifted loose. "You're giving me too much credit. The boys are restless, that's all. If they don't rip a few Di-Luca arms off every now and then, they get bored and start breaking things. Nothing to do with me."

"Don't bore me with modesty. Actions have consequences. If you want to play, you've got to be prepared to lose."

A pleasant buzz drifted in my head, whether from the wine or Dante I couldn't tell. He was right. I'd said my lines and taken my chances. Shit, if Ange wanted to get hormonal, so much the better. I sipped and swallowed, steadying myself against the bar. I felt warm, pliant, agreeable, and through a distant fog of apathy, it occurred to me that maybe Dante had put something in my drink.

He slipped his hand around my waist and tinkled the rim of his glass against mine again. "So do you want to play, Jade? Or are you just a spectator?"

For a moment I wanted to protest, to say, *What the fuck? How dare you?* but the truth was, I didn't mind at all. He made me feel safe, wanted, protected. That bottomless blue gaze flooded mine, his fingers harmless on my waist, and gratitude immersed me, overwhelming. "Umm . . . what did you have in mind?"

He put his glass aside to grip my chin, gentle but inexorable, as if he needed to make me look at him the way I was staring. "Be mine, Jade." His whisper was comforting, warm and sweet like honey, mesmeric. "Forget Angelo. Forget Rajahni Seth. Give yourself to me. You know you want to."

My lip trembled. I did want to. So help me, I did. Some distant warning of wrongness clamored deep in my skull, and my thrall bangles heated, urgent, but it seemed faint. Inconsequential. I ignored it.

Dante gave a soft smile and put a finger to his lips, as if to hush me. I watched, fascinated. Now, blood shone on his fingertip, rich dark blood with a coppery scent that made me faintly sick. Horror gripped me with sudden, burning claws as he brought the filth to my lips, but it was too late. I couldn't move.

Hot vampire blood ran into my mouth, coating my tongue with salt and rust. My will dissolved, and the first dark sexual glimmer sparkled in his eyes. "Come, Jade," he whispered, walking me backwards away from the light, "tell me everything."

Dante feeds her, just a single burning drop on the tip of his finger, and she sucks it down greedily, her eyes glazing, her tongue lapping and searching.

"More." Her whisper is husky and pleading, and Dante smiles softly as he walks her back into the dark. This is only the beginning of her addiction. She'll need more, crave it, beg him for it. But not now. There's too much to do, with her body limp and willing under his hands. She isn't really his type—too skinny, too many bones—but to take what belongs to Kane and Rajahni fucking Seth makes his teeth ache and his cock bend and strain.

He can't help but press his body against her, enjoying the pressure of her little breasts, the grind of her hips. Never mind the business with her and Angelo, so painfully transparent, it makes his head ache. She's so needy, so empty inside. For all her powers—and he can feel them, struggling deep within her like a starving beast—she's just a lonely, unloved little girl. Easy prey to a sly whisper of charm, a blink of hypnotic suggestion. And then a single drop of lust-drenched blood turns Kane's spy into Kane's weakness. It's all too easy.

He sniffs at her mouth, teasing himself with a taste of her bloodstained breath. "Tell me what Kane wants."

"Poisoned fae," she murmurs, distracted, her eyes rolling. "He wants to know why you killed them."

Irony stings Dante's throat, sour amusement stinging like bile. He laughs, and nips playfully at her chin, catching it in his teeth and shaking gently. "Fucking demons and their games. Well, it doesn't matter. Shall we get to know one another?"

Swiftly he folds her onto the soft white couch, her limbs still strong but pliable, persuadable. Her head falls back against the wall, listless, her forest-brown hair floating on her shoulders. "More," she pleads again, breathless, her lips shining.

The urge to take her throbs in his veins. Take her. Taste her. Skin breaking, flesh crushing in his mouth. Shake her throat in his teeth until the tendons rip and the burning blood runs scarlet . . .

But not yet. There's too much to be gained from waiting. With the blood already seeping poison into her wits, Jade will tell Kane exactly what Dante wants her to. And—the salty gravy on the feast—this willowy ingénue is in Rajahni's confidence. Rajahni is planning something. Plans can be spoiled. Jade's blood will speak to Dante, tell him the truth she won't dare whisper.

Dante snarls, hot saliva flowing over his teeth, dripping. Sweat dampens his warming skin. Her carcass is his. He'll suck blood from her throat, her ankle, the palm of her hand, the core of her dripping sex, tear her skin open wherever it pleases him and she'll beg for more while she's screaming.

But not yet.

He peels her skirt up to get his mind off her blood, pulling her legs apart and her skimpy black underwear away. Her sex smells fresh, clean, salty, blood pulsing gently in the vein inside her slit. He growls and drags his tongue over her, the hot slick fluid the next best thing. She presses against him, murmuring, offering herself, and he dives his tongue in, searching, tasting, feeling for that tempting pulse.

She writhes, her murmurs deepening to moans. Her clit hardens under his stroking, her flesh swelling. He burns to pierce it, twist it, feel the orgasmic gush of blood splashing the back of his throat. His cock swells in sympathy, urging him not to stop, to take everything, even if it's just to spite Rajahni. But if she comes, if he bites that tender little bud to feel it throb, he'll never stop until he consumes her.

He drags himself away, aching, his teeth stinging with thwarted anticipation. He cleans her up, wiping away the wetness, and pulls her skirt down before he leaves her to lurk in the darkness, stalking her with hungry eyes.

"What the fuck was that?" His skinny cousin Joey sidles up to him, black fedora tilted over one unblinking eye.

Dante grins. "That, Joseph, is an opportunity."

Joey's narrow hands morph to scaly black fins, and he snaps curved talons together like he's still picking Valenti blood from them. "Don't underestimate Kane."

"Kane underestimates me. Fuck him."

"I told you that demon queen's been sniffing after you. We should do the deal, get her on our side before—"

"I already told you no." Dante crunches bitter teeth, his own blood stinging his tongue. Let Angelo fawn to the demon court if he wants to. No demon queen will own the DiLucas, not while Dante lives. He searches the crowd for Jade and steps away to follow her.

Joey grips his arm with snakeskin webs, the stink of rotten leather rising. "That one's poison, Dante. You're crossing the line. Why don't you let me handle her?"

Jealousy burns Dante's blood, and he snaps aching fangs within an inch of Joey's black-scaled nose. "No. She's mine."

Joey squirms backwards, his neck elongating swiftly like a serpent's. "Okay, dude. Whatever you say. Just don't say I didn't warn you."

Dante wipes his sticky mouth. "You always warn me, Joseph. It's never stopped me before." And he grins over his shoulder as he slinks away.

9

I sat up with a start, blinking. Unseelie Court hove into view, crowded and smoky, lights glowing, music throbbing. My fingers found soft suede upholstery beneath me, my short skirt still in place, my purse mercifully unstolen. I didn't remember sitting down. Those tequilas must have really gone to my head. I'd vagued out for a minute. Beside me on the pale couch, two girls kissed, spit shining, one's hand planted firmly between the other's legs. Looked like I was lucky no one had jumped me while I sat here in a daze.

I swallowed, my mouth sour, and stood, my legs a little weak but not so unsteady as I'd feared. I wasn't wearing a watch, so I had no idea what time it was, but the club was still pumping. I had time to do what I'd come for. Detective Quinn would be here somewhere, and his soul was mine. My guts warmed as I thought about it, my pulse quickening, and rapture awoke, snarling within me like a caged tiger.

I weaved around the ring of sofas and shouldered out onto the floor, through glitter-eyed banshees and rainbow-haired fae, struggling to silence my simmering rapture so no one would notice me. Unseelie Court was owned and run by some faceless corporate conglomerate, but the DiLucas hung out here with predictable regularity and Quinn was up to his speed-shiny eyeballs in their graft. He'd be here, and he'd be in the shadows, watching, waiting for some simple, unsuspecting wallflower to try his shallow charm and rough good looks on.

I climbed metal steps to the shadowy mezzanine. Fae and mortal alike tumbled and giggled on the floor in a haze of chemical mirth, or slumped sluggish against steel chairs, hallucinating, fingers straining for things only they could see. A fat black spriggan waddled among them, stealing, her gnarled fingers crawling into their pockets or snapping off chains and shiny earrings.

I ventured deeper into the green neon darkness. Against a wall, a muscled vampire in leather nuzzled a naked, groaning mortal boy's cock, tongue and teeth trailing over the soft-veined skin inside his thigh. That little romance was going only one place.

Above the narrow doorway to the back room drug shop burned a single ultraviolet fluorescent, bathing smokers, lovers, and junkies in weird violet light—and against the doorframe leaned Killian Quinn, alone, tense and twitchy, a cigarette burning in his hand. I could only hope he hadn't already gotten off tonight.

He saw me, and his eyes focused, unmoving. I walked up, letting him survey me with that chilling half disgust, half lust that made me squirm. "Hello, Killian."

He eyed me sullenly, his gaze traveling over me, up, down. He didn't look very drunk, and his bloodshot brown eyes gleamed dully over a falling high. An almost imperceptible green mist hummed around him, shining sickly.

I glanced around in the dim purple glow. No one watched us. Excitement tightened my skin, and I tried to keep my breath steady. He knew what I was, of course, so I had to be careful with the rapture. Subtle. I shifted, crossing one foot over the other, letting my hair fall on my shoulder with an oh-so-gentle shimmer of persuasion. "Look, I wanted to say sorry about the other night. I didn't mean what I said. I just . . ." I let my head drop, hiding behind my lashes. A real blush burned my cheeks, but it wasn't from modesty. Lust for his soul writhed inside me, threatening to break loose and smother him.

"You just what?" He drew hard on his cigarette, the ash flaring bright, and held the smoke for a moment before releasing it away from me.

I wandered closer, twisting my fingers together like I was embarrassed, and breathed another tiny whiff of rapture into the air. No more, or he'd get suspicious. "You want the truth?"

His pale gaze slipped to my breasts, then back up to my face, and he swallowed and dragged again. "It'd make a change."

Watching him move was okay, actually, now he wasn't threatening to rape me with a .38. He was a big man, tense, barely contained. I could see his muscles straining beneath his shirt, sweat trickling along his throat, the dark aura shimmering like a second skin. A hot body, overwhelmingly male. Probably had a big cock. I'd bet he was quick and rough in bed, a good hard ride if you could keep up with him.

Pity he was such a woman-hating asshole that the thought of doing what I'd have to made my stomach turn, even as my yearning for his soul made me want it bad.

I slid my hand onto the wall beside him and shifted even closer. Now I could smell him, fresh sweat and scotch. I looked into his eyes, letting my gaze flicker downward. "Truth is, I don't know how to behave around you. What you did, the way you touched me . . . it got me thinking." I licked my lips to tempt him. "I've been thinking about it all weekend."

His aura rippled, thickening like murky green treacle. He turned toward me, his shoulder against the wall, his breath deep and husky. "Yeah?"

I didn't back off. "Every waking moment."

Insolently he stroked my hair with the hand holding the cigarette, smoke drifting. He wound a curl around his broad thumb, pulling until it hurt, watching me gasp. "You look hot, with that tight dress up around your sexy ass."

It was hard to smile at such an evil compliment. But I did, and my trapped rapture made me ache, hungry now as I traced a seductive finger down over his shirt to his belt buckle. "I wore it for you."

"Why?"

To make me look like the slut he thought I was. I moved my finger lower, teasing. "I wanted you to like me."

"Is that all you want?" His aura flared, bright, and he tossed his cigarette away and grabbed my hand, his eyes flashing. For a moment I thought he'd shove me away, and my heart skipped, but instead he wrenched my hand over and pressed it into his lap, his breath short.

Oh, yeah. He had a big cock, all right. Big and hard like a stone. Angry heat sizzled off him to burn my palm, his fingers digging into my wrist.

"God," I whispered, widening my eyes, "you're so . . . I never thought you'd let me . . ."

His eyes flashed, ravenous and filthy with hatred, that aura writhing bright and evil. My pulse thudded in my ears, triumphant. My thighs tingled, and rapture clawed within me, my body screaming with lust. I was wet, my flesh throbbing with anticipation. I wanted it, and I hated it as much as he did. If he rammed that hot, massive thing inside me, I'd come, and that would be too humiliating.

So I slipped to my knees on the iron floor, gazing raptly up at him, letting my lips part and shine. God, I was glad it was dark and no one else could see me. "Can I? Please, Killian. Let me."

Swiftly he opened his trousers, freeing his cock, the musky smell of aroused male sweat overpowering. He leaned on the wall over me, his head on his forearm, one hand twisting in my hair, tight so it hurt. "Suck me, bitch. If I see you pulling any rapture tricks, I'll break your fucking neck."

We'd see about that. Until you've experienced the rapture, you don't really understand how helpless you are.

His hateful aura swam around me, tingling my skin with delight and danger. I took him in both hands, triumph and dread swilling together in my guts. A drop of liquid already glistened on his tip, and I licked it off, hot and salty, making him sigh. I slipped the head into my mouth and closed my lips over it, letting the saliva flow to dilute his sweat, sliding one hand down to grip his heavy balls. They were tight, hot, the veins pulsing rapidly. It wouldn't be too long before his soul was mine.

I slid my lips down farther, grazing him with my teeth, applying suction with my tongue. He groaned and pressed forward. "Yeah. Take it. Take it all, you horny slut."

God, how romantic, you fucking shitball.

I moved down as far as I could—he really did have a huge cock—and pulled back, sucking. He watched me hotly as I worked him, and I watched him back, sensation building inside as rapture sizzled over my every nerve ending, stinging to be free. And then he made his last mistake.

He closed his eyes.

I sucked down as hard as I could, dizzy with triumph, and let the straining rapture gush out.

The air shimmered, crackling hot with seductive energy. His swirling aura fled like a storm cloud, screaming, but it was too late. He gave a gasping groan, and I swear his cock swelled even further as he pushed it deeper into my throat. "Oh, Jesus, Jade, you're good. So hot . . ." He crushed his fist in my hair, leaning over me, his heavy thighs straining, thrusting harder and faster until he let out a throaty cry and emptied himself into my mouth. His hot seed spurted into me, sweet and salty, and with it came his soul, a dark struggling mass of seething emotion that boiled down my throat like hot tar. I swallowed, and swallowed.

Color drained from his eyes, his face slackened, and it was done.

I let go and scrambled aside before he fell. I collapsed panting against the wall beside his lifeless body, wiping my wet mouth with the back of a shaking hand. Victory burned in my heart even as my stomach churned with what he'd left there. I had him. He was mine. One down, three to go.

But Jesus, I'd just sucked off Killian Quinn. That qualified as a new low, even by my standards.

Nausea clutched my guts, and I scrabbled in my purse for the brass soultrap bottle, popping the cork just in time. My stomach heaved, and the black mess spewed out stained with white froth. It poured into the bottle, plopping like hot black soup. Tears scorched my eyes, my face burning. My guts clenched again, and more foul liquid choked me, splashing out over my hand. I wiped my dripping lips, but still more came up, and by the time I finished spewing, I'd filled the bottle to the very top.

I spat one more time, jammed the cork back in and shoved the bubbling bottle back into my purse. My guts ached, my mouth sour and stinging with acid. I wiped my mouth again, black grime smearing with what was left of my lip gloss, and scrambled to my feet. No one watched me in the dark. No one saw anything. All too intoxicated to care. Even forensics wouldn't lead to me. They didn't have my DNA on file, and even if they did, going down on a guy isn't illegal. Without Quinn, the cops didn't believe in succubi. And Quinn was a speed addict, a hypertensive accident waiting to happen. I'd get away with it. I always did.

My knees buckled as I descended the mezzanine stairs, and I had to grip the railing to keep myself upright. My rapture crackled angrily, robbed of its treasure, and swollen glands ached between my legs. That was to be expected, but all wasn't well inside me. I could feel it. Part of Quinn's energy still festered within, not yet dead or consumed. It feels strange, another person's soul jabbering in my mind, terrified, thrashing against the bars of its new and eternal cage.

It occurred to me for the first time that I'd have to drink the whole thing again to be free. As well as three others, whoever they turned out to be. I'd be lucky if I didn't come out a raving lunatic.

I reached the bottom of the stairs and searched through the backlit smoke for the exit. My rapture gnashed frustrated teeth, making me squirm. I didn't want to feed it, not now. I wanted to go home and sleep it off.

"There you are. Are you okay? I've been looking for you." He hurried up to me, his dark blue eyes clouded with concern.

"What?" For a moment I had no idea who he was.

But he slipped his arm through mine, and warm contentment flowed over my skin, calming my restless heart. Dante. I remembered now. I was supposed to pretend to like him. Thing was, I did like him. I felt like I'd known him for years. We'd had such an interesting conversation . . . about what, exactly? How exactly did we meet?

I didn't remember, and for a moment confusion rippled my nerves, uncomfortable.

But I knew he'd charmed me, intrigued me, treated me like an equal instead of like an object. That was enough.

He smiled, handsome, and my heart fluttered. I dropped my gaze, sure I was blushing like a girl. "Oh, sure. I'm fine."

"Can I get you anything? You look hot." He paused, and swiped a hand over his dark curls, embarrassed. "Shit. Flushed. I mean you look flushed. I didn't mean it that way." He touched me shyly under the chin, his fingers warm and safe.

I liked how he spoke without thinking, said what was on his mind. How he didn't try to touch me sexually, even though I could see he wanted to. Though right now I wouldn't have minded if he had tried something. I wanted to forget about Quinn, get rid of the greasy shadow of his hands in my hair, his salty sweat on my lips.

I grabbed Dante's smooth hand, slipping my fingers into his. "I'm fine. Really."

"How about another drink?" He made as if to lead me away.

"How about you come here?" I pulled him back, closer, facing me, and his body brushed mine, warm. I'd let Quinn make me his whore. Dante could wash me clean again.

He smiled, his heartbeat quickening against me. "Okay. I'm here. What now?"

He felt lean, muscular, controlled. Not massive and frightening like Quinn. I needed Dante to touch me, needed to know I was still here, not in some crazy dreamland where I gave blow jobs to men I despised and cried in the arms of men I lusted after, where everything was turned upside down, where it was even possible I could be free.

"Well, generally you go like this." I slipped his hands around my waist. "And this." I slid my arms around his neck, crossing my wrists.

"Mmm." He dared to pull me closer, a sparkle in his eyes. "I'm beginning to get the idea."

"Thought you might." I wanted to look at his mouth, tempt him to kiss me, but I couldn't look away from those wonderful, bottomless indigo eyes. All my secrets seemed to swirl there, everything I'd ever wanted a man to understand. My head swam, my thoughts melting in warm, adoring enchantment. I wanted to tear my heart out and give it to him. Lie beneath him and whisper *I love you* while he stroked my face, played with my hair, made love to me.

He drifted his mouth closer, his teeth glinting. "Is this okay?"

I swallowed, cool fear coating my nerves even as my heart raced. Angelo and his vicious moods had kind of turned me off the whole vampire sex thing. I wanted so much for this to be different. "Umm . . ."

"Don't be afraid. I won't bleed you unless you ask me to." His warm whisper brushed my lips, and desire wrapped me like a hot velvet blanket.

Trepidation piqued my need as I remembered I'd just vomited, and probably wouldn't taste too good, given the contents. But Dante didn't seem to mind. He closed his eyes, his lips hovering so close to mine but not touching, waiting for me to go to him.

And I did. His mouth was soft, gentle, warm, tasting faintly metallic, and trust glowed in my veins along with smoldering desire. He wasn't like Angelo, crude and demanding and careless of my pleasure. I wanted to share myself with him. I tried to get him to part his lips, tracing my tongue over them, tempting, but he shook his head to break free, his fingers tightening on my hips. "You shouldn't."

"I don't care." I captured another kiss, sinking my fingers into his crisp curls, and he groaned and caught my tongue with his, tasting me, letting me in. He crushed me against him, his rapidly hardening cock pressing into my belly, and ravished me with his tongue, testing every corner of my mouth. My sex ached, wet and burning, not just because he turned me on but also because I trusted him. I wanted him to touch me, slide his fingers into me, rub me and make me come. Reckless, I flicked my tongue along the crisp edges of his front teeth, daring him, daring myself. I brushed the razor point of his fang, my tongue stinging. He gasped into the kiss, and sensation ripped into me, not agonizing or frightening but glorious. I pressed the tip of my tongue harder, and the delicate skin broke, his fang piercing me like a sweet knife. The taint of coppery blood twinged my tongue, but not for long.

Dante's body flushed, sudden heat radiating. His arms tensed around me, and I could feel him holding back, trying not to crush me. Slowly, delicately, he sucked on my tongue, the salty burst of blood warm and gentle, flowing into him. The intimacy overwhelmed me like a dark flood, and I longed to be closer. The barrier of clothing between us maddened me. I imagined us kissing like this but naked, my thighs gripping his on his lap, his sensitive vampire cock buried deep in my flesh.

Such erotic thoughts about a man I'd just met warmed me, and I flexed my tongue, giving him more. I could have released my rapture, tasted his energy, consumed some, but I didn't. I wanted to be with him, not use him. If Dante wanted my blood like this—not a demand but a desire, not a rape but a shared pleasure— he could have it.

Dante swallowed, groaning, and the flesh between my legs swelled, painful. Surely, this was how thrall ended. Not in the rotting skeletal agony of energy starvation or flickering out after a thousand horrible, never-ending years, but in the dark, damning passion of a vampire's kiss. Life bleeding out, red and burning, not lost on the wind but savored, relished, consumed. The ultimate orgasm, death.

Hot tension gripped me, my thighs trembling with longing, and I whimpered.

A different, hotter hand touched the back of my shoulder, startling me out of my spell, and I jerked back.

"Jade, I've been . . . oh. Shit. Sorry." The touch snatched away, but the fine scent of cardamom drifted, laden with memory.

I swallowed, my mind overflowing with sudden confusion, and I couldn't help turning my head.

Rajah stared at me, black hair drifting free, a crease deepening between his fine dark brows. He looked mouthwatering as usual, in a loose white shirt that glowed in the nightclub lights and soft blue jeans that caressed every firm curve. He sucked on that luscious bottom lip, his gaze flickering away. He looked mystified. Hurt. Confused.

Jesus. What was I doing? My hand drifted to my throat in embarrassment, and I shifted away.

But Dante smiled softly, his tongue brushing the tips of his teeth. "Always late to the party, Rajahni."

Rajah's gold-flecked eyes glinted with rage. "I'm sorry about his manners, Jade. If this is about you and me, DiLuca, leave her out of it."

Suspicion hardened like a hot stone in my guts. I opened my mouth to ask, but Dante touched my hand, making me look at him, his ultra-blue eyes flashing a warning. With a sick stomach I remembered how Rajah had seduced me, first taking advantage of my rapture and then with some horrid attempt at empathy, fooling me into thinking he cared about me when all the time he only wanted sex. God, the way I'd behaved with him. Like the slut he'd treated me as, like they all said I was. A tear misted my eye, and I blinked it away.

Dante squeezed my hand, and I didn't pull away. He slipped his arm back around my waist, protective, and glared coolly at Rajah. "Always so arrogant, assuming everything's about you. Miss Jade and I are having a private conversation. I don't remember either of us inviting you. Any questions?"

"Just one." Rajah focused on me, his gaze dark and candid. "Are you sure you know what you're doing?"

Rajah was dangerous. Dante was safe. I looked Rajah in the

eyes, uncomfortable warmth swelling in my belly. Damn, he had beautiful eyes, the bastard. I swallowed. "Perfectly sure, thanks."

Pain swirled for a moment, and then his eyes glassed over, hard. "Fine. Sorry to bother you." He walked away, biting his pretty lip. I watched him go, my eyes stinging.

Dante touched my chin, breaking my gaze away. "Are you okay?"

Looking at him, I felt better already. I smiled. "Sure. It's nothing. What is it with you and him, anyway?"

He shrugged faintly. "Vampire fixation, I guess. He wants it pretty bad. He's got quite a temper. You should be careful."

Doubt slid a cold finger up my spine. Rajah lied to me about not wanting immortality, then. "What do you mean? He'd never hurt me."

"Don't be too sure." He hesitated, like he didn't want to say more. "I saw him last night, with a fae girl. He killed her, Jade. Just like that. I tried to help her, but . . ."

Nausea roiled. I'd seen Rajah last night, and he certainly hadn't lacked for energy. Sex had poured off him in waves. He hadn't needed to consume any.

I'd turned him down, and he'd taken out his anger on some poor fairy.

"Don't let him bother you. He's just jealous of me. And he should be, tonight." Dante brushed my hair from my shoulder, a smile curling his lips. "How about that drink? You can tell me more."

"Okay." I smiled back. I couldn't remember what I'd been telling him, but it didn't matter.

He slipped his hand into mine, and we walked up to the bar. He whispered to the bar girl, and she poured thick ruby-red wine that stained the inside of the glass. I lifted it to my nose, a dark, fruity, musky smell rising.

Dante's eyes glinted. "Drink up."

Jade puts the glass to her lips, and Dante watches greedily as she sips, blood staining her mouth. She's already senseless, her eyes distant and euphoric like a fae junkie's. Her slender throat bobs as she swallows, one gulp, then another. His pulse flows quicker, anticipation whetting his taste buds.

Such a seductress, charming that fucking idiot Quinn. She really knew how to suck a man, too. He'd watched transfixed as she'd taken Quinn to the hilt, his own cock full and aching in sympathy. No wonder Rajahni wants her.

Well, Rajahni can't have her.

Dante takes the empty glass from Jade's fingers and slips his arm around her thin waist, leading her away. He's never seen any reason to play by the rules, never laid stock in dusty centuries-old clan traditions. Follow the rules, get screwed by the rules. He learned that with emphatic force as a boy, the day Mussolini marched the Blackshirts into Calabria to shoot and kick the shit out of hundreds of the people who'd voted the fucker into office in the first place. And he'd sucked up another powerful dose when the Reds strung the aging Il Duce up from a bloody meat hook in Milan. The spoils go to the strong, not the nice or careful. Stop kicking for an instant, and you'll sink.

Dante is young, delirious on his power, not old and stale like Angelo Valenti, or Sal DiLuca, Dante's predecessor. Who squealed like a squashed rat as he bled to death, thank you very much, a sound Dante still remembers in hot blood-soaked dreams. He always swore he'd bathe in Sal's blood, and a mighty fine bath it was. He orgasmed as he held the struggling old man down, hard and long and breathtaking, burning blood and come splashing his skin. He's not afraid of that, doesn't shirk from what it says about him. Hell, if it feels good, bring it on. That's what power's for.

Fuck 'em if they can't take it. And fuck the demon lords, too. All jealous of his freedom. Dante's got no time for useless courtesies or ancient clan bullshit about territory and suitable mates. And now he's on his own in the new world, with no crusty elders controlling his every move.

So let the world drown in blood and chaos, and all these craven liars who pretend they're so goddamn civilized will eat each other alive to stay afloat. Let them sink deeper into brutality with every dying thrash, and Dante and those he deems worthy will watch and laugh. His own dark hell on earth, so much tastier and more fascinating than the one below.

Pity Jade won't like to watch. He's rather enjoying her, even if it's just to spite Rajahni. He offered Rajah everything once, and Rajah turned him down, saying he didn't want to live forever. Laughing at the very idea. No one laughs at Dante DiLuca and stays happy. Dante will fucking well make sure the smug bastard lives every last excruciating moment of his thousand years with Kane. Just thinking about it makes him hard and ready.

He pulls Jade onto the couch with him, distant strobe lights flickering in drifting white smoke. Her gaze smolders as he tells her silently what he wants her to do, the blood connection between them crackling in the stale air. As she stretches onto her back and slides her fingers between her legs to open herself for him, he smiles. Vampire blood, the date rape drug from hell.

He rips her panties away, opens his trousers, and plunges

inside her. She's tighter than he expects, coating him like hot honey, and he has to push hard to enter her fully. She cries out, weak, but thanks to the blood, her rapture is stunned and useless. He nuzzles her breast through her soft dress as he thrusts, tugging the flowering nipple with his front teeth, saliva running from his mouth to soak her. She moans, her muscles rippling around him, and he grins, curiosity a pleasant throb in his balls. "So who are you thinking of, Jade, now I'm fucking you?"

"You," comes the answer, faint. "Rajah. Killian."

"All three? Ambitious. Still, you won't remember any of this, so go right ahead." He laughs, his urgent breath wetting her dress more. "Now tell me what you really want from me."

She shudders, resisting, her head jerking from side to side. "Kane—"

"Not Kane. You." He likes it when she fights. "And don't tell me you want to be loved. No one loves hell's whore. Believe me, I know." He captures her mouth, driving in his tongue, and lets blood-tinged saliva flow, another sly taste of persuasion. "What is there without love, Jade? Tell me."

She sighs, sensual, tilting her hips against him to slide him deeper, and the words he's waiting for slip at last from her shining lips. "I want to die."

Desire thickens his blood, and a growl wells up in his throat. "Say that again."

"Kill me."

His cock swells, painful. He could kill her, too. Vampire blood can erase her fragile immortality, wash it away like dirt whether she knows it or not. But he won't grant her wish, not yet. Not until it suits him, and she begs him properly. But he can't wait any longer to taste her, and he drags the shoulder seam of her halter dress inward, revealing one small white breast with a hard, puckered nipple.

"You know this'll hurt. Don't scream." He stretches his jaws, snarling, and with a growl of hungry desire he fastens his mouth over the peak and sinks his teeth in deep.

Blood, boiling and glorious, flowing over his tongue, rich with her salty stink. She moans and writhes. He sucks, filling his mouth. He drives deep into her as he swallows, but the pleasure of rapidly nearing orgasm is pale compared to this.

Her lifeblood pumping into him, her soft skin trembling in his mouth, the dirty, gritty taste of pain against the hardness of her nipple yearning for more sensation. Complete submission, and with it come her thoughts, fragments of memory, ecstasy, fear. Whispers of scent and sensation, a thousand different men, the succulent brush of lips, the slick taste of skin and pressure of teeth, hot hardness filling her, hurting her, pleasuring her, all together in a heady rush of life. And most recently, the luxuriant fall of midnight hair, slick swollen lips teasing hers, the enthralling scent of spice.

Jealousy burns Dante like acid, overboiling his desire, but triumph steals his breath away. He can see into her mind. He knows what Rajahni's up to, wanting out from Kane's thrall. And he knows exactly how to fuck it up.

Hot tension grips his balls, explodes along his cock. Desperate, he sucks hard and long, one last delicious mouthful, and comes with a deep groan, jerking into her.

He laughs as aftershocks steal his breath. Come inside a succubus. Not many men get to do that and live. But she can't steal a vampire's soul, at least not with rapture. He licks the last of her blood away and pulls her damp dress back to cover the seeping wound on her breast. She didn't come, and her flesh twitches in protest as he withdraws.

He crawls up to her face, his breath hot and coppery, wetting her ear. "Sorry, darlin'. Maybe next time. Now listen carefully, and I'll tell you how you can find Vorenus Luna."

10

I pushed up on my elbows in my sweaty bed, squinting at the afternoon sun pouring in the open venetians. Dust motes swirled, glinting, and my body sweated and burned in the sun-cooked bedroom air. Jesus. What time was it?

The digital clock on the bedside table said 3:25. I groaned and flopped the damp sheet aside.

I dragged myself up to the bathroom, a throbbing ache in my temples. My stomach hurt. I leaned on the wall next to the toilet, fumbling knotted hair from my face, and waited for the nausea. I was naked, sweat running in rivulets over me, and I smelled like a seldom-cleaned distillery where someone had died. My wrists felt swollen, my thrall bangles tight. I had no idea how I'd gotten home. At least the other half of my bed was empty.

My stomach churned at last, and I bent lower and let the spew heave out into the bowl, stinking and stringed with scarlet. I wiped my mouth with a hot sticky hand, tasting acid and copper. God knew what I'd drunk last night.

I turned the shower on and stumbled under, grateful for the cold water soothing my skin and running through my hair, blissfully icy on my pulsing scalp. I rinsed sweat from my limbs, gingerly lathering soap everywhere. I rubbed absently at a tender bruise on my breast I didn't recall getting. Not only did I not remember getting home, I didn't remember much at all, beyond tramming it to Unseelie Court, a few tequilas, seeing Killian Quinn. . . .

Goose bumps constricted my skin, and I snapped upright, the soap slipping from my fingers to bang against the cracked tiles. Quinn. Jesus.

I sprinted into the lounge, not minding about a towel. Water sprayed from my soaked hair as I scrabbled on the floor for my purse and rummaged inside. My heart stopped as I felt nothing—but then my fingers closed around the cool brass neck of the bottle, and I drew it out, my pulse thudding. I held it up before my eyes, water dripping, and something heavy inside *shifted,* like it wasn't happy to be there. If I listened hard, I could hear a hissing whisper of fury.

The message tone on my phone squeaked, and automatically I fished it out, the soultrap still seething in my other hand. A mobile number I didn't recognize. I pressed View.

Dont 4get 2nite eureka tower cy@9 xx Dante.

Pleasant memories stirred. He'd invited me with him to a party, with a handsome blush when I teased him by asking if it was a date.

Dante DiLuca, the most feared man in Melbourne, blushing for me.

I wanted it to be a date. We'd barely kissed—I remembered that now, his baffling blue eyes, the way he'd savored my taste, and my spine prickled, pleasant—but I felt he knew me better than almost anyone I'd ever met. I wanted to bask in his attention, even if it only lasted for a while, until he found out I was Kane's spy and chewed my throat out. Was that so wrong?

Rajah certainly thought so. I recalled the distant look in his gold-flecked eyes when he'd seen Dante and me, the tight lines around his perfect mouth. Hurt. Confused. Sick. Like I'd betrayed him.

Well, I hadn't.

My heart somersaulted, and I swallowed firmly on guilt and regret. There was nothing to betray. Rajah didn't own me. He had no right to control me, just because we'd kissed. Just because we'd burned for each other, breathless and sore with desire. Just because if I thought about it I could still feel Rajah against me now, his glorious scent wrapping me, filling my senses, making me long for his smile, his cheeky laugh, the warm feeling of his hand in mine.

The doorbell clanged, jagged.

Absently I put the phone and the soultrap on the table, and twisted the dead bolt before I remembered I'd just stepped out of the shower.

Shit.

My skin burned all over again. I poked my dripping head into the gap, trying to keep the door closed as far as possible and hoping to hell this wasn't anyone I knew. The door stuck to my wet breasts, uncomfortable.

A teenager in a blue cap stared at me, blond hair sticking out. "Jade?"

"Yeah. What?" Only then did I notice what he carried, and my breath caught.

"These are for you." He handed me the basket, the heady scent of roses rolling over me like a wave.

A couple of dozen scarlet blooms, curling petals still dotted with water drops, green foliage shining. No one had sent me flowers for at least a hundred years. Apart from Nyx's daisy chains, if you counted those. I inhaled, dizzy, and plucked off the note, the door still awkward as my shield.

Still working up the courage. D.

A foolish lump swelled in my throat, and my eyes stung. God, I'm so pathetic. A little romance and I'm anyone's.

"Is everything okay, miss?" The delivery kid's gaze darted to my bare shoulder and away a few times.

I swallowed, and smiled despite my aching head. "Yeah. Everything's fine. Thank you."

I pushed the door shut and put the flowers on the table, burying my face in velvety petals. My nose tingled with sweet fragrance. Glorious. A man who didn't think I was easy. Who thought he had to work for me. Someone should bottle this guy . . . Okay, bad joke.

I laughed, but my gaze kept drifting to the soultrap, and the pleasure soured a little. What would happen if I earned my freedom? Lost my immortality? Just as things were starting to look up.

I glanced at Rajah's phone number, still scrawled in the thickening dust on the opposite side of the glass. *Primordium.* For once, ten years of the Bible shoved down my throat in Latin came in handy. The origin, the beginning. But whose origin? The beginning to what? I was even more mystified by the others, *terminus* and *animus*. The last one especially was a lousy clue. Soul. I mean, duh. And *terminus*, the dividing line. Who was that supposed to mean?

And even if I figured that out, what was I supposed to do? Drink Quinn's soul now? Or wait until I'd trapped all four and guzzle them all at once? I was feeling drained, drawn, tired, even apart from my hangover. Did it matter if I fed on other souls in between? And what if Kane found out? Rajah had earned a split lip, but he'd kept Nino's soul. How had he done that?

Frustration and embarrassment stirred a prickly cocktail in my queasy stomach. There was too much I didn't know, and I had only one chance. I couldn't let my pride screw it up.

My fingers strangely clumsy, I picked up the phone, entered the digits, and pressed Call.

It rang three times, four, five. Blessed relief washed over me. It'd go through to voice mail, and I wouldn't have to talk to him.

But then he picked up, and my tender abdomen clenched. I heard a muffled clunk while he switched the phone from hand to hand. "Yeah. Rajah."

His voice made me think of rogan josh, spicy and mouth-watering. Great. I was talking to him naked. I swallowed, my mouth crusty. "Umm . . . it's me. Hi."

"Jade? Are you all right?"

The animated concern in his tone made me bristle. "Of course. Why wouldn't I be?"

"No reason. Just after last night, I thought—"

"Well, don't think, okay? I'm fine." Irritation at his posses-siveness crawled on my naked skin, and I stalked into the bed-room, scraping damp hair from my face.

"Hey, you rang me. If you've got nothing to—"

"Okay, I'm sorry, all right?" I realized that he now had my number, and cursed that I hadn't thought to call him from a public phone. "Listen, I need to talk to you. About this . . . thing you told me about. You know."

"Sure." He hesitated, like he swallowed or bit his lip. Or ran his tongue over them. Making them wet. *Jesus, don't think about his lips.* "I'm at home. You want to come over?"

"What, now?" More bumps shivered my skin, my bare nipples tight. But it wasn't such a dumb idea. I'd probably be safe from my lustful fixation with him today. Between the gut ache, the headache, and fatigue—the physical kind—I'd never felt less like having sex. "Okay. Where is it?"

11

His address was the top floor of a refurbished apartment block at the casino end of Spencer Street, where plane trees blew lazily in the summer breeze and the distant sound of trains rumbled. I hopped off the tram at about five, the hot sun turning golden and the streets starting to fill with tired, sweaty commuters dressed in business suits far too warm for the weather, coats tossed over their shoulders and damp patches showing on their shirts and blouses.

The glass security door was unlocked. A sleek fountain trickled in the marble-tiled foyer, and the silent lift gleamed inside with chrome and mirrors. I pressed the button for five, trying not to look at my reflection. I'd put on a thin white cotton skirt and sleeveless top, and left my hair out to dry. It curled around my shoulders, wild. I wished I'd brought something to tie it back with, or at least a brush, but could find neither in my purse. I combed my fingers through it uselessly, just making more knots.

What did I care, anyway? Right? I was going out with Dante tonight. I'd dress to kill for that. For someone who gave a shit.

Daylight shone in a broad skylight in the top-floor lobby, glistening on slate floor tiles and pale clay-rendered walls. Air-conditioning hummed softly, the air cool and refreshing. It was a change from my place, where the summer sun baked everything to boiling in five minutes flat. Especially if you crashed until three in the afternoon and didn't close the blinds.

When he opened the door, he was wearing those same faded black jeans he'd worn the night I met him, soft as a baby mouse's skin and as touchable. Not much left for the imagination there. Top button undone. A glimpse of smooth brown hips. I'd bet no underwear.

I flushed, my guts warm. Honestly. There's only so much a girl can take. At least he had a shirt on this time.

"Come in." He turned immediately. Was he avoiding looking at me? Maybe I'd embarrassed him by staring. I'd sure as hell embarrassed myself.

I followed him down a short carpeted hallway into the living room, where the sun filtered through half-closed mini venetians over the broad windows. A sweet, smoky scent drifted, like incense or an oil burner. Books stacked a dozen high on his low glass dining table, and above it hung a frieze of the Hindu god Shiva, multiple arms gesturing. The couch lay sprawled in front of the plasma TV, and a console game showed in pause, some first-person shooter set in a swamp, green slime dripping into swirling gray water littered with alien bodies. Looked like he was kicking ass. I smiled. "Busy, huh."

He shrugged, sheepish, clearing magazines off the couch. "Can't work all the time. Umm . . . can I get you a drink?"

I wanted something to do with my hands, but I didn't know what to ask for. I hadn't seen him drink alcohol. I glanced over the marble island bench and noticed an ice tap in the door of his stainless fridge. "Water?"

"Sure. Have a seat."

I sat on the cool cushions, velvet fluffy under my fingers. He returned with two tall iced water glasses and handed me one, his gaze drifting away as he realized he'd have to sit next to me. He settled finally a few feet away, silent.

I sipped, the icy water stinging my tongue, aware that we were avoiding each other's eyes. This was ridiculous. I put my glass aside. "I wanted to—"

"Jade, I—"

We'd both spoken at once, and he grinned, bashful. "You first."

I licked my lips, dry despite the water. "I wanted to say sorry for snapping at you last night. I don't really remember, but—"

"You've nothing to apologize for. It was entirely my fault." He took a deep swallow of his water, his long hand tense and pale on the glass, fingertips slipping.

I tried again. "No, really. I was rude, you surprised me, I didn't mean to—"

"You did mean to, and I deserved it. My question was totally inappropriate. It's none of my business what you do, and it's I who should apologize."

Well, bullshit. He was so obviously lying, the way his fingers shook and whitened, his gaze sliding all over the place but not on me, the ever-so-slight quiver of tension in those strokable thighs. So obviously repeating what he thought I'd want him to say.

He probably thought I'd slept with Dante already. Sorrow and anger tightened my jaw as I remembered how I'd thought Rajah understood me, wanted to know me. Jesus. I'd been so stupid. He might be an incubus in thrall, but he was still a man like all the rest, focused on his own need and not giving a stuff for anyone else's. Why didn't he just say, *You're a cock-teasing slut, Jade,* and be done with it?

I forced a smile, sure I looked as insincere as he did. "Sure. Fine. Forget it."

He swallowed the last of his water, ice clinking, and set his glass on the table with a clunk. "Fine. So what did you want to talk about?"

Unease tickled my spine, and I couldn't help glancing over my shoulder. I knew Kane couldn't hear me, but I dropped my voice to a whisper anyway. "I got one. *Odium.*"

I heard Rajah catch his breath, and he looked at me in spite of himself, a little smile turning his lips. "No way. Already?" He inched closer on the couch, cheerfully conspiratorial. "When? Who was it?"

I swallowed. "Last night. Before you . . . before I saw you. It's a guy I know, a cop. He's always hated me."

"You don't mean our charming friend Quinn?" Sultry admiration sparked in his golden-brown eyes, and the tip of his tongue touched his teeth, delicate. "Well. I'm impressed."

By what? My audacity? My technique? My willingness to humiliate myself with men I despised? "It's at home. I didn't know what to do now. Do I keep it, or what?"

He nodded, animated. "I think so. I mean, I have no idea, but it makes sense, right? Remember the day you got these?" He brushed his finger across my thrall bangles, just for a moment before pulling away, his lips tightening.

I felt it deep under my skin, even though he hadn't touched me, and I squirmed. Maybe I'd been wrong about the hangover.

But I did remember the day of my thrall. Sick terror, flowing over me like choking black mud, golden manacles pinning my fists against the floor, hot stone rough beneath my naked back. Burning demon blood, sticky on my lips, coating my tongue. Kane's sweet mouth on mine, hot, ravenous; distant flames crackling, scarlet sunlight glaring in my eyes, the crisp ashen stink of hell. My soul screaming, ripping from me in a thick acid rainbow like vomit, flooding into him.

For an instant, I died, agonizing. Then it slammed back into me, writhing in the grip of a twisting, gnashing thing that ripped and tore its way into my heart, burrowing deep. A fragment of Kane, inside me forever. The chains popped free, and the golden bracelets shrank onto my wrists, immovable. And then Kane's breathless *thank you,* the hesitant brush of his fingers in my hair.

I nodded slowly. To break the thrall—to excise that vicious, whispering Kane-parasite for good—one soul at a time would never be enough. All four at once . . . Well, that might be a start. Excitement thrilled in my veins, warm. "So what now? What does *primordium* mean?"

"It means 'origin.'"

"I know that. I mean, what origin? Whose origin?"

"I've thought about that. *Primordium,* 'origin.' *Terminus,* 'the line that separates.' Where you start, where you finish. It's your origin, Jade. The one who made you what you are."

"Kane?" My vision blurred for an instant, overcome with confusion. "Kane doesn't have a soul. How does that work?"

"Not Kane. Kane does what he does. You can't blame him."

Realization slammed into my chest, sucking my breath away.

Vorenus Luna, my golden-haired god. An immortal sorcerer, bound to Kane with blood. My blood.

I imagined it. Luna's misbegotten soul, sparkling with power and grace, free of the encumbrance of conscience. And Quinn's vile hatred, thrashing and spitting vitriol. Mixed up, furious, lashing out. Maybe I did have a chance against Kane's nasty little cancer.

Rapture shimmered in my flesh just thinking about it, and I gasped, energy sizzling all the way to my fingertips. So much for not wanting to think about sex. The energy felt cooler than normal, weak and sputtering with my fatigue, but it didn't stop me. Immediately I was hyperconscious of Rajah, just a foot away, his warm lean body, the sound of his breath past his lips, the wonderful fragrance drifting from his skin. The way his hair just brushed his shoulders, soft and sleek. The hard muscles of his thighs, moving beneath those second-skin jeans. "But . . . he's . . . he could be anywhere. I can't possibly . . ."

Rajah's gaze slipped, and he tucked his hands beneath his thighs, shifting. "You might be surprised. Things happen when they happen for a reason. Why do you think these auras burn now?"

My nerves twitched. I wanted to squirm, but I didn't want to leave a mess on his couch. I wanted to grab that silky hair and drag his mouth onto mine, and it wasn't only the rapture drawing my gaze to his lips. I coughed, struggling to keep my mind where it should be. "You don't mean because they're all here?"

"Precisely." His gaze met mine, dark and driven, and I couldn't help but stare, enraptured in more ways than one. My pulse thudded, my flesh aching and thick, but my heart ached, too, and for a moment I wished that none of this were between us. Not thrall, not rapture, not Dante, not the vengeful search for corrupt and hideous souls to drink. Just a man and a woman who liked each other. He'd said he wanted a mortal life. Was this what he had in mind?

Then he let his beautiful head fall back on the couch and laughed. "Oh, Jade. It's so near. It's just a matter of searching. Asking around. We'll find them, both of us."

I laughed too, grateful for the release in tension, though my body still screamed at me to act, move, touch, take. "Asking around? You're so cute. You might have missed it, Rajah, but this is the twenty-first century. Ever hear of the Internet? It's quite popular."

He shrugged, sheepish. "I'm not so good with computers."

"You have an Xbox and the world's biggest TV but not the Net? Shame on you."

"I have it. I buy stuff on it. I just don't get the rest of it. What am I going to do, blog about thrall and luring souls to hell? That'd be a hit." He knelt to rescue his laptop from beneath a pile of books on the floor and handed it to me. "Be my guest."

I took it, careful not to let his fingers brush mine.

He sat again, closer so he could see the screen, resting his arm on the couch behind me so it almost—but not quite—touched my shoulders. "Do you mind?"

Oh, I minded. That he was too close. That he wasn't closer, on me, all over me. That he wasn't Dante. That I didn't want him to be.

"Of course not." I tugged my skirt straighter, flushing, and flipped the shiny white laptop open. The wallpaper showed the Taj Mahal, white marble glowing golden in the sunset, and the desktop was littered with e-books.

If I knew anything about Vorenus Luna, it was that he craved the limelight. He wore his vanity like a prize. If he was in town, everyone who was anyone would know about it.

Rajah shifted next to me, cautious. "You really think you can find him with this thing?"

"Watch and weep." I launched the browser and typed *www. myspace.com*.

In five minutes, I had him.

I stared at the pictures, my stomach writhing. He was calling himself Luna, just one word like Beyoncé or Madonna, but he hadn't changed a bit. Gorgeous golden hair flowing, face like an exotic catwalk model, body copied from a Michelangelo. Dressed like an S&M rock star, black velvet, leather and lace, studs and diamonds and bright steel. Dating movie stars, models, celebrities. Here he was in black tie at some dreadful television awards ceremony, showing that stunning smile for the camera, an up-and-coming starlet clinging to his arm.

And he'd lived in Melbourne these last few months, in the penthouse of a high-rise city tower. His perfect face no doubt scattered through those glossy gossip magazines Kane adored so much. Just went to prove that I didn't get out enough.

My rapture had evaporated, but my blood throbbed, sick and hot, revitalizing my faded headache. He was . . . decorative. Dazzling. Spectacular. I wanted to smash my fist through the screen, break him into glassy shards. The idea of touching him made me want to rip off my skin to get rid of his filth. Sucking out his soul would be worse than anything I'd done with Quinn. Whatever his grotesque faults, at least Killian was honest. Luna was a seething asp's nest of lies with beauty's face. I'd vomit buckets before I was done with him.

This wasn't going to be easy.

Scrolling down the page, I saw from the inane comments that he was throwing a party. At his place, tonight. Invitation only, but my rapture could take care of that, no problem.

I looked at the address. Eureka Tower, Riverside Quay.

My heart skipped as I remembered Dante's message. I wouldn't have to glamour my way in. I already had an invitation. Coincidence?

I looked away, discomfort coiling inside, and realized I hadn't asked Rajah the obvious question. "So have you found yours?"

He stared at the screen, chewing his bottom lip absently. "I'm sorry, what?"

"*Primordium*. Have you found them?"

He grimaced and stood, shoving his long hands into his pockets and walking away from me, turning only when he reached the window. "I have a confession to make."

His dark expression sent a shiver of apprehension along my skin, and I smiled uneasily, trying to shake it off with a joke. "That you're in a hot fog of lust for me? Yeah, look, I figured that one. . . . Damn it, Rajah, you're scaring me. What is it?"

He laughed, helpless, shaking his dark head. "This is so unfair. Remember the student I told you about? The one who traded me to Kane?"

Black dismay stiffened me. I realized I knew what he was going to say, and horror clawed up my throat, nearly choking me. "You're joking."

"Afraid not." His gaze flicked to the screen on my lap, where Luna gleamed out at me, beautiful and horrible.

I swallowed, my mouth dry. "How long have you known?"

He didn't look at me. "Since the other night. When you told me how you ended up in thrall."

Anger burst into my blood, sizzling with rapture to make a seething mess of fury. I pushed the computer aside and bounced up, my nerves jerking. "And when were you going to tell me? When you'd already stolen his soul behind my back?"

"I'm telling you now, aren't I? I'm sorry. I didn't know what to do." He walked closer, reaching out a hesitant hand.

I shook him off. Disappointment soured my rage, and I berated myself for my stupid wishful thinking. Everything Dante had told me about him was true. "Don't touch me. I can't believe you lied to me like that."

He frowned, his mouth tight. "I never lied to you—"

"You omitted, then. Whatever, okay? It's the same fucking thing."

His golden-brown eyes stormed, dark. "Well, shit, Jade, you were pretty fucking preoccupied last time I saw you, what with your tongue down Dante's throat and all. Not like I had a chance to mention it."

Fury made me laugh, short and dry. "Oh, so now we get to it. You're jealous."

Hurt clouded his face. "Of course I'm jealous. He's a gold-plated asshole. I thought you were smarter."

Heat burned up my body, scorching my cheeks. "No, you thought I was easier. Well, I'm not easy, okay?"

"I never thought that. But I bet he does."

I almost hit him. My fist clenched, indignation sizzling in my bones, and I took a step toward him. "What the fuck does that mean?"

He didn't back off, just fixed me in that inimitable stare. "Don't you think it's weird, how you're acting around him? What did you drink last night? Do you even remember?"

Uneasiness wriggled inside me, a flash of disquieting memory, but I laughed it off. "My god, you've got an ego. Just because I'm with some guy who isn't you doesn't mean I'm up to my eyeballs in Rohypnol."

"Oh, so you're 'with' him now?" He dragged a frustrated hand through his hair, black locks spilling so close, I could have touched them. "Funny. I could have sworn I remembered you begging for it from me."

My skin crawled with embarrassment and memory even as I bristled at his arrogance. I could still feel that amazing kiss, the way he tempted me, pleasured me. "You're a fine one to talk. Taking your frustration out on fairies now?"

"Is that what Dante told you?" He laughed, humorless. "I can't believe I'm having this conversation. That fairy was sick. She wanted me to kill her. She came to me for help, Jade, and I shouldn't have but I did. Haven't you ever done someone and regretted it later?"

I remembered Nyx melting in my arms, and sharp guilt pierced me. But I didn't want to hear Rajah's explanations, no matter how reasonable. He'd deceived me. "Oh, yeah. I'm regretting almost doing you more and more every minute."

"Really." He drifted closer, and his eyes flashed, daring me.

Despite my fury, my mouth watered. God, he smelled incredible. Clean, hot, sinful. I lifted my chin, defiance tightening my jaw even as I trembled. "Really."

He slid his tongue over his bottom lip, just because he knew it drove me crazy. "So you're not tempted now."

My gaze glued itself to his shining mouth, inches from mine, and warmth crept up over my skin. I wanted to touch him, to trace my fingertip over those swelling wet lips, slide it inside into his warmth. I dug my nails into my palms to keep my hands still. "No."

He bent closer, his breath hot on my cheek, and drifted his hand over my hair, barely touching. "Are you sure?"

"Quite sure." My legs weakened with desire, blood rushing to my tender, yearning flesh. Nerves flowered and tingled between my legs, moistening me. I should have pulled back, slapped his hand away, but the intoxicating flavor of his closeness maddened me beyond sense or anger. I couldn't breathe. I couldn't think. How did he do it? Only this man had ever turned me on with a glance, made my sex weep and ache with a lick of his lips. Well, only this man and Luna. But I didn't want to think about Luna right now.

Rajah brushed burning lips across to my ear. "Not a bit?"

"Not even a bit." My breath caught as he flicked his hot tongue around my earlobe, slow and tantalizing, sparking delicious shivers that started at my neck and tingled all the way down. When he nipped me, I nearly moaned. I wanted to crush my breasts against him, feel his mouth on my nipples, his hands on my thighs as he spread them and feasted on me. And there wasn't a scrap of rapture swimming in the air. This was pure, honest need. Helpless and dizzy, I leaned into him, on fire for his kiss, accepting his victory.

But he pulled back, his lips twisting in a smile. "Me either."

Embarrassment seared my skin right to the top of my scalp, and I whirled away, spinning full circle to face him. My skirt clung to my damp legs, pulling tight. "You bastard."

He stared me down hotly, his chest heaving slightly with

short breaths. What I could see of his skin above his shirt buttons gleamed with fragrant sweat even in the cool air. Those soft dark jeans revealed the clear evidence of his desire, wrapping around his swollen cock and showing every quiver. "Tell me now that you want to be with someone else. That you could bear to be with someone else. He's tricking you, Jade. Think."

I tried not to let my gaze slip below his face. My eyes stung with unshed tears, my throat aching like the rest of me. "I don't want to hear it."

"I bet you don't. Feeling a bit tired, are you? Did you spew this morning? Was it red?"

"Just don't say anything else, okay?" I yanked hair from my burning face and walked away, my nerves seething and my body still flaming with desire and frustration. "See you at Luna's. Or not. I've already got an invitation from Dante. Maybe you can just fuck your way in."

12

From the eighty-seventh floor of Eureka Tower, I could
see the whole of Melbourne in a panoramic 270-degree
view, darkened glass gleaming from marble floor to ceiling. Golden lights glittered as far as I could see, broken at my feet
by the dark snake of the river striped with bridges. Blue and
green lights rushed up and down the arts-center spire like an iridescent inky fountain, and farther afield the bright white spot-
light towers of the cricket ground blotted out the stars. High-rise
buildings festooned with neon advertising jutted up below us,
dwarfed, and to the north and west, traffic-bright freeways slashed
red and white through light-studded suburbs, the slow arc of the
Westgate Bridge garishly backlit in orange.

I swallowed, dizziness swirling gently in my head as I stepped
from the glass lift. Fatigue still washed me out, and a warm hollow stretched my stomach like I hadn't eaten all day, which I
hadn't. I'd gone straight home from Rajah's, too shaken up to
want anything.

My reflection shone dimly in the sepia-toned glass, showing
my hair curled up on my head with a few wisps hanging free,

shadowy glitter around my eyes. My sleek crimson silk dress pushed my breasts up and brushed my thighs as I moved. I'd wanted to stand out, to make Luna look. There was no point in hiding, or expecting him not to remember me. I'd need all my powers of seduction tonight.

My skin burned faintly, and my breath heated my throat, like I had a fever. Maybe I was getting the flu, or just needed a fix. Once I was done with Luna, I'd get one, some poor guy who'd never understand why he felt sick, staggered, passed out. . . .

A bit tired, are you? I remembered Rajah's words, and a scowl tensed my forehead. He knew nothing. Just seething with jealousy and a bruised ego.

Did you spew this morning? Was it red?

Dante gripped my hand, warm, leaning over to brush his lips against my cheek. "Don't worry. You look gorgeous." He sure sounded like he meant it, all breathy and intense.

"Thanks." I smiled, as best I could, straightening the thin golden rope holding my purse over my shoulder. He didn't look so shabby himself, dressed neatly in some designer as usual, light pleasant aftershave drifting, dark curls brushing his open white collar. Something comforted me about a vampire who wore white. Like he didn't expect to make a mess tonight. Maybe he was just a careful diner.

We walked up to the wide black glass doors, and a big bald security guy with no evident sense of humor gave Dante a thick-necked nod. I laughed inwardly, satisfied. Rajah would need all his imagination to get past that guy.

As we stepped across the carpeted threshold, my jaw dropped.

The walls, the distant vaulted ceiling, and half the floor were entirely of sparkling glass. The night sky glowed above like jewel-scattered mist, and where the pale lush carpet ended, the skyscraper fell away and the city sprawled below, twinkling. Gaps in the glass let in the breeze, smelling of wind and water and city decadence. The broad lounge stretched into the starry distance, scattered with couches, cushions, and chaises in the height of expensive modern style. Behind where we'd entered lay other rooms behind darkened glass—presumably where Luna went when he grew weary of outshining the stars—and a long black bar, serving fae-drenched drinks, sparkling white powder on slivers of mirror and colored glass eye droppers of shit most real people couldn't afford. Hidden somewhere, a diamond-clear sound system played something androgynous with sharp guitars and echo effects, maybe Placebo or My Chemical Romance.

The guests—a mixture of fae and mortal—looked like the cream of the hip, beautiful crowd at Unseelie Court, only the dresses were more expensive, the diamonds real and flashier, the drinks in crystal instead of thick glass, and no one was fucking over the wine velvet chaises longues, at least not yet. Some of these women were freaks, tall, perfect and big-breasted like supermodels in shimmering satin or drifting transparent silk, and the men weren't far behind.

I saw actors, pop culture criminals, musicians, sports stars, and littered amongst them all the silvery butterfly wings, lissome limbs, and wild rainbow hair of fae. I couldn't yet see Luna. No one I knew personally . . .

Shit. Over against the window. Skinny brown body in a black suit, bristly black hair like wire, a slither of forked blue tongue over jagged teeth. I let my gaze drift, but too late. He'd seen me. Tony LaFaro, Ange's crazy-ass fae-born cousin.

Happy carelessness warmed me. What the hell. I wasn't with

Ange anymore. Tony could stare till his freaky lizard eyes burned out.

"Isn't this place fantastic?" Dante's murmur warmed my ear, intimate. "I wanted to see you in it."

I laughed giddily, still gobsmacked. Like the moon at midday, I was totally outshone. "Lucky you can see me at all."

He caught my waist and spun me around, his indigo eyes glistening and intense as he grinned, his face close to mine. "I don't see much else tonight, sweet Jade. You've bewitched me."

My skin heated. Damn. Was I blushing? I slid my wrists around his neck, inviting him to press his body against mine. I didn't care what Rajah thought. Dante actually liked me. I could feel it in his gaze, intent and adoring. "Not true. It's all still in the can, I swear."

I felt him laugh against me, light and easy, and I laughed, too. His heady compliments still dizzied me, bringing back the delicious scent of his roses. He made me feel interesting, worthwhile, special. I wondered what it'd be like to touch someone who made me feel like that, let him touch me. Make him want me, slide him into me, make love to him.

He leaned even closer, teasing his lips across mine, his hands sliding warm over my hips. A cool sliver of fear pierced my skin, unsettling but tantalizing. "I dreamed of you," he whispered, "did you know that?"

"Didn't know vampires dreamed." I stole a kiss, sucking his bottom lip between my teeth, and a burning image flashed, steamy, sensation-soaked, of Dante inside me, deep and hard, my head thrown back on pale suede, his mouth sucking my nipple to painful hardness. I gulped, and jerked my head away a little, my thighs hot and tingling and my nipples scraping my dress in sympathy. Jesus. That was pretty real. I must really need a fix.

Dante smiled, his tongue flicking out to mine. Like before, he tasted coppery, metallic. I wanted to swallow, drag that salty essence into me. "Only when we want to. Want to know what my dream was about?"

"Love to." I meant it. I could listen to his compliments all night, and if it was a sexy dream that might put him in the mood, so much the better.

"We danced. We drank. We had dinner at some restaurant, and you pushed me under the tablecloth and let me go down on you."

Another sultry flash made me gasp. Dante's head in my lap, my legs apart and my black dress crumpled around my hips, his tongue sliding over me, into me, teasing my clit to ecstasy.

I closed my eyes on aching dizziness. God, it seemed so real, almost like a memory, that creamy suede under my thighs, the smell of cigarette smoke. . . .

No. It couldn't be. Could it? Unseelie Court?

Did you spew? Was it red?

Icy trails of disgust ran down my back like melting snow. He hadn't. Had he?

His thigh pressed against mine, hard. "I know, I should be so lucky. But it gets better. You gripped my hair and pulled me into you, and guess what?" He traced a warm fingertip over my hip, suggestive, and dropped his voice to a whisper. "You were bleeding. You tasted so delicious, so wet and hot. I slid my tongue into you and sucked you, and you came, but you couldn't scream because everyone was watching. That's what I dreamed."

Images of hot splashing blood washed into my mind like

waves on some hell-scarred beach. I could taste it, thick and visceral, coating my tongue, dripping past my tonsils. My fingers clenched behind his head, and I longed to pull away and slap him. But my thrall bangles burned, searing and insistent on my itching skin, and I couldn't move.

Never. Kane's rapture parasite spat acid denial in my heart. *Never defy me.*

I had to swallow so my voice wouldn't shake. "That's . . . pretty forward, Dante. Aren't you afraid I'll take offense?"

He pulled back, raising his eyebrows. "Not at all. I want you to know I want you, even if you deserve to be treated like a goddess. You're a beautiful, sensual woman, not a Barbie doll."

My gaze caught on the shiny tips of his teeth, just visible beyond his bottom lip. Hot saliva burst into my mouth, and wetness seeped between my legs in sympathy. My breasts ached, my nipples hard and tingling. My tongue slipped out to wet my lips. I couldn't look away. All I could think about was his kiss, his fine teeth piercing my skin and sliding inside, the blood welling, always the blood. Horror crawled in my veins, mingling with burning desire.

Dante watched me and smiled, teeth flashing. "Time to meet our host. You'll love him. Everyone does." He slipped his hand into mine and led me away.

I nearly staggered in my heels, my legs wobbly and unwilling but compliant. Bloodlust still raged in my veins, screaming, my body shuddering with macabre arousal, trapped with nowhere to go. I stung my rapture with a clumsy spurt of energy, but it wouldn't ignite, and fatigue weighed my heavy head down. Dante's delicate scent still filled my nostrils, stealing my attention, his fingers warm and possessive in mine.

Dismay wrenched my spine. I couldn't meet Luna like this. I needed all my wits. I unfocused my eyes, trying to clear my mind of Dante and whatever eldritch spell he'd wrought, trying to think of anyone anywhere who'd ever given a shit about me. I brought to mind Nyx, a rainy afternoon hunting antiques in Fitzroy, his long green fingers agile over dusty piano keys. Watching *Australian Idol* beneath soft downlights on Kane's couch, his golden head resting easy in my lap as we munched popcorn. Kissing Rajah in warm darkness on my doorstep, his savage lips claiming mine, my body longing for him, my heart carved open and bleeding, craving his love.

Golden rapture sizzled to life deep within me, invisible static sparking the air. The world swam back into sharp focus, my skin alive with awareness, the stink of blood fading. I felt revitalized, as if my spirit dragged its weary head from the dust. Fatigue still tugged at me, but I could handle it. I squeezed Dante's hand, breathing in his scent again, but this time fresh, feeding my soul with his strength. I clasped my purse closer with my other hand, feeling the hard swell of the empty soultrap hiding there. I could handle this.

We approached the bar, and I searched it with a quick glance, nerves tingling my fingertips. A pair of drunken banshees, giggling as they wobbled on their stools. A stony-skinned earth sprite, dusty elflocks dangling over her breasts, swaying her naked brown hips in a trance to the music. And a luscious sweep of long golden hair, glowing with a faint, sweet mauve aura.

I stared, trembling, as he turned. Tall, broad-shouldered, gorgeous like an airbrushed dream. Sharp amber-green eyes, deep and wise with experience. A long Chinese silk coat brushed his thighs, shiny black, the high open collar drawing attention to his bone structure, cheekbones and chin perfectly carved. Pale shirt beneath, almost translucent, showing off his impressive body.

I don't hate often. Not Kane, not Quinn, not even Angelo. But I hated Luna for what he'd done to me, and black disgust filled me like tar, sticky and vile.

"Glad you could make it, my friend." Luna kissed Dante on the corner of the mouth, their fingers touching briefly. His voice rang pleasantly, no trace of language problems or foreign accent. Luna adapted fast, always had. He switched his gaze to me, voracious. "And with such a lovely lady, too."

I pasted a sweet smile on my lips as I held out my hand. "Hello, Vorenus."

He eyed me speculatively as he swept my fingers to his lips, his perfect blond brows contracting a millimeter or two, fingers of violet aura flickering over his flawless skin.

I fought a flush, my skin crawling. He had no idea who I was. He didn't even remember me.

And then his lips parted in a perfect smile, his eyes brightening with delight. "Jade! My god. You had me there for a minute. Dante, my friend, you're a dark horse."

I fixed my smile in place. "You haven't changed."

"Oh, go on. It's been so long. But you! You look fantastic. Hell, you always looked fantastic." He grasped both my hands, laughing, and pulled me into a hug.

Black silk pressed against my cheek, warm. The contours of his body brought a wash of vile memory, his hands excruciating in my hair. His dark otherworldly scent filled my nose, and I swallowed, gagging.

"Still chasing the dangerous ones, hmmm?" His breath whispered on my cheek, his closeness nauseating, but before I could react, he released me. "So how'd things work out with Kane, eh? I swear the bastard cheated me that night. Can't say I blame him." He winked at me, handsome.

I forced a little laugh. Unbelievable. He had no idea that I hated him. No clue why I might resent him even a little bit. "I don't think you can cheat at faro."

"Nonsense. If you try hard enough, you can cheat at anything." He flicked an inscrutable glance at Dante. "Perhaps we'll have a game, see who wins the prize."

His arrogance made my stomach curl. But confidence could be his weakness. Let him think I didn't mind, that I'd forgotten about that cold, dank dungeon, the rusty iron chafing my wrists. I breathed a tiny shimmer of rapture over him, tempting him to look, move closer, touch.

Luna's smile froze, and my warm tendril of glamour slapped hard into a frigid wall. Static shocked up my arms, zapping my skin with pain, and fragrant rapture evaporated like summer rain. I caught my breath, my eyes wide. Jesus. He'd seen me coming a mile away.

He flicked the tip of his tongue over his teeth, his lips curling in amusement, his stare a haughty challenge. "Well, well. You should keep your wildcat chained, Dante. I think she bites." He trailed his elegant finger under my chin, teasing. "We'll talk later, eh? Enjoy yourselves."

Luna swept away to greet other guests in a perfumed swirl of silk, and Dante laughed and led me up to the bar, his arm flung casually around my shoulder. I went, still stunned, my mind racing. Luna had brushed my glamour aside like it was an annoying insect. How could I ever get close to him?

Dante ordered wine, leaning his elbow on the glossy black bar. "So when did you ever meet Luna?"

I shrugged, trying to keep it casual. I hadn't seen Rajah here yet, but I couldn't imagine he'd have any more success than I. It didn't make me feel better. "It was a long time ago. I'm surprised he remembered me."

"Who could forget you, my love?" He slid a long-stemmed glass toward me, thick ruby wine glimmering.

I shuddered and pushed it back, sick copper echoes twinging my nose. "I'll have a white, thanks."

He captured my hand, preternaturally swift, and brought my palm to his lips, burning me. "Are you sure?"

My vision swirled and blackened. I inhaled sharply, dizzy, my stomach lurching, blood rushing away from my head. Blindly I gripped the glass bar, nausea frothing in my guts. I felt weird. This whole night was weird.

"Jade? Are you okay?" Dante's voice drifted over me, and the world shimmered back into focus, a glimpse of pale carpet, the black glass bar near my face smelling sickly of lemon disinfectant. How long did I faint for? A few seconds? A minute?

I wiped damp wisps from my face, my skin burning. I needed space, cool clean air where I could think. I needed to concentrate, to come up with a plan, and Dante wasn't helping. "I just need the bathroom. I'll be back in a moment."

He smiled, sweet and dangerous, and sipped his wine, long teeth glinting. "Don't be too long."

Shadowed in sepia-drenched starlight, Tony LaFaro watches Jade through transparent inner eyelids as she weaves into the ladies' room, teetering on her high heels, her titties just about falling out of that tiny excuse for a dress. Tarty little whore, trying all the flavors before she buys. Never mind them bangles, if he was Ange, he'd fuck some goddamn sense into her.

The slender yellow fae girl beside Tony grins and trails her glittering hair on his shoulder, reaching with her long tongue for his cheek. Her crystal-tainted gin fizz lolls half-empty in her hand. Now this pretty lady's no whore. Wouldn't hafta spike her drink if she was a whore. Told him to fuck right off, she did. She ain't saying that no more.

Tony wipes remnants of bright banshee blue from his flat nose and slips a scaly hand around her hip, eliciting a sigh and another besotted lick to his cheek. With his other hand, he slips out his phone and dials Ange. "Hey, it's me. Yeah, nothing much. Listen, I've got a thing for ya. Guess which bangle-wearing thrallslut I just saw with Dante DiLuca?"

He grins, his forked tongue slithering, and holds the phone away from his ear to muffle Ange's curses. "Yeah, mate, he sure did. . . . I dunno, she looked happy enough about it to me. . . . How the hell would I know if he's fucking her? I don't have my hand around his cock, I'm just tellin' ya what I saw."

He holds the phone away again and nibbles at the girl's sugary lips, tasting her sleepy kiss while he waits for Ange to shut up. "Will you calm the fuck down and listen to me? I'm trying to tell ya this could be a thing for us. Kane could be up to something. I mean, I woulda dumped ya greasy fangwhore ass, too, but she can't just . . . Okay, so now ya real brain's workin'. Whaddaya want me to do? . . . Well, I'd let it run, see what we catch. . . . Yeah, okay. I'll let ya know."

He debates telling Ange what else he's heard—that there's a

certain curry-munching incubus with his queerboy hand up Jade's skirt, too—but decides he'll save it and ruin Ange's night again another time. Vampires. No sense of humor.

The yellow girl sucks on his pointed earlobe, her lithe body falling against his. He stretches webbed fingers to squeeze her perky little breast and cuts Ange off in midsentence. "Yeah, mate. Whatever. Gotta go."

13

I clutched my bag in front of me and walked to the end of the bar, where an open doorway led to a candlelit bathroom, the mirrored walls leaping with reflected flame. My shoulder itched above my collarbone, and I brushed at it irritably. I leaned my forehead on the cool mirror above the creamy porcelain sink and closed my eyes. Tears pressed behind my eyelids, stinging. I felt unprepared, alone, helpless.

A choking gasp made me lift my head. A fae girl huddled in the corner, pale blue arms clutched around her scrawny midriff. I palmed my eyes clear. She retched again, a dry heave that made her gasp, blue water welling from her silvery eyes, long white tangles spilling forward over her face.

I wiped my nose. "Are you okay?"

She started to wave me away, but choked again, her face crumpling in pain. This time she did spew, jets of dark stinking mess riddled with blood. I held her hair for her while it all came up, her jerking body thin under my arm, the long silver dress she wore staining with vomit and blue saliva. "I can't keep it down," she gasped, bloody bubbles frothing from her sharp nose. "Some snort it with sugar. Live forever. Blow your mind, that will."

I eyed the rainbow vomit suspiciously. Bright, thick, cherry-colored blood that clotted and writhed like a living thing. Not fae. Not human.

Vampire blood. Was it Dante's? I shuddered, jealous and disgusted at the same time. "You'll kill yourself with that stuff."

"Doubt it. You should know." Gamely the fairy grinned at me and grasped the wall with long padded fingers like a frog's to pull herself to her full height, inches above me. Her beautiful long face shone translucent in the candlelight, blue-veined skin glowing.

She traced a splayed finger over my collarbone and licked the tip, tasting. Her delicate fingers flowed to my chin, lifting it so she could look at me, black pupils slitting wide like a cat's in silver irises. "You look lost. Want to try something? How about oblivion? I can do you a mean forgetful. Or some fresh abandon, let yourself go, sweet child. What do you say?" She sniffed my mouth, lascivious, flickering her long forked tongue over thin blue lips.

Her fruity river scent drifted, faintly rotten. "No thanks."

Her fingers on my chin held me fast, her shiny eyes pleading. "You sure? You look like you've memory to spare. How about a hit of curiosity? It's my most popular. Broaden your horizons."

Her body heat radiated, her curved hipbones standing out like beaks, silvery cotton flowing around her slender bare feet. I shook my head and made to turn away, but I hesitated, thinking of Luna, the challenge glinting in his tiger's eyes. "What about confidence? Can you bottle me that?"

The veins in her face pulsed azure. "Oh, yes. Assurance to

stand you up reckless in death's face. One bottle, one fix. But worth my price." She licked her lips again, artful. "I'll need a memory. Something bold and gallant."

A shot of recklessness might be just what Luna needed. "Knock yourself out. But just one."

I closed my eyes, thinking of that warm spring night on the Bosphorus when I met him, lanterns shining over the barge-laden water, the fragrance of pomegranates sweet on the stinging oriental breeze. We danced, silk scarves flowing from my hair, our bodies pressed together, his fingers insistent in mine, his desire for me already pushing his cock hard and ready against my belly.

The fairy giggled and sniffed my face, her warm breath tickling over me. "Mmm. More, please."

I'd wanted him that night like I'd wanted no other. We'd stumbled through a dim stone doorway, our lips glued together, his tongue mashing mine, my hands already hungry inside his clothes. His body was a revelation, smooth, muscular, strong. I pushed him against the wall and took him there, first with my mouth and then when he could take no more I climbed onto him and he brought me off with his last frantic thrusts. We came together that first time, and later that night when he tied me to his bed with those same silken scarves and tortured me with sweet desire, I thought I'd found life itself.

"Yes. That one." The fairy glided her lips across mine, salty, parting my lips with her scaly tongue and slipping it inside. My throat constricted as it probed and writhed like a wet snake, and I reeled as the energy dragged up over my tonsils, forcing from me. I gagged, saliva flowing.

"Mmm. Just the thing. Memory food." She withdrew, her eyes shimmering, and drew out a shiny glass tube. She whispered a puff of breath across the opening, misting the glass. A tiny cloud of golden sparkles showered like fairy dust, drifting down into the tube. She popped in the cork and handed the tube to me between two bony blue fingers. "Take care, lonely child."

I took it, plastering the back of my hand over my sick mouth, and mumbled indistinct thanks as the fairy glided away, freshly healthy on the energy I'd lost.

Golden ether shimmered in the vial, inviting. I thought once again of the night I met Luna, but I couldn't remember a thing, and a weak grin spread over my lips despite my nausea. Now, I was armed and dangerous. But Luna wasn't stupid. He'd be wary of anything I offered him, even hot fresh fairy score like this.

I thumbed the cork aside and sniffed, cautious, careful not to bring the glimmering stuff too close. Icy freshness sparkled up my nose, citrus and stinging like cocaine, tingling my palate as it wafted down. My pulse strengthened, bold despite my fatigue. Sure, I'd get him to take it. Why not?

I slipped the corked tube into my bag and stepped out of the bathroom, trying to feed on that magical confidence. But they were my memories she'd crafted, my essence she'd trapped and tortured, and I knew it for a false high. I tossed my head back, game, but for some reason my ankle buckled and my wobbly legs wouldn't hold me. My shoulder thudded into the shiny wall as I staggered, pain spearing my guts. Jesus. What had I eaten?

Dizzy, I gripped my stomach with both hands and folded. Red waves shimmered before my eyes, sickening.

Rajah hops up the stone steps and through the automatic glass doors into Eureka Tower. Cool air slides pleasantly over his skin after the heat outside, and he scrapes sweat-damp hair off his neck. The foyer glistens, bright yellow downlights reflecting on warm clay-colored marble. He hangs back awhile, waiting for his chance, but his nerves wriggle, and it's nothing to do with the rapture tricks he's about to pull. He just hopes Jade and Di-Luca are already inside. He doesn't want to see her with Dante, watch her smile for him, touch him, look at him that way.

The cold words they'd exchanged still scratch at Rajah's skin like jagged ice, and the shocking heat of their almost-kiss only sharpens the pain. He won't hold back if he gets that opportunity again, but the chance of that is slim. Maybe he's just wishing her mesmerized. Maybe she wants Dante more. Hell, she's probably already swapping more fluids with him than blood.

Jealousy burns his throat like bile, but sorrow taints his mouth, too, sweet as well as bitter. Fuck. What does he care, right? Not like it'll matter once he's got Luna's poisonous soul thrashing in a bottle.

People walk in and out, residents, visitors, and tourists, but he's interested only in those going in. Three girls and their boyfriends, a glitter of golden bangles, eyeliner and silk. Too many, too difficult. Two guys holding hands, beautiful in smooth expensive shirts, designer stubble, diamond earrings. Too conspicuous. A pair of young women, jeweled chokers sparkling at their throats, long blond hair carefully blow-dried. Satiny party dresses, one pale yellow and one purple, and strappy heels show off long tanned legs. They laugh together as they step into the glass elevator.

Now that's what Rajah's waiting for. He slips into the elevator with them, offering a smile. Their perfume drifts, sweet and sexy. "Eighty-seven?"

"Of course." They eye him up and down, sly painted lashes dipping. One whispers in her friend's ear, and they laugh.

Rajah leans over to touch the button and releases a silent waft of rapture. The shimmer caresses the girls, brushing over their limbs, creeping along their smooth skin. The one in yellow inhales, a hazy wisp drifting up her nose like a delicious scent, and she flushes, biting her lip as she watches him with smoldering eyes. The second girl is more wary, her frosted eyelids narrowing, but her gaze, too, is drawn, her breath shorter as she shifts on her feet, squirming.

He traps his hands behind him as the elevator door slides shut, his bangles clinking against dark glass, and gives the yellow girl a come-hither look, laced with none-too-subtle glamour.

She practically purrs, her body stretching luxuriantly. His gaze follows the delicate line of her throat, down to her swelling cleavage. Her nipples harden beneath the thin yellow silk, tiny peaks poking, begging for his touch.

Rajah's blood heats, rapture tingling beneath his skin, but faint sickness sours his mouth, too, and he wonders why. This is just work, just a job that needs to be done. There's no reason he should feel guilty. It's not like he's promised her anything.

His nerves twitch, uncomfortable. Damn it. When did Jade become *her*?

He shoves his unease away and concentrates on his task, letting glamour flow over the yellow girl, caress her, lick her nipples, trace invisible fingers up her thighs, flood her senses with wanting. She fidgets, lips parted, chest heaving.

He taps his fingers softly on the glass, tense, as the elevator rises with a hiss. "Care to join me?"

"Don't mind if I do." The yellow girl can't stand still a moment longer. She stalks over and plants her glossy lips on his in a desperate, rapture-drenched kiss, her hands already tugging at his clothes. She tastes of vodka and the bitter sherbet of cheap cocaine.

Rapture ripples lust into his blood, warming his thighs, filling his cock. He lets her ravish him, opening his eyes in mid-kiss to skewer her purple friend with a dark spear of glamour. The purple girl gasps, her muscles jerking, and he grazes his free hand along her jaw and pulls her close, sliding his thumb into the warmth of her eager mouth.

By the time the elevator slows and the door whispers open, they're entangled in a three-way embrace, unsure of who's kissing whom and who wants whom more.

"Let's go inside." The yellow girl teases Rajah's lips with her teeth, stinging. He can smell her juice, hot and salty, her sex sore and weeping with too-sudden need, and his rapture gnashes urgent teeth, wanting. He reaches around her to squeeze the purple girl's narrow ass, pulling both girls closer.

The purple girl squirms and drags hungry hands across her friend's breasts from behind, playing with swollen nipples, her breath leaving wet marks on the yellow girl's shoulder. "How about we fuck right here?"

Rajah's cock jumps in anticipation, and he swallows a smile. "Inside," he whispers, and they tumble into the penthouse foyer, limbs tangled. The yellow girl simpers at the security guy, digging one-handed in her bag for her invitation, the other hand occupied in sliding up between her friend's thighs, while Rajah bangs teeth with the purple girl, her kiss rough and desperate, shaking fingers yanking his hair.

"Uh-huh." The big bald guy squints casually at the gilt-edged invite. "What about him?"

"He's with us." They both say it at once, breathless.

Rajah winks at him, and the security guy scowls back. "Half his luck. Don't make a mess." He jerks his head gruffly at the black glass door, and they stand straight for just long enough to pass through.

The penthouse is amazing, a vast glassy space suspended above starry nothing, the sea of dazzling men and women glittering like jewels, but Rajah barely has time to look before the girls yank him onto a soft couch in a dim corner, a pile of supple limbs, breasts, silk, soft blond hair. The sweat-drenched perfume of their sex and the sweet mixture of their moans heats his blood, his balls tight and his cock hungry for contact. His rapture crackles, pure lust searing inside him, and it's an effort to drag himself away. He extricates himself, sliding one girl's hands onto the other's body, one girl's mouth onto the other's throat. "Knock yourselves out. Gotta go."

The yellow girl whimpers in displeasure, but the purple girl cuts off her disappointment with a sensual growl, pulling her on top and dragging her smeared mouth downward, blond waves tumbling.

Rajah grimaces and walks stiffly away, forcing air into his lungs to slow his pulse. His thwarted rapture snarls, bitter heat stinging his skin, and an angry shimmer swells the air around him. Beside him, a slender blood fairy in white velvet glances up from his drink, scarlet pupils dilating with desire, and Rajah curses and flickers out of sight before he spreads his damn glamour all over the fucking place.

Glassy music fractures the air, a happy little song about dying from cancer treatment. Still invisible, Rajah heads for the bar, stepping carefully around people who can't see him. He scans the crowd for Jade, but he can't pick her from the mass of color and beauty. His stomach tightens with disappointment, and he realizes he misses her. Nerves clench in his spine, uncomfortable. If he sees Dante touching her, he might not be able to contain himself in his current mood. There must be a way he can make her see sense, instead of seeing just another self-absorbed male who thinks he owns her.

Truth is, he burns to own her. His blood rushes again, painful in his already aching cock, and guilt only makes him want harder. To be the only one allowed to touch her, kiss her, penetrate her sweet body and obsess her mind. To be the one who teases her into a laugh, puts that glorious smile on her pretty face, sends her eyelids fluttering closed with bliss. It's not what she thinks, not just jealous possession. It's more like . . . Well, he doesn't want to think about what it really is.

A mortal couple stop talking abruptly as he passes and fall into kissing, and he grits his teeth and clamps down harder on his glamour. The cool air eventually soothes his twitching skin, his rapture sulking in a tight frustrated coil. The fierce ripple in his blood dims, his pulse slowing, and the boiling shimmer in the air subsides to an occasional dirty spark. When he pops back into sight at the black glass bar and orders lemon, lime, and bitters, he gets merely a sultry glance and a lick of glossy lips from the bright-eyed bar girl.

He sips, citrus fizz cooling his throat, and dark prescience prickles the back of his neck.

He spins, his nerves jerking, but sees nothing, no one who stands out from the crowd. He takes a deep breath, calming. Probably DiLuca, showing off.

Or maybe Luna. Rajah gulps his drink, ice and all. If Luna sees him first, and realizes his intent, it's all over. He has no idea how to steal Luna's soul. Overt rapture won't do him any good. Luna is far too clever to let him get that close again. He'll need his most artful fakery even to get in the same room.

Dark challenge heats Rajah's skin again, and he has to bite his lip to halt a mischievous smile. Dismay makes him sigh, but it can't extinguish the old reckless spark in his blood. Trapping Luna shouldn't be impossible. His biggest weakness was always his ego. Maybe a confidence trick, a clever sham. Rajah has nothing to lose.

Except Jade.

Cold sensation spears his guts. His spine crawls, and he realizes he's afraid.

He swallows, overcome. His longing for her cuts deep, the pain sharper than he can ignore or explain away. But his freedom demands her sacrifice. He can't have both.

Well, why the hell not? What's more important—to live free? Or to live in love?

The idea stops his breath. Her freedom, his thrall, her love. Everything he's ever wanted . . . Well, almost everything. He can never give her a child, not in thrall, even if she could conceive. Would she forgive him that?

Shit. Did he really just think that? He flushes, reality souring his mouth, and shakes his head at his own stupidity. She'll never love him. The way he's acted, all jealous and possessive and lustful, he's everything she's ever loathed about men. She'd rather go with a vicious blood-hungry vampire than be with him. And if she were free, just a regular woman, how long could she stand a lover who screwed other women for a living?

He clinks his glass back onto the bar, skidding it away from him in frustration. His crush on her will pass. It always has before, such idle covetous impulse. It has to.

Beside him, a tall water sprite in a slim silver gown winks at him, white hair flowing to blue-veined shoulders. Her diamond eyes twinkle as she sniffs the air, wet wings shining. "What's that I smell, incubus? Regret?"

A reluctant laugh twists his lips. "Sad but true."

She sways closer, remnants of a forgotten song crooning in her throat. She smells of the river in summer, warm and tainted. "You've no such sorrow from me, I'll bet."

He eyes her, curiosity warming his palms. She does look familiar. Maybe he's fucked her. Something about her bow-shaped lips or the pale line of her chin puts him in mind of St. Kilda Beach at midnight, salty summer breeze, waves lapping, the warm grittiness of sand on his skin. She tasted of sea salt, not sweat, and water rushed beneath her skin in rivulets, warm like blood but blue.

"The penny drops." An artful smile, blue pointed teeth glinting.

He can't help another rueful laugh. "Sorry, sweetheart. My mind's elsewhere."

She runs a splayed fingerpad around the rim of his empty glass and slips it into her mouth. The forks of her scaly tongue flicker, lascivious. "Want something stronger, pretty? A splash of sweet forgetful? You'll regret nothing then."

To forget Jade would be sweet relief. Temptation slides crafty fingers over his thighs, and he's about to caress the fairy's chin and ask what sordid favor she wants in return, when a flash of scarlet satin catches his eye. Slender shoulders, soft brown wisps, a vicious splash of . . .

Urgency slams pressure into his racing blood, and he doesn't even bother to excuse himself.

14

I staggered against the glass wall, and a dark shape materialized, warm hands on my stinging shoulder.

"Bring it up. Come on." His voice was soft, compelling,
and despite my agony, I smelled a whisper of familiar oriental
spice.

"Rajah . . ." Relief choked me, and another spasm twisted
my guts. "I don't feel so well." I leaned against him, shivering,
and he wrapped his arm around my shoulder, gently but insis-
tently forcing me back to the bathroom. I went, stumbling, my
ankles tangling. My thrall bangles hissed and sparked, the hot
metal tightening painfully on my forearms, but I didn't care. I
wanted to pass out, sleep forever. Candlelight gloated on dark
mirrors, the metallic stink of the fairy's vomit still souring the
cool air.

Rajah gripped my shoulders. "Look at me. Jade. Look at me,
please."

With an effort of will I dragged my swimming head up, and
he cupped his hands around my face, his thumbs caressing my
cheeks. "You have to bring it up. It's making you sick."

"What?" My lips fumbled, clumsy. "What d'ya mean?"

He spun me around to face the mirror, leaning over to press his head against mine, his hands gripping my waist, forcing me to look. There I was, fatigue drawing lines around my mouth, mascara smudged on my lashes, my red satin dress twisted where he held me, my bare shoulders gleaming golden in the flickering light. He'd shown up in his full glory in a sleeveless black shirt and jeans, showing off glistening muscles and perfect poise. His dark hair mingled with mine, his beautiful lips tense and close to my ear. A faint shimmer of his rapture flowed over me, warm, probably the remnants of whatever he'd done to get in here.

I couldn't feel the glamour, of course, but I wanted to swoon anyway. His body moved against my back as he breathed, swift and short, but he didn't seem concerned with rapture. His reflected golden gaze bored into mine, unrelenting. "Look," he insisted, harsh. "Can't you see what he's done to you? Can't you feel it?"

I blinked, straightening my nodding head, trying to filter my glaring vision. My reflection goggled back at me, dumb. I twisted my neck, aching. My shoulder stung. I rubbed it, wincing, and my hand came away wet and warm.

I looked down. At fingers smeared with sticky blood.

Horror crushed my heart with an icy fist. Wildly I stared up at the mirror, my pulse galloping. Scarlet streamed over my shoulder, pooling in the hollow above my collarbone, dripping, staining my dress. A bruise already blackened on the soft flesh between my neck and shoulder, a ragged red gash freshly torn open by rapacious fangs. Blood welled in the holes, dripping, fragments of scab already crusty.

When the fuck did he do that? I remembered my fit of dizziness by the bar, that few seconds I'd blacked out.

I wanted to scream, but no sound could escape from my parched throat. My body shook, helpless, my stomach shriveling. Dante had lied to me. I'd been an idiot to believe him for an instant, to imagine for a moment that a man who had everything could be the slightest bit interested in me. And Rajah . . . I didn't want to think about the things I'd said to Rajah. God, what a fuckup.

Rajah gripped me tightly, his warmth enfolding me. "It's okay. I've got you. Did you swallow any?"

I shook my head, my mouth dry with terror.

"Did you swallow any?" Rajah repeated, shaking me lightly to get my attention, his hands tense and hot.

"I don't know!" I forced out at last. "Maybe. I don't remember." But memories squirmed to the surface like worms, of Dante's body on mine, pushing inside me, his hot coppery warmth tingling in my mouth, down my throat. He'd fed me. Mesmerized me with his blood. Licked my clit, made me like it. Fucked me. Probably came inside me, and I didn't know anything about it. And all the time I'd believed he wanted more than that.

God, I'm so dumb.

Blood rushed to my face, burning. Claws of nausea slashed into my guts, and my stomach heaved. I scrambled for the toilet, hanging my head over the bowl, and stinking scarlet bile erupted onto the porcelain, scorching my throat. Pain punched into my abdomen, my body spasming over and over until nothing remained.

I dragged back damp wisps of hair, my eyes streaming. Dark vampire blood steamed in the bowl, thick and clotted. Disgusting. I wiped my mouth, blood smearing on the back of my shaking hand.

The rush of water made me turn. Rajah flipped the tap off and handed me a glass of water, wordless, his eyes dark and inscrutable.

I took it, my gaze slipping away. Embarrassment crawled on my skin. He must think me so gullible. I swilled cool water in my mouth and spat into the spotless porcelain sink. Twists of bloody phlegm swirled down the plughole. I shuddered, and washed my mouth out again and again until my spit ran clear and the foul taste was gone, but it still didn't feel clean.

I touched my aching shoulder gingerly, trying not to flex it and reopen the wound. My own blood stained my skin, crusting darkly on the red satin, streaked with viscous vampire spit. My fingers shook, desperate. I wanted it gone. I fumbled for paper towels, frantic, smearing my skin as I tried to wipe the mess away.

Rajah's hot hand gripped mine as he reached from behind to steady me, his body warm and firm against my back. "Careful. Let me."

Unwilling, I relented. He pried the bloody paper from my fingers and got some more, wetting it under the hot tap and pressing it gently to my fouled skin. His fingers were delicate, tender, soothing, the hot tissue fresh and cleansing. I closed my eyes, relaxing, letting him take care of me. He brushed a stray curl away from my neck, sliding the wet paper over me, dabbing gently. Warm tingles spread across my back, climbing my neck, and I shivered, letting my head fall to the side so he could touch me.

I could feel him breathing, tense against my back, and I realized his rapture probably wasn't helping the situation. I opened my eyes. "You don't have to—"

"What if I want to?" He tossed the mess in the bin and soaked a fresh lump of towel, moving down over my collarbone where sticky clots still formed. Hot drips glided down to my breast, soaking into the soft low neckline of my dress. I imagined his fingertips following, sliding the fabric aside, tracing the shape of my breast, teasing my nipple to hardness. I didn't want him to stop. His gentleness unnerved me, made me yearn for more.

He dabbed at the dress's stained edge, hesitant, his fingers brushing the top of my breast. "I can't get this off."

"It's okay." His touch flooded tingling sensation into my guts. My nipple strained against the wet satin, and I struggled to keep my breath slow and regular. Had he noticed? He must have noticed.

I felt him swallow, and slowly his fingertip slipped down over my breast, tracing a deliberate circle around my tight peak. I shivered, my lips parting. His thumb joined in, and he pinched my nipple, delicate, pleasure shooting deep inside me.

I closed my eyes. "Rajah . . ."

"Mmm?" He bent his lips to my neck, his tongue flicking out to pleasure me with a long slow lick toward my ear, his thumb and finger making delicious wickedness at my breast, rolling and tugging until my nipples swelled, tight like pebbles, yearning for his palms, his mouth, his teeth.

His cock pressed into the curve of my back, long and hard, and I trembled, the air pregnant with his energy like an imminent storm. He was right. I didn't want to be with anyone else. Not Dante, not Luna, not anyone but my beautiful Rajah, who cared who hurt me and how. I didn't mind if his arousal was just rapture this time. For once, I'd take what I wanted.

"Kiss me," I whispered, turning my head toward him.

He dragged his lips over my throat and my chin, sinking

hot trails of desire into my skin. I caught his mouth with mine, and his tongue delved into me, tracing my teeth, seeking my own tongue and stroking it until I moaned. His energy mingled with mine, pure and arousing. He cupped my breast, palming the nipple through wet satin, the friction delicious. I leaned back into him, finding a place for his cock in the hollow of my bottom, sliding him against me. My sex swelled and moistened in sympathy, hurting. I wanted his length driving into me, pressing against my limit, stretching me until I was full of him.

He pulled me back onto him, strong fingers gripping my hip, his mouth sliding reluctantly from mine. His voice husked, hot on my cheek and thick with need, his touch still alive on my swelling breast. "This is impossible."

I leaned my head back on his shoulder, burying my nose in his dark fragrant hair, my body aflame in his arms. I wanted to trail kisses over his throat, down his chest, bite his smooth brown nipples. How was I supposed to keep him at a distance? He was too alluring, too wonderful. "I know. What are we going to do?"

"Well, there's this." He teased his fingers under the satin, tugging my bare aching nipple. I gasped from pure sensation, my teeth grazing his throat. He crept his other hand beneath my skirt, feathering a shiver up the hot inside of my thigh. "And this."

I willed his touch upward, shifting my stance to let him in. "I meant about . . . Oh, god." He'd slipped his fingertips inside my underwear, finding hot wetness. A bolt of fierce need shot up into me, my clit swelling for him. He teased my entrance, sliding over me lightly, maddening, and I thought I'd explode with boiling desire, heat pouring off me in waves. His fingernail brushed my sensitive clit, and I whimpered, nerves afire all over my body.

I reached up to crush his hair, gripping it tightly, pulling his lips back onto my neck. This was worse than rapture. This was heaven.

"Do it." The words burst from my lips, strained with lust. I was begging before he'd even undressed me, and I didn't care. "Please, just do it."

He slipped a long, smooth finger inside, all the way in. I groaned in pure delight, my flesh quivering and clenching. He buried his face in my neck, his mouth gentle but ravenous, and crept his other hand down to massage me, two clever fingers sliding around my clit, rubbing while he pushed inside me. Tension gripped me, pleasure building rapidly. But fear tinged my sensation with hot edginess. I was too raw, Rajah too overwhelming. "No," I panted, "it's too much. Stop."

"Must I?" His breath burned my skin, heavy. "I want to feel you come."

"I can't. There's still Luna . . . no. Stop it." I grabbed his wrists and dragged him from me, my flesh whimpering in protest. I'd need all the energy I could muster to seduce Luna. I couldn't afford to waste it now, no matter how much I wanted to.

Yeah, okay. I hadn't made him stop because he frightened me, or anything. Not because when he touched me I forgot who I was. Not because he made me feel like a woman instead of a machine and I didn't know what to do.

He leaned his damp forehead on my shoulder, closing his arms around me, and gave a deep shuddering sigh. "I'm sorry. I didn't mean . . . Oh, Jade. What are we going to do about Luna?"

I wriggled away, his closeness too much to bear. "I don't know. I've tried rapture and he just shrugs it off."

He eyed me darkly. "That's not what I mean."

I swallowed, the mirrored wall cold against my shoulder. Luna was one thing we couldn't share. But I didn't want us to fight, not now. "Well . . . he's no good to either of us still alive, is he?"

A tiny smile turned Rajah's lips. "Fair enough. First trap our soul?"

"And bicker about it later?"

"I'm game if you are."

"Okay."

"What did you have in mind?" He licked his shining fingers delicately, and I blushed when I remembered they were still wet from being inside me.

"I've got this." I fumbled in my bag for the fairy's sparkling drug. "Confidence. He's not afraid of me. We can use that."

"It might take both of us to break his defenses. I don't see him letting us get him alone."

"Both of us? Not a chance." I thought hard, trying to ignore the ache still burning deep inside me, and an idea glimmered. "But he doesn't have to see both of us, does he?"

Rajah grinned slowly, a hint of centuries-old malice lighting his eyes. "I like the way you think."

My mind raced. "Give him the drug. Make him think I want him. Get him alone . . ." Fear pricked my skin with icy needles. I never wanted to be alone with Luna again. The way he'd scattered my rapture into thin air scared me. I'd never realized I relied so much on my glamour for self-confidence. Was this how I'd felt as a mortal? Defenseless, weak, helpless? I bit my lip. Damn it.

"Only you won't be alone. I won't let him hurt you, Jade."

I closed my eyes briefly, shuddering, letting my head fall

back against the cool mirror. "I can't. He's too powerful. He'll know—"

"No, he won't. You're good. One weak moment is all it takes and he's ours." Rajah gripped my hand, sliding his damp fingers between mine. "Then one orgasm, he's dead, it's over. Improvise. You'll be fine. I'll talk you through it."

"How? If you make a sound, he'll know you're there."

Trust me.

His voice resonated in my head, caressing me like a warm feather. His lips hadn't moved. I stared. "How did you—?"

He smiled, cheeky. *It's magic. How else? Another of the few things he couldn't steal from me.* He brushed my cheek with his knuckles, tender. "You ready?"

My sex was still slick from his caress, and I considered going to the toilet to clean up. But I might need that wetness later, to convince Luna my skin wasn't creeping at the thought of him touching me. I tugged my damp underwear off over my heels and tossed it in the bin, and heaved in a breath. "Okay . . . oh. Wait a second."

I popped the cork on the vial and leaned over to wipe my finger in the stained toilet bowl, wrinkling my nose at the metallic, acid stink. A drop of Dante's blood quivered on my nail, still warm. I tapped my finger on the rim of the glass, and a single scarlet drop plinked in, dissolving in golden sparkles. I jammed the cork back in tight, pressed the flush button and wiped my stained finger on a paper towel as water gushed into the bowl, frothing away the stink. "A little persuasion. Just in case."

Rajah watched me, grinning. "You have a real talent for this, you know."

I grinned back in spite of myself. "Don't be too happy about it. It's my bottle his soul's going in."

His smile twisted. "We'll see." He blinked out like a popping lightbulb, his reflections vanishing. *Can you still hear me?*

"Sure." His disembodied voice unnerved me, but knowing he'd be there kept me warm inside. I slipped the blood-tainted vial back in my purse, straightened my shoulders, and walked out of the bathroom.

My heart leapt, blood throbbing hot in my veins.

15

Dante smiled at me, leaning against the mirrored wall with his arms folded, his reflection copied in infinite corridors on either side.

I swallowed, flushing, wondering how much he'd heard. "Shit. You scared me."

"I worried about you. Taking so long and all." He straightened and reached for me, his hand warm and gentle but somehow unyielding in the bend of my arm. His blue eyes glowed bright and intense, dizzying.

I wanted to look away, to break his stare, but my gaze slid inexorably back to his. My wits thrashed, sluggish. Bastard. How had I not noticed this before?

"You look tired, sweetheart. Can I get you a drink?" His soft whisper shot straight to my skin, cold shivers rippling. My thrall bangles buzzed, distant but definite, my wrists itching.

Don't, Jade. Remember. Rajah's voice slid into my head, gentle but insistent, the smell of his skin still warm in my nostrils.

"No." My lips slurred, and I had to force the words out. "No thanks."

Dante's fingers slid delicately over the twin scarlet dents in my shoulder where Rajah had cleaned up the mess, and he slipped his fingertip into his mouth, tasting. "My, my. Defiance. It doesn't taste good. Someone whispering poison in your ear, my sweet? Maybe you need another taste of my antidote."

Darkness smeared the air, crashing Dante back against the mirror. Rajah materialized, his fingers squeezing Dante's throat, muscles rippling and male bodies crushing together as Rajah forced him against the glass. "Take your filthy fingers off her."

Dante hissed, pink spit flecking, and broke free, his movement a blur. Effortlessly he threw Rajah against the opposite mirror, glass creaking under the impact. He bared shining wet fangs an inch from Rajah's face. "Careful where you piss, puppy dog. It might get you into a fight."

"Go on, then." Rajah gritted his teeth but didn't back down, challenge ripe in his flashing eyes. "Do it, in front of everyone. I'll die in a noisy mess they can't possibly miss. You really want that?"

Mad relish swirled in Dante's ultra-blue gaze. "You'd better be sure I give a shit."

Apprehension wrenched my long-suffering guts once more, and I forced a laugh. "Steady on the hormones, guys. Not in front of a lady, huh?"

Rajah stared Dante down, raising a defiant eyebrow, sweat trickling down his perfect temple.

Dante shoved him aside, swallowing a snarl in an effort to keep his dignity. "I'll not make demands on you, Jade. Do what you like. I only ever asked you for trust." He turned his deep blue eyes on me, hurt and distant. "Only I care for you. Only I

understand you. Come back to me when you've realized that."
And he was gone, air rushing in to fill the sudden space.

I let out a pent-up breath, blinking to empty my mind of
those horrid, hypnotic eyes. My thrall bangles yipped and stung,
angry like insects. I ignored them. I was well rid of him. I'd just
have to find some other way to satisfy Kane's demand. The scarlet stink of that fairy's spew drifted once again in my nostrils,
and I suspected I knew the answer to some of Kane's questions
already. Dante was poisoning the fae with his own blood. But
I still didn't know why.

Rajah cracked his neck, rubbing scarlet scratches on his throat,
and sighed. "Yeah, so I handled that well." He scraped a tense
hand through his hair, fury still tightening his muscles, and gave
me a lopsided smile. "Sorry. Couldn't help it."

His bashful gallantry shone on my heart like sunshine, and
I wanted to kiss him. "It's a wonder you've lived this long, Rajahni Seth. Leaping to girls' defense like that."

"Not girls. Just you." He winked, and disappeared. *Don't
worry. If Luna tries anything, I'll stay invisible while I throttle him.*

I straightened my purse on my shoulder, scaly dread coiling
in my bowels. "You'd better be kidding."

His invisible lips brushed mine, burning, and his tongue
flicked my teeth, the unexpected sensation shocking through my
core. *We're in this together. I'll help you when I can.*

I nodded, anxiety still raw on my skin like a rash, and stepped
from the corridor, trying to look like my legs weren't shaking. I
could trust him, right? He'd never fool Luna on his own. So he'd
keep his word, and help me. Wouldn't he?

The glittering party still mingled and laughed, the bar still
festooned with drunken fae and improbably perfect mortals. At

my end a muscled football player I recognized chatted up a golden-skinned fae girl, trying to ease his hand down the front of her dress while she giggled and snorted a line of sparkling blue dust off the glass bar, spiky green hair flopping. On a pile of white cushions an identical pair of sly blond fae boys shared a sleepy-eyed vampire girl, thin silvery limbs entwined, their tongues flicking together as they kissed her, her long black hair fluttering on the pale carpet.

I walked up to the bar and asked for cognac and absinthe on ice, two of. I glanced around while the girl mixed my drinks. I couldn't see Dante, and I hoped he'd left without me. But there stood Luna at the massive window, golden hair flowing over his silk-clad shoulder in a haze of mauve aura. Talking into his phone. On his own. Perfect.

Nauseating. Are you really going to drink that stuff? Rajah's amused whisper slipped softly into my head like a caress, but I couldn't feel him near me, and I wondered about the range of his sexy little mind tricks. I resisted a nervous smile, and the girl eyed me strangely as I took the two cocktail glasses.

My heels clicked softly on the dark glass floor, and my guts lurched at the heights, the city impossibly distant beneath. I approached him, the stems warming in my trembling fingers, and my nerves twisted as he turned. Had he heard me coming? Did he feel my body heat? Sense me? I had my rapture under control; I wasn't emanating anything. Hell, maybe he'd smelled me. I wouldn't put it past him. I could smell myself, warm and salty, the hot fluid still coating me from Rajah's touch. My cheeks warmed, my pulse swelling in my temples.

Luna looked me up and down with sharp amber-green eyes, still speaking into his little silver phone. "Yeah, well, I told him a hundred and fifty or he can go to hell. No pun intended. Listen, I really gotta go." He flipped the phone shut and vanished it away with a twirl of long fingers.

I swallowed and offered him a glass, ice clinking in clouded green vapor. "To old times?"

He studied me, cool, before giving me his shattering smile and taking the drink from me, his hard fingertips shocking mine with static. I struggled not to flinch. Was that a tease, or a warning?

He clinked his glass against mine and took a mouthful, rolling his eyes in a caricature of pleasure as he savored and swallowed. "Damn, that's good. You know what I like. But I'll drink to new times and screw the old."

"That's fair." I sipped, the fiery alcohol zinging on my tongue, fumes dizzying. I'd need it, to stomach his charm.

"Eminently. Anyway, were we really that long ago, you and I?"

"Long enough. Aren't you afraid I'll poison you?"

He smiled, beautiful eyes flashing. "You don't smell like poison, wildcat."

"Really. What do I smell like, then?"

He slitted his eyes, pretending to consider, but ruined the effect with a cheeky turn at the corner of his mouth. "I'd say . . . regret. Frustration. Angsty shit like that, you know. But poison's a coward's weapon, and you were never afraid. Besides, you've something better now. Those sexy bangles." He let his gaze travel over me, cool.

My nerves stung a warning. "Not that I ever needed such a thing with you."

He laughed, dropping his arm around my shoulder and

gesturing to the window with his half-empty glass. "God, I'll never tire of this. Never. Remember those nights in Sultanah-met, the torchlit barges on the bay? We swam in the warm ocean naked and swore we'd live forever. And here we are." A laugh rumbled his chest, his mauve aura whispering warm and hungry on my skin. "Not totally what you had in mind, I guess, but still."

Intentional or not, his barb skewered my heart. Bastard. I'd forgotten his carelessness, his reckless disregard for feelings. No wonder he and Kane got on so well.

His scent of orange blossom and cloves drifted, too close, unpleasantly disarming. Warm silk-clad muscles pressed into the back of my neck, tempting, but his familiarity sickened me. I tried to concentrate on the sensations, forget our history, ignore the screaming impulse to rake my nails down his face, choke him, smack his head into the glass until he bled and tear home to scrub myself clean. Just a man. A handsome, powerful man, a candy feast for my eyes and a snarling feline god in bed, but just a man. I'd had hundreds. I could surely have this one.

His fingers lay slack against my upper arm, casual, like he'd no intention of letting them stray elsewhere. We'd see about that. I tilted away, sliding my hand into my bag. "I brought you a gift."

"Oh, you shouldn't have—" His tone changed when he saw the vial, his pupils dilating, and when I slipped it into his hand, he swallowed, golden glitter reflecting in his eyes as he held it to the light. "But I'm so glad you did. What is it? No, don't tell me. Let me guess."

He put his drink aside on the metal window frame and loosened the cork, tracing his fingertip around the vial's lip to collect a sparkling drop. As he touched it to his lips, the air shimmered around him, so slight, I thought I'd imagined it, and my stomach clenched in anticipation. Rapture, while I distracted Luna's senses with the drug. My admiration for Rajah slipped up another notch. That was good. That was very good.

Luna's eyes sparkled, and he sucked his fingertip with relish. "Not sure if I'm flattered or disappointed. You gave up the night we met for this?"

I wetted my lips, delicate, and the shimmer flashed again. "I wanted you to have it. She asked for something . . . fierce."

His gaze fixed on mine, entranced. "Never mind, then. We made plenty like that, eh?"

I held his stare, daring him. "Hundreds."

He watched me, and electricity stung my skin as he searched, suspicious.

I didn't let my gaze slip. The rapture was all Rajah's. He'd find nothing.

Finally he gave a soft laugh and popped the cork, bringing the vial to his nose. Golden glitter swirled as he inhaled deeply, savoring the fresh fae essence. His face colored, his green eyes glazing, and he let out his breath in a rush. "Good god."

More, murmured Rajah, and Luna's aura writhed and rippled under the slow caress of rapture.

I smiled, careful. "Like it?"

"I love it." Luna sniffed, swallowed, and offered me the half-empty vial, his tawny lashes shimmering. "Try some."

My heart thudded, my fingers clenching on the hot stem of my glass. I hadn't anticipated he'd want to share. The last thing I needed with him around was a head full of reckless fairy shit.

Take it. Rajah's whisper was urgent, tense. *I'm watching. You'll be fine.*

He was right. I couldn't back down now. I took the vial, willing my fingers not to shake, and snorted.

Lemon-splashed fire exploded in my skull. My pulse leapt into a sprint. My vision tumbled, drenched with falling stars, and I swayed, water stinging my eyes. Holy shit.

Luna laughed, gripping my shoulder so I wouldn't stumble.

I steadied myself, acid citrus searing my palate, air fresh and cold in my nose. My body warmed as the drug rushed into my blood, sweat seeping onto my skin. I felt a foot taller, stronger, my hips curvier, my breasts bigger. Rapture kindled deep inside my womb, and I clenched it tight so it couldn't escape. Not yet.

His gaze slipped to mine and stayed there, his fingers gentle now on my shoulder. "Now that's worth an old memory, eh?"

Cloves stung my tongue, seductive, my drug-washed sense of taste heightened. I hadn't realized he was so close. I tucked the empty tube away in my purse, and it clinked on the waiting soultrap, surely audible. I swallowed, my lips parting. "Want to make a new one?"

He raised his fine eyebrows, amused, but his lips shone wet, and he slipped hot fingers up my cheek, tucking away a loose curl. "Well, well. If I didn't know better, wildcat, I'd think you a trickster."

I rubbed my cheek against his palm, letting my eyelids flutter as if I lost myself. His silken cuff brushed my collarbone, warm. "You know all my tricks," I whispered. "You liked them once."

"More than once, as I recall." He traced his thumb over my bottom lip, speculative.

Excellent. Jade, you're a genius. Rajah's wicked rapture twinkled over us like snowflakes.

Luna's gaze darkened, scorching. He twisted my glass from my fingers, drained the drink in a single gulp and dropped it. It shattered at our feet, green-stained fragments scattering. "Let's see if you've learned any new ones."

He slid his perfumed wrist around my neck, pulling me toward him. His lips came down hard on mine, tilting my head back, filling my mouth with his strong taste. I gasped, triumph and seductive memory burning deep holes in my composure. He forced my mouth open and slanted his head to get his tongue in deeper, and for a frightening instant I remembered how I'd loved him. He'd broken me, burned my life to endless ash with a careless shrug, humiliated and hurt me like no one else ever had. But I had loved him. My body singing with it, my senses drenched in it. I'd whispered it in his ear, screamed it to the world, gasped it into his mouth with my legs wrapped around his hips and his hot length buried deep inside me.

My heart ached with loss. I stretched my tongue deeper into his warmth, searching for anything that remained of what we'd had. His long fragrant hair flowed over my hands, silk raw on my palms as I slid them up his spine.

My front teeth scraped against his, and the shock hauled me back to reality. He'd said he loved me, too, and I'd ended up chained to a filthy wall in his dungeon. Fingers of nausea curled in my stomach that I'd enjoyed touching him again even for a moment. Maybe Luna had rapture spells of his own.

He smiled, his lips curving in our kiss. "Didn't think I'd leave this to chance, did you?"

My throat swelled in alarm, but he spun me around, forcing

me against the window, pinning my wrists to the glass, his body unyielding against my back. My breasts flattened on the window, my taut nipples compressing. He was hot, his heartbeat strong and quick, his cock pressing hard and inviting into the base of my spine. He dragged ravenous lips across the curve between my neck and shoulder, his tongue savoring the sticky fang marks. "Mmm. You still taste good."

He released one of my hands to crush my skirt in his fist, pulling it up over my thigh, fingers grasping for my skin. The glittering city loomed below, dizzying, and I pressed my cheek against the cold glass, my hot breath misting in a damp cloud over my hand. He'd take me here, in front of everyone. My heart pounded, the drug dilating my vessels. I've never fucked eighty-seven floors above nothing.

I folded my head back against his shoulder, breathless and squirming for more reasons than nausea. "Not here. Take me to bed."

He forced my thighs apart with one of his, and his urgent fingers traced the curve of my naked ass, tempting. "Never so shy in Constantinople, wildcat."

I resisted the urge to thrust back onto him, get him inside me any way I could, get this over with before he could screw with my mind. "No phone cameras in Constantinople."

"True." He released me and slipped his hand into mine, tugging me away toward a darkened doorway beside the bar.

An amused, lustful tingle along my spine made me jump. *Pity*, whispered Rajah. *I was getting hot watching that.*

I swallowed a smile. So Rajah liked to watch, did he? Well, he'd get an eyeful pretty soon. My insides heated at the thought of him watching us, those gold-flecked eyes molten with lust.

Luna dragged me into the dark corridor, grating electric music fading, and my nerves wriggled, shaking off my levity. The fairy's drug sharpened my vision and put a sway into my hips as I walked, but deep-seated unease still dragged me down. Luna was dangerous. Forgetting that could hurt me.

We emerged into his vast pine-scented living space, the tall glass ceiling distant and star-flecked, pale carpet glowing under soft spotlights. On a low table by the window an old-fashioned brass oil lamp gleamed beside tortured blown-glass figures in black and scarlet. Bizarre art decorated the walls, dark scrawls and bright painted slashes of color, stunning nature photographs of sunsets and waterfalls digitally warped and stained to look like scenes from hell. Slate tiles covered an alcove in one corner for a bathroom, with a shower, a wide white bathtub, and a mirror over the sink.

Luna nipped my ear with wet lips, his seductive tongue curling. "Make yourself at home," he whispered, and shoved me backwards.

16

I stumbled, flinging my arms out for balance, and thudded into soft whiteness. My purse slipped from my shoulder, tumbling to the floor, and he was on me, his lips crushing mine, his hard thigh insistent between my legs. I shivered beneath him, icy apprehension and hot desire chasing each other over my skin. He already had me on his bed. Luna wasn't one to mess around, especially not with rapture whispering lustful thoughts inside his head. Triumph tingled my thighs, adding to my pleasant discomfort, and I writhed, pressing myself onto him. I could do this. One orgasm, he's dead and it's over. Right?

He sat astride me and fought for my wrists, pinning me down, his long silk coat flowing over my bare legs. Reflexively I struggled, and he held me tighter, his eyes gleaming. His beautiful golden hair tangled over his wide shoulders, an unsettling smile creeping about his lips.

He released one of my wrists, and without so much as a flicker of his hot green eyes, he conjured a mass of bright silk into his hand, the energy release tainting the air with ozone. He wrapped my wrist tightly, and tied it fast to the rail at the top of his bed.

The scarf bit into my pulse, making it throb, and swiftly he did the same to the other wrist, stretching my arms over my head. "Wouldn't want you wriggling away."

I swear I heard Rajah catch his breath. *Oh, now that's too much. Do you have any idea how hard it is to stand back and watch?*

My nipples tightened, and I squirmed, enjoying Luna's weight pressing down on me as much as I relished the thought of Rajah watching. Have to admit, the tying-up thing still turned me on. My sex awakened, the pleasant ache growing, new moisture thickening. If I had to let him fuck me, I might as well get into it.

Now that I lay immobile, Luna shrugged off his coat and tossed it away. His ultrafine silk shirt didn't even pretend to hide the brutally masculine shapes of his chest, the way his waist narrowed and tightened, the steel piercing at his nipple. That was new. He'd always had sensitive nipples, a hair-trigger for his arousal. I imagined my tongue flicking that sharp stud, teasing the hard peak of flesh, sucking it. It'd drive him crazy. If I could reach, which I couldn't.

When he unbuttoned the shirt and let it fall, I got an even better view, his pale skin taut over naturally toned muscles, that sexy serpent tattoo curling around his biceps, assorted scars across his chest still showing after all this time. Some of those were probably from my teeth, and I recalled the citrus tang of his skin, the silky stone of his cock on my tongue.

He leaned over me, soft golden hair brushing my breasts, and trailed his wet mouth up the inside of my silk-shackled forearm, leaving shivering heat in his wake. His scent filled my mouth, triggering bittersweet memory. I recalled the games we'd played, how he teased me until desire threatened to boil my blood, until I whimpered and pleaded for him to fuck me. My stomach clenched even as he pleasured me. Would he make me beg?

I hesitated at the thought of Rajah watching me humiliate myself. But there wasn't much left of my dignity as far as he was concerned anyway, not after he'd nearly made me come screaming in about three seconds flat with just his fingers.

Still, the sooner this was over with, the better. I was already liking it too much. Daring, I flexed muscles deep inside my abdomen and let loose a tiny ripple of that pent-up rapture.

Luna's mouth claimed mine again, and I gave in, tempting him, letting him dominate me. He nudged my chin up, his lips wicked on my throat, and unwillingly I strained against the silk, wanting to crush his hair in my hands, drag his mouth farther down to my puckered nipples, my belly, my sex. God, I'd forgotten how good he was, how effortlessly he turned me on. The things he was doing with his tongue shot burning bombs of desire straight to my clit, and he was only kissing my neck.

Rajah's sigh sparkled over my skin, intense. *You are so hot. I could come from just watching you.* Warm breath burned my ear, shocking me into a hiss. He was right there, at the edge of the bed. Watching me gasp, smelling me, inhaling my pleasure. I tossed my head toward him, stifling a groan, longing to feel Rajah's beautiful swelling lips devouring mine while Luna slid that talented tongue between my legs.

Too late I smelled ozone, the telltale stink of conjuration. A cold metal blade stung my collarbone, tipping icy water over my need.

I choked, tugging helplessly at my bindings. Luna leaned over onto one elbow and traced the knifepoint across the sensitive bone, leaving a smarting trail, heat seeping slowly as my blood trickled. I kicked, but he trapped my legs with his thigh, heavy and strong and impossible to move. His cock lay hard against me, and my wriggling only got him harder. He ground against me with a slow sigh of desire.

My heartbeat quickened, and I tried to swallow, fear gripping my throat like a tight fist. I'd seen him torture girls, cut them, burn their nipples with glowing iron, tease them with his tongue and his cock in the most sensitive places while they sobbed. His imagination was staggering, his patience never-ending. It had amused me, back when I hated the world and everyone in it except him. But he'd never done it to me. "What the fuck—"

He clamped his other hand gently over my mouth and clicked his tongue. "Did you really think I'd forgotten those curses you spat at me? I've never heard such filth come out of your sweet mouth." He trailed the warming knifepoint into the hollow of my throat and pressed gently, his gaze fixed on mine.

The spot stung, my pulse throbbing, and dread parched my mouth. Rajah's invisible fingers brushed across my hair, reassuring. *It's all right, I won't let him hurt you. He's still enraptured. Just do what he wants, and wait for our moment.*

I knew Rajah was right. Luna's face still glowed warm from the fairy's drug, his eyes glazed with unnatural rapture-borne sensuality. He was still ours. So long as I could endure this.

God, I hoped that wasn't just the drug rushing around my own head talking.

Luna watched me, his lips quivering apart. "You want to be careful who you curse to hell forever next time. It might come back and bite your pretty ass. We can still be friends, Jade. I can forgive you. But not until you've repented for your mistakes."

The knife's wide blade glinted, and for a moment he admired

the light catching on the sharp edges. Then he slid the cold steel beneath the satin shoulder strap of my dress. The blade sliced through the thin scarlet fabric as if it wasn't there, only a tiny hiss of friction. He slit the other one, too, and undid the side zipper on my dress so he could drag it down. He slid the slick satin under my ass, over my trembling thighs, down to my ankles and off, slipping the straps of my shoes over my heels so they came off, too.

His hungry stare raped me, raking over my body like rough hands. I'd never felt so naked. I quivered, the scarves cutting into my wrists, desolate helplessness washing away my confidence.

You are so beautiful. Rajah's whisper felt thick with lust on my ear, and for an instant something wet and burning brushed my nipple. His invisible fingertip, wet with his saliva.

Desire flooded me, hot and fast, shooting under my skin. My clit ached, aroused too quickly, a rush of blood so fierce, I cried out. *Jesus. Don't do that. He'll see.*

But Luna just smiled, oblivious. He stripped naked, down-lights gloating over the perfect shapes of his thighs, the sweet curve of his ass, the soft satiny sheen of his magnificent cock. His aura glowed violet, a rippling, eerie second skin. A beautiful man with a demon's cold heart. Not that I wanted to insult demons. At least Kane eventually figured out he'd hurt you, even if he didn't understand why.

He crawled back up over me, muscles gleaming with light sweat. Delicately he flicked his tongue out to my nipple, savoring it, adding to Rajah's heat. "Good girl. Already so hard." He reversed the knife in his hand and licked the sharp point, wetting and warming it. A drop of his shiny saliva collected on the wicked tip, and delicately he lowered it to my straining nipple.

The hot sting tore into my breast, and bumps broke out on my skin. I gulped, my thighs straining beneath his. To have pain where I'd just felt burning pleasure was exquisite and horrible. He twisted his wrist, digging the point in farther.

He moved the knife away and nudged me hard between the legs with his cock. I wriggled my thighs apart, hoping the bastard would just get on with it. But he smiled, cruel. "So you can still handle a little pain? Let's see how you cope with pleasure."

He slid down my body, opened me with deft fingers and fastened his hot tongue right over my clit. Treacherous pleasure shot to my core like a bullet, hard and painful. My breath left me in a rush, hot juice flooding from my womb to soak the sheet, and my rapture ignited in a burst of flame, filling me with shuddering, pent-up energy.

Rajah's groan inflamed me more. *You're killing me. Come, my love. Let him bring you. Fake it if you have to, and while he's distracted we'll have him.*

Fake it? He had to be kidding. Luna's tongue worked harder, swirling over my most tender spot, and burning tension rippled through my abdomen. I gasped, traitorous tears welling in my eyes. It had been so long since any man had bothered to go down on me—I certainly didn't count Dante raping me with his tongue while I sprawled in a blood-drenched stupor—that I'd forgotten how good it felt. So hot, so perfect. My inner muscles rippled, foreshadowing my release, and metal stung my swollen flesh there, cold and frightening.

Jesus. He had the knife there. Millimeters from my soft insides, so I couldn't move, not unless I wanted to skewer myself. The sick son of a bitch. Nausea and disgust crawled cold fingers over me, spoiling my pleasure, and I was glad.

"Uh-uh," Luna murmured, and I felt him smile. "Don't move." He sucked me, delicate, drawing my swollen clit deeper into his mouth, and raw sensation gripped me, but all my enjoyment in the act had fled. I couldn't come like this, not with that sharp steel threatening to slice me and the air dripping with Luna's breathless malice. Guess I'd have to fake it after all, and I'd better make it good.

I closed my eyes, willing my body to stay still, and thought of Rajah, pretending he was doing what Luna was doing, tonguing me softly, then hard, teasing my flesh into spasms, his gorgeous dark hair spilling like warm water over my thighs as I locked my ankles around his neck. I thought of how I'd react, and I groaned, tossing my head back. I imagined his tongue sliding inside, fucking me, drinking my hot fluid straight from the source, and I struggled to remain still. My breath quickened, my thighs quivering, straining. My imaginary Rajah replaced his tongue with that smooth finger, more fingers, sinking them deeper, stirring, stimulating that magical spot. I moaned, my nipples hardening again without any help. "Oh, god, that's good."

"Mmm." Luna pulled back a little, softening his tongue. "Good girl. Can you come without moving? Bet you can't."

You're doing great. Don't let him see this. Invisible fingers plucked at my wrists, loosening the scarves. Silk whispered over my forearms, and I was free. I cried out breathlessly so Luna wouldn't notice, curling my toes and making my thigh muscles jump like I couldn't take much more. "No, please, don't."

Rajah's hot palms slid over mine, and I gripped his unseen hands so tightly, my knuckles ached. I wanted to grab Luna's hair and drag him off me, gouge my nails into his eyes and rip them out. I wanted to grab Rajah and take him, sink him into me and never let go. Rapture swirled in my abdomen like a dancing fireball, threatening to explode.

My mouth watered hard, painful, and I swallowed. Okay, enough thinking about Rajah fucking me. The point was to make Luna fuck me, to make him come, not me.

I made my body shiver, panting. "Please, don't make me. I want to come with you inside me. Please . . . oh, god, no." I cried out, digging my heels into the sheet, pressing myself against Luna's horrid caressing mouth, trying not to wince as the knife blade brushed my skin, stinging. I contorted my thighs, letting my muscles shudder and heave. Luna groaned, covering me with his tongue, his fingers digging into my thighs.

Yeah. Now let it rip. Rajah released my hands, and his dark shimmering ripples slammed down over us, soaking the air like a rampant heat haze. I gritted my teeth in anticipation and let my own straining rapture erupt.

Agonising relief burst in my guts, like its own kind of orgasm, and my body burned with magical sexual energy. Sparks arced in my hair, crackling, the smell of ozone spreading.

Luna shuddered between my legs, his heavy shoulder muscles shaking. He whipped the blade away and tossed it onto the floor, diving onto me and pulling my thigh around his hips with a hot, strong hand. His cock jammed into my pubic bone, painfully hard. "Wildcat, you gorgeous thing, I can't pretend. I want you so bad," he breathed, and rammed himself into my swollen flesh in a single powerful thrust.

My rapture sizzled. Rajah laughed darkly in my head, and I felt like laughing, too. I locked my legs around Luna's hips and wrapped my hands in his hair, dragging his head down to me. I had the bastard exactly where I wanted him. I flexed, gripping his cock with practiced muscles, and he clenched his teeth, thrusting deeper, again and again. It felt good. But not so good, I couldn't enjoy his powerlessness. Cold magic fists grasped, crushing, searching for my glamour, but it was too late. The rapture was too strong, flowing over us like a sparking volcano.

Absurdly, a breathless smile parted his lips. "Shit. You're good. I figured I'd see this coming. I didn't see a damn thing." He pushed into me again, helpless, groaning, his glittering mauve aura licking over me. He knew what was happening. He just couldn't do anything about it.

Victory flushed me, and I tightened my thighs, urging him on. "Confidence in a bottle, Vorenus. You should be more careful what you snort."

"Guess so. Still, it was good, wasn't it?" His movements quickened, sweat beading on his handsome forehead. His breath came shorter, his lips shining. "Oh, fuck. No way. You won't get me like that." He pushed away, triceps straining, forcing my legs down and away from his hips, trying to pull out of me before he came. I struggled, despair clenching dead fingers in my guts. He was too strong. I couldn't hold him.

"No, you fucking don't." A dark shadow flickered above us. Gold-speckled brown eyes flashed into view over Luna's shoulder, wild black hair, gleaming brown skin.

Luna choked and slammed back into me, crushing me, a painful gasp escaping his open mouth. He struggled to press up onto his elbows, panting, and with an effort sniffed the air like a cat. "Rajah," he gasped, a smile tugging at his lips. "There's two of you. No wonder. Look, we can talk about this—"

"No talking. Not for you." Rajah stared at me, smoldering, and reached down to grasp my hand, bracing himself. His forearm strained in his shining thrall bangle, his long fingers clenched in mine. He slipped his other hand beneath him, and I felt his fingers slide delicately around where Luna and I joined, collecting slick wetness and spreading it. "It's been a while, Luna. Sure hope you don't mind."

Luna tried to catch his breath, sweat glowed on his face. "You crafty bitches."

"That didn't sound like a no." Rajah gripped Luna's hipbone tightly, where Luna's body pressed into his beautiful naked flank, and shifted his hips, gritting his teeth, working his way in. Luna gasped again, his cock swelling inside me.

I couldn't see what Rajah was doing, but I had a pretty good idea. Delicious images flooded my rapture-soaked senses, and I shuddered, pleasured, sure my eyes were glazing over. The night I'd met him, I'd imagined a threesome. This wasn't quite what I'd had in mind. But my heart overflowed to look at him, damp hair falling in his face, his lips wet, gazing raptly down at me while we both did something—someone—we abhorred. He squeezed my hand, his thumb teasing my burning wrist, and his luscious lips formed a kiss, just for me.

Rapture licked over my body, raising lustful gooseflesh on my skin, and my loins ached for him, my flesh scorching with friction. I knew it wasn't Rajah my muscles clenched around in longing. But it didn't matter. He was here, with me, making love to me as we murdered our oldest and most deserving enemy. My heart ached, a lump swelling in my throat, and I fought back sweet tears. It was the most romantic thing anyone had ever done for me.

I tilted my hips up against Luna's, urgent now to get this over with. Luna groaned and filled me, and to my surprise a tear glimmered on his mauve-lit lashes too. "Well," he breathed with a gentle smile, "might as well enjoy it while it lasts." He pushed backwards, grunting in pleasure. Rajah thrust deep into him, driving them both into me. My breath forced from my lungs, delicious sensation rippling deep inside me. We moved together, slick skin sliding, muscles rubbing on muscles, dark hair mingling with golden, and the whole time Rajah's gaze never left my face, desire burning in his eyes, his fingers crushing mine.

Luna's breath deepened, ragged, his eyes squeezing shut as he tried to hold off his orgasm, to prolong the pleasure and his life. But Rajah pressed again and again against some deeply pleasurable place inside him, and I milked him, squeezing and releasing his cock until he shuddered, every breath a groan. "I can't," he gasped, a helpless laugh tearing from him. "See you both in hell."

He thrust hard into me one last time, muscles straining in his thighs, and his cock jerked and throbbed, filling me with his seed and his soul. A long painful cry forced from his mouth, dampening my face with his last breath, and his beautiful bright eyes faded to gray and rolled back. His arm muscles juddered and loosened, and he fell on me, lifeless, his weight crushing what was left of my breath away.

17

I lay stunned, my limbs rigid. Luna's soul rushed around inside me, laughing madly, filling my veins with burning mirth. My mind distorted and stretched, brimming with insane, alien intelligence. I shuddered, uncontrolled. Luna was crazy like a blood-mad raptor, and I wanted to scream, cackle like a madwoman, let the bubbling thing froth up my throat and choke me.

Rajah dragged Luna's heavy corpse off me. Golden hair tumbled onto the sheet, limbs tangling. He caught me in his arms, crushing me to his chest, smoothing sweaty hair from my face. "It's done, princess. You got him."

The carnal smell of our sex churned my stomach. Luna's soul writhed in my womb, kicking, scratching at my walls with hateful nails, and my rapture hissed and fought back. I retched, spit flecking, my eyes watering, but nothing came up.

Rajah pulled me closer onto his lap, my legs folding over his knees. The air still shimmered and roiled around us. His heartbeat throbbed rapidly against me, his damp cock still pressing hard beneath my thighs, but he wasn't bothered with rapture now, and neither was I, not really, not with this evil soul energy still raping me. I dry-heaved again, my face scorching, and he stroked my back gently, small circles from the base of my spine up. His hand shook a little, burning to do more, but I couldn't blame him for that. "Come on, sweetheart. Don't keep it in."

"Always telling me to be sick," I muttered, nausea gripping me again, the lust burning within me from unsated rapture only making it worse.

He grinned softly, charming, and scrabbled on the floor for my bag. He dug out the soultrap, folded my fingers around its warm brass neck, and resumed stroking my back, willing the grotesque thing out of me.

And out it came. Pain stabbed through my veins, cramping like a vise. Acid seared up my throat and poured out onto my tongue, bubbles stinging my nose. Hot purple froth gushed into the soultrap. I choked, spitting up the last of it, sweet and horrid in my mouth, and when I was finished, Rajah jammed the cork in tight. The bottle sizzled in my hand, the metal thrumming. Rabid laughter echoed faintly from within.

I dropped it on the bed and clung to him, my limbs stiff and sore, sticky fluid leaking between my legs. He folded his arms around me, resting his cheek on top of my head. Cheated of its prize, my rapture flared hotter, angry, heating my skin. My senses ignited to Rajah's quivering body, his warm muscles moving against me, the stony length of his cock pressing against my leg. But the sickly sweet taste of Luna flowered on my tongue, a shady remnant of his soul still chuckling deep in my heart. His sweat still greased my skin, his saliva still running between my legs, his hot semen still coating my insides. Filth smothered me, clogged my hair, my nails, made me stink. Sluggish worms of loathing coiled in my innards. Disgusting. Filthy. Useless. Whore.

I shoved Rajah away, my legs scything on the wet sheet. I didn't want him to have to touch me. Why would he want to touch me? I stank. I wept refuse. Shudders racked me, and I wrapped my arms around my curled legs, sick, even as my rapture screamed at me to push him down next to Luna's cooling corpse and impale myself on him.

Rajah's warm hand touched my shoulder, hesitant. "Princess—"

"Don't touch me!" I shrugged him off, furious.

But he held me, and a moment later I felt his arm slipping beneath my bent knees, my shoulder thudding into his hard chest as he lifted me effortlessly. I wriggled. "What are you—?"

"Hush." He carried me across the carpet, cradling my head on his shoulder, his warm cardamom scent a temptation and a scorching reprimand at the same time. His bare feet snicked on hard tiles, and I heard the splatter of rushing water. He put me down, the slate cold beneath my feet, and pushed me under the shower.

Hot water splashed, running over my face, into my mouth, soaking my hair, flooding down my body. Steam clouded, misting the air with warmth. Scalding freshness sloughed over me, but filth still clung like fungus. I scrubbed at myself, frantic, my bangles scraping, water stinging my eyes as I tried to see. My arms, my breasts, my belly, between my legs, the hot friction of my wet hands tearing at my skin, digging into the dirt, my nails scratching.

"Slow down." Rajah gripped my wrists and gently pulled them away. Water splashed over his gleaming brown body, rinsing away sweat and stickiness, and he reached for the soap. "Let me wash you clean."

Tears spilled from my eyes, cold in the steaming water, and

my hand shook in his. Was he reading my mind now? God, I'd been raped enough already for one night. But I looked up into his eyes, and his bleeding torment floored me. He chewed his lip, his mouth tight and quivering, and his fingers strained white where he clutched the pale soap. It was okay between us; he didn't despise me. His anguish was for me, and it was all his own. He wasn't reading my mind. He just knew.

My giddy heart tipped over a precipice, falling forever, and the clang of warning in my head came too late.

Barely able to move, I nodded. He touched my shoulder and turned me gently, and I felt the smooth soap rubbing over me in his palm, slow circles over my shoulder blades, down my spine, up to the base of my neck. My hair stuck to my shoulders, and pine-scented soap suds slid down my back, over my hips, into the cleft of my ass, washed away by the rushing water. Now he used both hands, massaging me, sending new blood to my worn, aching muscles. Bumps crept over my scalp. I shivered, flexing sore shoulders, and my still-unsated rapture sighed, urging me to press backwards, slide his cock between my legs.

He folded strong arms around me, holding me gently against him. My skin slid over him, slick, the friction delicious. I could feel his erection pulsing against my bottom, his body heat searing even in the shower, but he didn't seem to care. His soapy hands slid to my belly, my ribs, leaving a fresh, clean feeling behind them. He washed the undersides of my breasts, hesitant, and I wanted to thrust forward, rub my nipples into his palms, feel the hard lump of soap against them.

"Touch me." My voice scraped my throat, hoarse with wanting. I needed Rajah's hands on me, to erase the memory of what we'd done, of Luna's body on mine, the smell of orange blossom, his mouth invading me, the hard thrust of his cock, his groan as he came and died.

Rajah bent his head against mine, black hair dripping hot water onto my face, and his gentle touch moved higher. My breasts slid like gel in his hands, slippery with soap. He delved his hands between them, around them, over them, up around my shoulders and back down, and soft pleasure flooded into my body, washing away the tension and the dirt. He caught my nipples between his knuckles and tugged gently, and when his fingers slipped off, twin bolts of desire jammed deep into me, my breasts aching.

Now I did press back against him, rubbing my head on his shoulder. Water flooded down, over my face, washing hot waves over my breasts, trickling between my legs. I parted my thighs, and the water stroked my swollen clit, teasing, making me want more. My soap-slick back skidded on his chest, the twin hard nubs of his nipples dragging over me. He sighed, and reckless need ignited in my heart. I flexed my hips. He pulled me onto him, his fingers digging into my hipbones, his cock burning in the drenched furrow between my buttocks. I shivered to my core with longing. My body wanted more, wanted to bend over and push him into me, make love to him, fuck him hard and fast until I exploded. I clenched my ass, squeezing his cock, and the throb of his flesh and his soft groan told me he wanted the same.

But my mind wouldn't let go. Fragments of insane soul energy still giggled inside me, wicked. I couldn't forget the feel of another man fucking me, making me wet, sticky, filthy with desire and come. And it wasn't just Luna. It was Dante, Quinn, Angelo, every man I'd ever touched without emotion, every man

I'd let soil me with lust. Rajah touched my heart and my pleasure in ways that delved deeper than I wanted to admit. If we were going to love, I wanted it to be special, and it wasn't.

"I can't," I whispered, but something deep inside me cracked.

"It's okay. Let me care for you." He slid the soap down over my belly, into the curls between my legs, rubbing me gently until it lathered frothy and white. Easing his hand lower, he slid soap into the creases at the tops of my thighs, washing sticky residue from the hair. Despite my upset, my flesh twinged and strained under his touch, and my thighs drifted apart of their own accord. When the soap in his palm brushed the hood of my clit, sensation shocked my nerves, crinkling my skin with pleasure.

"Don't," I gasped, but I didn't mean I didn't want it. Just that I didn't deserve it. He shouldn't have to touch me, not like this, while I still reeked of other men.

"Hush." The dark intent heating Rajah's whisper sent anticipation shivering into my bones. The soap slipped from his hand and plopped onto the slate. Pounding water washed the lather away, the suds sliding over his hand and down my legs, but it didn't matter. His fingers glided into me easily, my hot entrance soaked from within. I couldn't help but moan. My flesh ached, lumpy with overworked glands and swollen tight from fucking, but having him inside me again felt so damn good.

He parted his fingers gently, twisting them, opening me. My muscles worked against him, pleasure flowering. Warmth gushed down in my channel, Luna's fluid and my own seeping out over Rajah's hand to be washed away. Clean hot water flooded his palm, washing up inside, sluicing the mess from me.

He slipped his other arm around my waist and bent his

head to my shoulder. "I don't care, princess," he whispered, water trickling over his lips onto my neck, his hair dripping hot trails over me. "It doesn't matter to me what you've done, who you've been with, whether it's for thrall or for energy or because you wanted to. I don't care. I just want you. Not only your body. You."

I shuddered, my heart slashed and bleeding. His fingers still stroked gently inside me, cleaning me. But he stroked my desire, too, making my nipples yearn for his mouth, my body long to be filled. His empathy ripped me open, exposing my deepest wounds, and impossible words like *love* and *forever* caught on the aching lump in my throat.

I gripped his wrist, pushing him deeper, and his forearm tightened in my grip, urgent. Our bangles clinked together, water spraying. He groaned and pulled his fingers away, and I groaned, too, in protest. But he spun me around, out of the water against the steam-wet wall, and dropped to his knees before me, his eyes fixed on the shiny slickness coating my thighs. "I have to taste you. I can't not . . . oh, Jade." He leaned forward and plunged his hot tongue between my folds.

My palms thudded into the slate wall lest my knees buckle. Sensation exploded, waves of excitement rippling my thighs, my abdomen, all the way along my limbs. He wrapped his arm around my legs, caressing my eager clit with the hottest, sweetest, most perfect sensations. My nerves erupted, heat flashing out like lightning to every part of my body. Energy swirled inside me, rapture shocked into burning upsurge. I quivered, helpless, sighing with pleasure.

I resisted letting my head fall back or closing my eyes to revel in this insane bliss. I wanted to watch Rajah go down on me.

Watch this impossible, beautiful man who cared so much about my pleasure, giving it to me with an intensity I hadn't known for years. Maybe ever.

His eyes lay closed, dark lashes a fine mess on his cheekbones. Steam clouded around us, and water sluiced over his back, his drenched hair dripping in his face. He dipped lower, bringing out more moisture, and he was probably licking Luna as well as me but he didn't give a damn. My clit swelled so hard, every movement was perfect agony. He parted my flesh with his fingers, and I watched his tongue move over me, swirling, flicking, tasting. . . .

Sweet Jesus. Watching him just made it worse. I groaned, my thighs contracting. Tension gripped me, tightening, more, more. My hand fisted itself in his hair, squeezing tight. "I'll come," I stammered, breathless, probably the most unnecessary warning ever.

He just sucked me, hard, flicking my sensitive tip over and over, torturing me. I just had time to see his eyes flicker open, smoky with desire, before pleasure slammed into my guts. I shattered, the blood rushing away from my head as energy tumbled out of me, reckless. He held me, roughly prolonging my pleasure with his tongue until I fell against the wall, limp and breathless, my legs refusing to accept my weight.

He wriggled up against me to his feet, hot water sloughing down between us, and kissed me, soft and sweet, scraping wet hair tenderly back from my face. "Okay, princess?"

Weariness drained me, his speckled brown eyes glazed bright with my energy, but I didn't care. I laughed, no breath in me to make it sound properly. "You've had four hundred years to practice that. I'd say I'm okay."

He leaned in for another kiss, this time long and hard with desire, our tongues sliding together. His cock burned my belly, thick and full, and the taste of my juices on his luscious lips inflamed me, making me want more of him.

I sucked on his tongue, and he made a sexy little growl in his throat, energy flowing back into me from his arousal. How I needed him now. Not just to feed me the energy he'd stolen, but to squeeze him deep inside me, claim him, let him claim me. To prove this wasn't a dream. I slid my foot up his strong calf, hooking my ankle around his leg, but my other knee gave way and I staggered, falling against him with a giggle. "Oops. Can't stand up."

"Then don't." He gripped my ass and lifted me, my back slapping against the tiles. The back of my head cracked into the wall and I squealed, wrapping my legs around his hips and my hands over his shoulders so I wouldn't fall. His fingers clutched me, desperate, like he couldn't get enough, his hard chest glistening as he panted. "Fuck. Sorry. Did that hurt?"

I loved the way he needed me, the way he lost control like that. I wanted him to lose control because of me. "I don't care."

He groaned, helpless, and bent to suck my breast into his mouth, the head of his cock nudging my aching entrance. He caught his teeth on my nipple, the sting shocking me with delight. Tension twanged, tight from my ravaged nipple to my sex. My breath caught, membranes of pleasure ready to burst all over me, all over again. I'd never been so ready. "Yes, Rajah, do it."

He turned his head to rest his cheek on my wet breast, shuddering, and pushed into me, long, powerful, all the way. "You're perfect."

A cry forced from my lips, the sensation more than I'd

expected, more than I could bear. He relaxed and thrust in again, this time slamming me down hard, his fingers bruising my ass. My flesh swelled, stretching, accepting, enfolding his burning length, the friction beyond belief. And then he gazed up into my eyes, and I thought I'd die.

He tilted his chin up, offering his mouth, and I dived in, entering him with my tongue in time with his thrusts, tangling my fingers in his sodden hair. I tried to move, but with my back jammed against the wall I couldn't, and in the end I crushed him to me and let him take me how he wanted, how he knew I wanted, hard, slow, as deep as he could go.

Energy flowed between us, swirling in our mouths and down my throat from his kiss, pouring into my insides where his cock filled me over and over. Rajah-scented steam soaked my nostrils, his taste drowning my mouth, his fragrant wet skin rubbing all over me. I couldn't get enough. I wanted this to last forever.

But it couldn't, of course. Not the way my muscles spasmed around him, bunching tight, not the way his cock swelled even harder, his thrusts fiercer, more urgent. My deepest nerves thrummed with pleasure, my most secret flesh sparking alive with tension, clenching harder, tighter. He gasped, his lips sliding on mine. "What are you doing to me, princess? I swear I'm in love."

Too much.

I erupted, burning deep inside, waves of throbbing heaven welling from our joining. He captured my mouth with his and swallowed my scream, soon matched by his own breathless cry as he came, deep, pressed up against the bone deep within me. Energy surged into me, searing like molten metal.

My skin sizzled, delight rising like fresh perfume, and my rapture coiled like a cat, sleepy and sated. He withdrew and let me slide to my feet, pulling me back under the hot shower. I clung to him, my heart still hammering and spasms of pleasure still racking my body. Damn, that was fantastic. He was fantastic. I don't know how he let me feel so good, but I wanted more of it.

My nerves sang with vigor, my muscles strong and lively. My spirit crackled, energy spitting like fireworks. I felt like I could run all night, vitality streaming through my veins. I wanted to sprint from here to Princes Bridge, climb hand over hand to the top of the blue neon spire and lean screaming into the wind with bats flapping in my hair. I wanted to pin Rajah to the steam-washed floor and screw him senseless again, feed him with my orgasm, let him feed me, make him come so hard, he passed out.

But I also wanted to lie beside him and kiss all night, his warm limbs wrapped around mine, his fingers gentle in my hair. Fondle his velvety brown skin, taste his tongue, feel his heartbeat. Slide my mouth onto his cock and swallow while he moaned. Settle my chin on his chest and watch him sleep, kiss him awake and watch him smile for me. I wanted to do everything with him.

My heart swelled, hot water sliding through my hair, my body trembling in Rajah's arms. I'd screwed an incubus before, a sweet young thing with more rapture than talent, back when I was new to thrall and still trying to make Kane notice me by fucking everything that moved. I'd enjoyed the energy fix then, too. But this was better. Out of sight, over the horizon, rocketing into orbit better. More nourishing than stealing souls, more intoxicating than any fairy's eerie drug. It was like . . .

Like the difference between fucking and making love.

Oh, hell.

I flushed all over, my skin afire, and I buried my face against

Rajah's wet chest so he wouldn't see into my eyes. And as I rested there, the wrongness of it all speared into me. I couldn't forget Luna's soul, gabbling away like a mad turkey in my trap. And I couldn't forget Rajah and I were enemies, still after the same prize.

For a few blissful minutes, I'd forgotten everything except this extraordinary, compassionate, delicious man. *Please, God, if you're there, if you haven't turned your face from me in disgust, let this just be afterglow from incredible sex. Let me just be crushing on him like a naïve convent girl. If this is your way of getting back at me, you win.*

Rajah wiped dripping hair from my face and bruised my mouth with his. His lips slid on mine like he couldn't bear to pull away, his tongue desperate to taste me. "Come home with me," he murmured between kissing, his breath tantalizing my mouth. "Say you will. Please. I need you again."

"God, yes." I couldn't believe the words spilling from me. I should go home, walk the streets and calm down, go out and pick up some anonymous hot body to work this unbearable intimacy out of my system. Go anywhere but to Rajah's bed, where I'd undoubtedly die of orgasm overload and a broken heart. Sure, he'd said the word *love*. Right when he was about to come. I'd heard that before.

But if he felt even a shadow of what I felt, I couldn't let this pass. I sought his mouth with mine, gripping his wet hair in tense hands. "Yes, tonight, now," I said.

Before it has to end. Before we remember we're going to damn each other for freedom.

He shut off the shower, reluctantly releasing me. My skin was shriveling up after so long in the water, and the tips of my fingers wrinkled. The sudden cool air shrank it further, beading my nipples. Rajah tossed me a fluffy white towel, and sweet orange blossom scent drifted. Unease shimmered through me, a distant cackle echoing in my head, but I brushed it away.

I wiped myself down, Rajah's gaze hot on my skin as I bent over. Flushing, I glanced at him. He smiled, dripping. I smiled back, warm and shivery, and a faint ache grew inside me, wetting me all over again. Damn, I was creaming from his smile now. So much for getting him out of my system.

I threw the towel at his head to stop him staring, and he caught it with a giggle.

As he toweled himself, I wandered back to the bed, wrapping my arms over my breasts. There lay dead Luna, his magnificence fading at last, his skin pale and waxy, his glorious hair spilling over crumpled sheets. As far as anyone would ever know, he fucked himself to death on too many drugs. Now that Killian Quinn was dead, no one at St. Kilda Road Homicide believed in magic or demons or soul-sucking succubi. They'd look for poison, and they'd find nothing but cognac and absinthe and elevated adrenaline.

Soft female laughter whispered, and I spun around, my nerves jerking. No one there. Just the starlight, gleaming softly on tortured glass figurines and glinting on the curved brass lamp etched like my soultrap, designs twisting like spiked vines. I wrapped my arms around my chest, shivering. I had to get out of here.

My shiny red dress lay crumpled in a pile beside Luna's body, the slashed shoulder straps tangling, and I realized I had nothing to wear. I picked up Luna's coat, and the smooth black silk caressed my skin with fragrant, memory-laden static as I slipped it on and fastened the knotted fabric buttons. It was far too big, of course, my shoulders slim in comparison to Luna's, but it fell to mid-calf after I pulled my high heels on. People might suspect I'd just come from Luna's bed, what with my hair dripping and everything, but no one would know for sure I was naked underneath except Rajah.

I tried not to stare as he dressed himself beside me. Damn, the man was beautiful. Beautiful, clever, compassionate, sexy as hell. I wanted to trace my finger on the perfect curves of his chest, bite his smooth brown nipples, slide my cheek over his taut abdomen, lick those luscious hips, nibble the insides of his sleek thighs, take his balls in my mouth and . . .

I looked away. *Get a grip, Jade.*

Slowly I retrieved the soultrap from where I'd dropped it, the living brass warm in my hands. The soul lurched inside, boiling, swinging the bottle against gravity as if drawn by a magnet. The cork trembled and I jammed it in tighter. I stared at the trap, emptiness welling larger in my stomach.

"Don't." A whisper behind me as Rajah fetched my purse. His smooth arms folded around me, and he twisted the bottle from my hands and stowed it away in my purse, slipping the cord over my shoulder. "Don't think about it. Not now."

I wanted to sink into his arms, forget about thrall and freedom and death. "Tomorrow."

"Tomorrow. You up to walking out of here?"

I squared my shoulders and stepped away from his embrace, turning to kiss him once more. "You bet. Just watch me."

He kissed me back, tentative, exploring. Shy, like we hadn't just come together in the shower with the dead guy we'd murdered lying eight feet away. Emotion welled up inside me, suffocating. He still didn't think he owned me, not even after everything we'd done. Astonishing. Humbling. Heartbreaking.

Tenderly, he grazed his thumb across my lips, his gold-flecked eyes warm. His mouth quivered, words about to spill out, but then he bit his lip and vanished. *See you soon. I'll be the invisible guy jumping you in the lift.*

"So you say. It's an express, remember. The fastest elevator in the southern hemisphere."

Unseen lips brushed my ear, delicious. *Don't relax too much. I can accomplish a lot in forty seconds.*

18

Hours later, I shuddered, dazed, aftershocks still rippling through deep, impossibly rising pleasure. "No, I can't. Not again."

"You can." Rajah pressed his long body against my back, his thigh sliding along mine. He glided his cock in and out, massaging the shuddering knot of nerves deep inside me to unbearable tension. His arm slipped over to embrace me, his lips warm and loving on my cheek. "Come, princess. Come on my cock. Let me feel you."

And I did, trembling, breathless, thrusting my breasts into his warm hand as I spasmed with insane delight. Tears slid down my cheeks, slipping salty into my quivering mouth. He was amazing. The things he did with his cock were amazing. And everywhere he touched me, every crevice he licked or sucked or stroked, memories sloughed away, wiping away years of disgust and brute, loveless contact. Our sweat and body fluid soaked his pale sheets, the heady smell of our coupling heavy in the air. He'd understood my need to cleanse, to use him to erase my shame, and offered himself freely to everything I'd asked. We'd done everything. He'd

covered me with kisses, sucked my nipples, slid his tongue and
his fingers inside me, pulled me up to my knees to bite my ass
and push his tongue into the entrance there. I'd trailed my tongue
over every curve of him, tasted his skin with my teeth, rubbed
the inside of my mouth with him, swallowed on his orgasm, felt
his thighs ripple in my hands and his cock pressing down my
throat.

Now, my eyelids flickered, and my body slumped against
him, my energy drained. A side effect of too many orgasms with
an incubus. Exhaustion had never felt so good. But the more
energy I lost, the more he gained. I could already feel him twitching like a speed freak, his cock straining hard in my dripping,
sated flesh. If he didn't finish again soon, he'd be biting his nails
and jerking around like he'd swallowed a bag of coffee beans.
And there was one thing we hadn't done yet, one place he hadn't
made me fresh and new.

I shifted my tired hips, slipping him out of me, letting his
wet cock slide between the curves of my ass. "Take me."

His fingers tightened on my breast, his breath short. "You
don't have to—"

"I want to." It was as much for him as for me. He'd had to
fuck Luna too. Still, I couldn't help but tense up. My experience
at this hadn't been friendly. Most men didn't see it as an act of
love.

But even before I felt him touch me, his gentle fingers spreading my slick fluid, opening me delicately, I knew Rajah would
be different. He guided himself to my entrance, pressing effortlessly into my ass, cradling my face close to his, rubbing his cheek
against mine. My muscles clenched, nervous. "Hush," he whispered, kissing me, and slid in farther, so slow, so gentle, I nearly

cried again. His compassion for me was intense, intimate, deeply erotic. He worked me, groaning softly as I accepted more and more of him, until he was fully inside, his warm belly flat against my ass. "You feel . . . oh, such a gift, Jade. Thank you."

His arm tightened around me and he rocked me against him, his cock moving in me ever so slightly, awakening nerves I never knew I had. The sensation was amazing, my whole body tingling. And then he slid his hand between my legs, slowly massaging my wet flesh, and I moaned. He pulled his cock out a little farther, drove it in a little harder. My clit jerked under his clever fingers, pleasure sudden and intense. I must have tensed, because he groaned and pushed harder. "Ahh. So tight. You perfect, beautiful girl."

He pressed my hard nub of pleasure, grinding it against the bone, and when I shrieked at the force of my impending release he sucked my earlobe into his mouth. My orgasm crashed over me, his merciless fingers making me spasm again and again, milking him as he lost control. He pumped me hard, my body welcoming his pleasure, seeking it, and when at last he buried himself and came with a long groan, his energy flowed into me, over me in a hot golden wave of pure perfection. Our spirits mixed, melded, rolled together in a breathless, loving surge. I shuddered, overcome. He was everything I needed, everything I ever wanted.

He buried his face in my shoulder, enfolding me in his warm embrace. "Thank you," he whispered again. "For everything."

I closed my eyes, tears pressing, the sheet warm against my cheek. His soft hair caressed my face, and I inhaled the spicy scent of his sweat, the taste of our endless kisses on his breath, the warm comfort of belonging. Emotion flooded me that I didn't want to analyze. Instead I let myself drift into a fuzzy dream of contentment, and as I lay there dazed, it occurred to me that the next 850 years might not be so bad if I could spend them here.

She's sleeping, and Rajah eases away from her, careful not to awaken her. His sweaty skin unsticks from hers slowly, reluctantly, leaving him cold and bereft. Her hair drifts on the pillow, caressing her sweet face, and it's all he can do to make himself let go. But let go he must, and it's no compulsion of time or hunger driving him but some all-too-telling burn in his heart.

He walks slowly to the shower, his limbs weak and unwilling, his feet sticky on the soft carpet. The energy they shared still prickles under his skin. Without her the bathroom is cold, empty. He closes the door, flips on the soft yellow light, and wrenches the water on hard and scorching. Once the steam rises he leans on his forearm against the glass and lets the hot water flow over his face, blinding him, dragging his hair straight and flat on his cheeks, streaking his body, washing her intoxicating flavor from his skin. He doesn't know whether he's desperate, or sorry, to be rid of it.

Anyway, the rough slough of scalding water only reminds him of loving her.

He can't get the images out of his mind. Her heartbreak, the shock and self-disgust on her face when she finally shook off Dante's tricks and saw her own blood flowing over her skin. Her courage, her mouth trembling and her fingers tightening around his while Luna tortured her in the most humiliating way. The anguish ripping from her gaze as she tried frantically to scrub herself clean, nails scratching like a captive animal's claws.

He'd longed for a good scrub himself after helping her kill Luna, though he couldn't deny that having Luna's muscles spasm around his cock in the throes of death had felt fucking good. But Jade's need was fiercer, the need of a lifetime of self-loathing, and he'd wanted to smash his fist into the tiles, scour the earth for the fucking pricks who'd used her, and rip their skin off. But the way she trusted him to understand, to help wash her clean with his touch, overflowed his heart with such dangerous wonder, he'd barely contained it.

Hell, he hadn't contained it. He'd sighed the L-word right into her mouth, and as he exploded with the hottest, most skin-melting orgasm he'd known for years, the truth of it slammed into his guts like a vicious elbow, so hard, he'd nearly dropped her.

Rajah bangs his forehead into the glass in frustration, his wet hair dragging clean streaks in the condensation. This isn't part of his plan. Not until he's sated his need for vengeance with the four magical souls and cut Kane screaming from his heart forever. Then, when he's mortal, he'll have all the time in the world for love. Not before, and certainly not with the woman he must cheat of her lonely, desperate dream in order to be free.

Madness, this flame in his heart. He wants it to sputter out, wants to shrug her off like countless others with a regretful sigh. But he can't deny what he feels. His hellbound soul zings with her, the taste of her pleasure still coating his lips. The burning instinct to keep her safe overwhelms him, the same blind compulsion that made him tempt Dante's wrath at Luna's. Heaven knew what he'd been thinking. Only a fool challenges a vampire, and Rajah's usually the guy who talks his way out of fights with a smile and a wheedling hint of rapture. But seeing Jade scared and hurt ignited his blood with rage, and the thought of Dante sliding his teeth into her—of any other man claiming her—inflamed his anger beyond reason.

The irony twists in his throat. After years of tricking lovers into wanting, he's the one yearning for some untouchable goddess. He never imagined she'd be interested in a guy like him— the words *easy* and *amoral* spring nastily to his mind, and he chews them up hastily lest he lose confidence—but something in the way she responded to his loving tells him her heart is vulnerable. Can he make a plan? Change her mind somehow? Buy some time to give himself a chance with her?

A chance to what? Fight over Luna's soul? Stand back and watch while his dreams die along with her?

The gleeful soul buzzing in that trap poisons everything, and icy reality pierces his core despite the steaming water. His throat swells, and he chokes as clarity shines, brighter and more lucid than ever before. She is his heart, his breath, the very taste of the air on his tongue.

And he can't have her.

Either way, it's impossible. Neither of them can bear staying in thrall. If he takes the soultrap for himself, she'll never forgive him. And he could never make up for the heartrending misery that is her thrall. She'll never give up her freedom, no matter how he loves her, and once she's free, she'll end it.

Without her, six more centuries of thrall stretch bleak and lonely. Excruciating. Unthinkable.

Tears scorch his eyes, and his muscles shudder, wretched, but he knows what he must do. What he intended all along, before his sentimental heart betrayed him.

Forget her. Take the soultrap and disappear. Find the last two souls, steal his freedom, and never come back.

Unwilling, he flips the water off, his nerves screaming. He can't bear the sight of her. Not now. Not her wounded gaze, the tremble of her sweet mouth when he tells her he's leaving. He'll do it now, before she wakes. It's kinder that way.

He steps from the shower, water plinking on smooth brown tiles.

A cold arm snakes around his throat, choking him into silence.

Shock triples his pulse, and instinctively he grasps for leverage to break free. But an impossibly strong male body slams him facefirst into the damp wall, wet leather creaking over his back. His cheekbone bruises, and his teeth scrape bloody dents into the inside of his cheek.

A crushing thigh between Rajah's legs jams his hips into the wall, grinding against his balls. A grip like iron yanks his arm behind his back, wrenching his elbow until a cold wedge of agony rips the joint apart. A whisper laden thick with copper drifts over the back of his neck. "I warned you, puppy dog."

Fury ignites Rajah's blood, sharpened to a burning edge by fear for Jade, and he jerks his head back, hoping to connect his skull with Dante's forehead. But Dante evades him easily, and scrapes stinging fangs over the crest of Rajah's shoulder, saliva dripping. The hot hiss of his breath slides like oil. "You stink of her. That's mine, her stink. Give it back."

Panic skewers Rajah's guts, his rage overflowing with images of Jade in Dante's blood-soaked embrace, but it's too late. Dante is too strong. Rajah struggles, his feet sliding on the wet floor, but there's nothing he can do to stop Dante's teeth from sinking into his shoulder muscle.

Agony flares, white-hot, and blinding dizziness rips through him. Dante's cool lips clamp down, and he shoves his fangs in harder, shaking his head like a dog. Muscle fibers pop, and vessels tear open with a slurp. Blood splashes, a hot scarlet mess diluting with water on the wall. Rajah jerks his arm helplessly, but Dante grips it fast, pulling harder to help the blood flow. And then he sucks, hard, sexual, and the pain is from hell, like nothing on earth.

Dante rips his teeth free with a snarl, and now his cock bulges hard against Rajah's naked thigh, water and blood thinning the fabric between them. "Think you can keep her, lover? A pretty fucktoy like you? Think again." His tongue slides a hot trail up Rajah's neck, searching for the soft vein below his ear. "Death is too kind for you, Rajahni. But you'll wish I killed you once I'm finished with her."

Rajah chokes, his skin crawling, and tries to spit out defiant words, but too late. Dante's breath stinks of meat, and his mouth fastens on Rajah once more. Wicked hot fangs pierce the soft skin of his throat with a horrible sweet sting. The vein bursts, exploding in a burning spurt of blood and pain. Dante sucks, then swallows with an orgasmic groan, grinding his erection harder.

Blood gushes under pressure, and Rajah's skin rips open further on Dante's tongue. Heat flushes Rajah's neck, bright blood splashing the wall. His tendons jerk, useless. He can feel his skin cooling, his blood vessels constricting. He wants to scream, to warn Jade, but he can't make a sound. His knees buckle, his muscles straining uselessly to hold him up, and his vision flashes with colored light like stars before fading to black.

Dante collapses, panting, his back against the blood-spattered shower wall. Rajah's blood still runs on his teeth, and he licks them, fragrant scarlet gushing down his chin to stain his wet shirt. His veins burn with bloodlust, his skin afire. His balls clench tight and heavy, his cock bursting. His gaze jerks inexorably downward, and his nostrils flare, dragging in the intoxicating salty flavor.

Rajahni has fainted, his beautiful naked body sprawled limp on the tiles. Wisps of steam caress his brown skin, black hair plastered to his elegant cheek. Scarlet-tinged water trickles onto the elongated muscles of his chest, over his sleek flank, down his shapely thighs, into the wet hair at his groin. The savage wound on the side of his neck exposes raw flesh, thick, salty blood dripping, pooling, congealing. . . .

Dante smacks his head back against the wall to distract himself, his skull smarting. Not really his thing. He'd much rather fuck her. Unless he can pin Rajahni down and feed him blood, force it down his throat, choke him with it. Come inside him and drain his life away once more, only to fill him again. Over and over, until there's nothing left but infected vampire blood, and—surprise!— here's irresistible hunger and eternal life, only it's not so everlasting when some sadistic demon lord already owns your soul.

A vampire incubus, ha ha. Try your fucking glamour then. But there's a better way to make the bastard suffer. To make Rajahni pay for taking what's his.

Rajah's memories hiss like a lunatic's whispers in Dante's mind, and his pulse throbs, glorious. Now Dante knows what it's like to love her, worship her, surrender your heart to her.

Well, screw that. He'll settle for fucking and eating. Not necessarily in that order. Maybe with a little subtle torture thrown in.

He wipes blood from his chin, steadies the shake in his hands with a few gulping breaths, and creeps like a shadow toward the bathroom door.

It opens without a creak, and there she lies, limp and slender in Rajahni's bed, pale sheets draped across her hip. Her hair tangles on the pillow, her fingers slack by her cheek in slumber. Her small breasts gleam in the crack of bathroom light, and he recalls the clean taste of her nipple, her flesh springy in his mouth, her blood thick and hot in his throat.

He leans over her, inhaling the sweet stink of sex. He can smell what they've done, how she's let Rajahni take her, how she's taken him. Dante's mouth waters, lubricating his teeth with slick spit. He wants to feel her come, scream, die, feel her rip apart in his mouth and bleed.

He savors her, sniffing her throat, her lips. Her breath whispers into him, slight and even. She's so full, of satisfaction and oxygen-rich blood. His balls ache with lust. He could have her here, drink her, eat her, spread her mess over Rajahni's bed, swallow her last heartbeat and leave her, raped and ravaged for Rajahni to find.

Or, he could make it hurt even more.

He grazes his fingertip on a wet fang and plinks a single glittering drop onto her damp bottom lip. "Jade," he whispers.

She stirs, murmuring. Her lips part, and her tongue slides out, licking the blood into her mouth. "Mmm." She sighs in her sleep, her body stretching in contentment. "More."

Dante smiles. "Not yet, darlin'."

19

I opened my eyes, and nothing happened.

Cool air shrank my naked skin, raising bumps. I blinked. Blackness, indistinguishable from the inside of my eyelids. Was it that dark? Hell, maybe you really can go blind from screwing.

"Rajah?" My voice sounded flat, close. No answer.

I lifted my hand, and my knuckles cracked against something hard. What the hell?

I spread my fingers, a hand's breadth above my face. Wood, flat and rough. Cold fear fingered my spine, and I splayed out my hands, searching. Splinters stuck in my fingertips, rough edges grazing my knuckles, clunking on my bangles, smacking into my elbows. A box.

A fucking box. My heart sprinted. I pushed upward, and the thing wouldn't budge. I kicked up, sideways, down, and met more unmoving wood. Bruises stung my knees, my elbows, my ankle bones. Swift hunger clawed at my stomach lining, insatiable. Panic rose like wildfire in my throat, and I choked back a scream. Maybe I'd died and gone to hell, and this was Kane's idea of fun.

A cackle rasped in my ears, hollow, and grasping fingers of malice squeezed my heart. *And now you know what it's like.*

My nerves prickled at that slimy, whispering voice. I fought to swallow, a frightened ache squeezing my breath away, and the weight of the word *eternity* suffocated me. I guess I never really thought it would happen. Not so soon. And now Kane had forever to torment me.

Not Kane, wildcat. The cackle writhed out again like wet tentacles, gripping my stomach with sick mirth not my own.

My head throbbed in confusion, hunger tormenting me. *What?*

I ate him. Well, I tried. Now he's hiding. Not talking to me. Fucking demons.

I licked dry lips, incredulous. *Vorenus, are you still here?*

Sweet, burning froth slithered up and down my throat, gagging me. *Trapped. Severed. Lost. Welcome to my hell.*

Frigid horror stiffened my limbs, my mind gibbering. My throat parched. I wanted to scream, but no sound came out. I'd almost rather Kane than this. How did this happen? Why hadn't my rapture chewed up what was left of him?

Luna's fragment chuckled, cold. *Rajah's quite a lover. You had energy to spare, so I took it.*

I shuddered. I should have known. Normal people couldn't survive being swallowed. But Luna wasn't normal. The sorcerer had powers I'd only dreamed of when I was mortal. He'd cheated death for this long, and he still wasn't giving up. Slimy disgust coated my mouth to think of him curled inside me while we loved, watching, consuming. . . .

No more than you deserved. A hot fist of rage clutched my guts, shaking me. I retched, and his voice hissed thudding vengeance in my head. *Now where's the rest of me?*

Heavenly light blinded me, painfully bright, and metal squeaked as someone wrenched the box lid free. I squeezed my eyelids shut, tears brimming, and Luna snaked into a tight coil inside me, quivering like a death adder's tail.

I forced my eyes open, squinting at first. Lightbulbs dazzling on metal claws, a distant ceiling of pressed lead, white paint peeling. The shadow of a face, flowing white hair, knotted in plaits with tiny flowers. Blue-veined skin, silvery eyes glittering, a familiar flicker of forked blue tongue. "Ooh, looky here. Bottle me confidence. Did you shine?"

I blinked, my head still spinning. The water sprite from Luna's. I was in hell with a fairy drug dealer? I struggled to sit up, fought to speak, my croaky voice stinging my throat. "Where am I?"

"We."

"I'm sorry?"

She laid a scratchy blue hand on my chest to push me back down, her froggy fingers too dry on my skin. I realized I was naked, and that she was still sick. Her skin peeled like week-old sunburn, her blue lips pale and parched. "Where are we, child. There's more than one of you. I see twinny, curled like a liver-worm. Sweet thing, too. Pretty hair."

Luna's imp smiled and unwrapped, lissome like slime leaching into my blood. *Why, thank you, beautiful. Dance with me sometime.*

The water fairy grinned, indigo ichor·staining her cracked gums. "Flowers for you, twinny. You smell good."

And I bet you taste good. Care to let me try?

Grudging admiration soured my mouth. He never gave up. Reduced to a gibbering soul fragment and still pulling moves.

I pushed the fairy's hand away and wriggled my hips to sit up, the wooden box chafing the backs of my thighs. My limbs felt watery, weak. Tangy furniture oil itched my nostrils, and I glanced around at tall windows draped with brocade curtains, lush green carpet, an antique mahogany dining suite, a stuffed pale velvet lounge.

My lungs clenched tight, robbing me of air. What kind of freak leaves space in their lounge room for a body-sized box? "What am I doing here? Why did you kidnap me?"

She laughed, hoarse, and the corner of her mouth cracked open, dust puffing from ruined skin. "I'm just here for the candy. For napping of kids ask the candyman."

Her mention of food watered my mouth, and my ravenous stomach growled. But I remembered the dirty blood in her spew, writhing like living flesh, and apprehension skewered me, sharp and hateful. Suddenly the box was a no-brainer. The kind of vampire freak who likes torturing people, maybe? And if I was in a box, what had he done with Rajah?

Urgency gripped me, adrenaline seeping warmth into my blood. "Is this Dante's place? Where is he?"

The fairy twisted her neck with a crack, listening to something I couldn't hear, and put a ripped finger to dry lips. She winked, her voice husking to a conspiratorial whisper. "Hush-hush on pretty twinny, child. He won't like it."

Luna's snaky shade thrashed, and cramps bit into my abdomen. *Pay attention, wildcat. Can't you smell him?*

Warm breeze puffed over my face. A dark blur severed the air and solidified into Dante, black-clad, raindrops glinting in dark curls, spit running on hungry teeth. He yanked the fairy's ragged hair back, forcing her chin up an inch from his face. "Don't meddle."

Dry white hanks broke off in his hand, and he grabbed more.

Her silvery wings flapped uselessly, their translucent membranes crackling like cellophane. Her lips stretched, more dust crumbling from her face. "I told nothing. Just a looky. No telling."

"I should hope not, if you want more." He slid his fingers into her ruined hair, making it a caress instead of a threat, and wormed his tongue over her broken lip, tasting her sickness. "Say please."

His whisper made her shiver, her black pupils slitting wide, her voice cracking. "Please."

Disgust crawled over my skin like a fat black spider. The air suddenly chilled. No doubt he'd made me beg like this, and humiliation seared like frost in my heart. I wanted to wrap my naked body in my arms, cover myself. "Jesus, Dante. Leave her alone."

He winked at me, malicious amusement glinting. "Your turn soon. Don't be greedy."

I wanted to scream shock into her veins, make her squirm away from his grip, but I realized I didn't know her name. "He's making you sick, darlin', don't go there."

But she ignored me, fixated on him. Dante scraped one wicked fang over his own lip, dark blood welling.

"Please, Dante. Give it to me. I need it." Her crusty lips trembled, and silver grit grimed her lashes, her tears thick and sluggish. "I want it."

"Good enough for now." He struck like a serpent for a kiss, rosy lips sliding on blue, his blood dribbling down her chin. She sighed and folded into his arms, deepening the kiss to suck out more. He groaned and cupped her breast, dragging her nipple to arousal.

Mmm. Luna's shade stretched, sensual. *Seems you like threesomes, Jade. Don't waste it.*

I looked away, nausea sliding in my stomach like a reptile's cruel fangtips bright. "Don't scowl at me like that. We're alike, you and I."

I folded my arms, trying to pretend I didn't care he could see everything. My fingers stung cold beneath my arms, my nipples tight and uncomfortable. "Sure, whatever you say. So what's the plan, Dante? I'm naked in a box. Are you just going to stare at me? Or will you poison me, too?"

"I didn't poison anyone." A fine imitation of hurt creased his brow, his eyes shadowing with candid disappointment.

His upset caressed warm fingers of remorse over my heart, and I hated it. But I'd seen that fairy blossom and heal with my own eyes. Maybe Dante spoke the truth this time. Just because he'd lied to me didn't mean he was guilty of everything.

But I couldn't forget how he'd invaded me, raped my will and stolen my secret heart. "Right. Sure. A captive audience for your 'antidote.' Why would you want that?"

He laughed, incredulous, and a flush sparked my cold skin. I'd liked his laugh, so easy and genuine, and it hadn't changed. "Listen to yourself. Why the hell would I want to poison fae? They're creatures of chaos. I'd fill this fucking city with fae and watch it crumble. You want poison, look to your own."

I stared. Glass splinters showering from a fluorescent tube, the hot gush of blood over Killian Quinn's face. Flames curling around Kane's fingertips, sparks lighting his hair. Nyx, color draining from his sweet face, his skin soaked in sick sweat when we'd tried to love.

Sick realization clamped my guts, and Luna slithered, giggling. Creatures of chaos. No one loved order better than Kane, so long as it was his order. I thought I'd drained Nyx's energy, only I hadn't. My rapture had. Kane's jealous fragment, indig-

scales. I didn't want to watch Dante fuck her, blee

her plead for more. It was too much like what he'd do

But Dante pushed her away with a blood-smea

"Enough. Leave us alone."

She murmured in protest, licking ravenous lips, and m

ached for her. She wiped her mouth with her frog-fingered

and it came away wet, not just with blood but also with wat

moment ago, her lips were crumbling. Now the wound

healed. She blinked, and moisture flowed into her gritty sil

eyes. Her dull white hair sprang, newly fresh and shimmerin

and her blue-veined cheek glistened damp and smooth, free o

crumbling decay. She stretched her fingers, the pads glowing

wet, and her smile shone clean, her teeth gleaming sharp.

I stared, confusion muddling my head like puzzle pieces tossed

back into the box. I remembered sweet Nyx dissolving into wet

rainbows on my sheets, Kane's pretty fire sprite with ice in his

hair. There was fae poison going around, all right, but it wasn't

Dante's blood. He wasn't making the water sprite sick. He was

healing her, at least for now. *Some snort it with sugar,* she'd said. She'd

spewed at Luna's through overindulgence, not from poison.

The fairy twirled, water drops sparkling from her fingertips,

iridescent fluid pulsing fresh in her wings. "Candy," she whis-

pered with a giggle, and fluttered away.

Dante licked his lips clean and sprawled on his lounge, a dark

inkblot on pale velvet. He eyed me coolly, his dark blue gaze

impersonal and bored. I recalled the way Rajah looked at me,

warm, besotted, like I was the other half of his soul. The contrast

made me shiver, gooseflesh crawling, my nakedness even colder

now. How had I ever thought Dante compassionate?

He watched me squirm, and dark interest parted his lips,

nant at what I was doing. The only reason Rajah escaped un-
scathed was that rapture couldn't affect him, not while he wore
bangles of his own.

What might Kane himself be capable of? His moods could
sizzle the sky with static if he didn't keep them under control.
Kane got pissed off, and people died. Fae died.

The lying prick was doing it himself.

So why the fuck did he send me to Dante in the first place?

Never trust a demon. Luna giggled again, and my stomach
frothed like vomit waiting to happen. I gulped, painful.

Dante grinned. "Like I said. We're alike, you and I."

"And how's that?"

"We hate being controlled. I've just got the guts to take what
I want."

"Yeah, that's so admirable. I've always wanted to mesmerize
people and enslave them with my blood but I've never had the
guts. And wow, you just go right ahead and do it. I'm impressed."

"Don't be flip. Blood is my power. Sex is yours. Don't tell me
you've never fucked someone just because you wanted to."

I thought of Rajah and flushed again, even though rapture
hadn't been a factor. "That's not the same."

Dante's eyes glinted. "And damning souls to hell for your
freedom. So unselfish of you."

The fact that they'd deserved it wasn't making me feel better.
"What the fuck would you know about unselfishness?"

He smiled, handsome. "No need to get defensive. I'm capti-
vated. That thing with Luna was beautiful. And the way you
used Rajahni . . ." He flicked his tongue over sharp teeth, saliva
shining. "Ingenious."

Shit. The soultrap. I'd left it at Rajah's. But I didn't care about that right now. I remembered the way he and Dante clashed at Luna's, my joke that one day that protective impulse would get Rajah killed. Icy fear hacked into my ribs like a blunt knife. "What did you do to him?"

Dante grinned. "Never mind that. Let's talk about us. Come here." And the bastard stood and held his hand out to me, courteous and charming like I wasn't kneeling naked in a coffin on his lounge room floor.

I stayed there, glaring at him, wishing for acid, a bee sting, anything to cause him pain. "You've got to be kidding—"

A dark weight crashed into me, knocking the breath from my lungs. I choked, my back pressed tight into the couch's warmth, my limbs flung out before me. His forearm jammed across my throat, and his lips quivered an inch from mine, showing razor teeth. "You're naked. I'm hungry. Don't try my patience." He let go and flung himself down beside me, glaring.

The brush of his coppery breath made my skin flinch, warmth crawling over me. The memory of blood filled my mouth, hot, arousing, and I swallowed. I didn't want to play his games. They were too dangerous. "I'm bored. If you're going to bite me, get on with it."

He leaned closer, resting his head on his hand. "I will. I just want you to beg first."

I laughed, trying not to stare at his teeth, the way the fangs brushed his bottom lip, delicate. "Never."

"Never say never." His gaze drew mine, hypnotic. "We've been through this already. I can help you. Just tell me what you want."

My stomach twisted even as I stared, transfixed. Snaky wriggles churned my guts, and I tried to stand up, but my legs wouldn't move, the muscles rigid and useless. *Don't,* Luna screeched, *don't want!* But I couldn't help it. My lips stretched, sluggish. "Won't."

"You will." He stroked my hair back, caressing, his tongue flicking out to clean his teeth. His voice growled softly, almost a whisper, but it drilled straight to my core and splintered my resolve, plumbing to the depths of my most reckless, hidden need. "You don't break my power over you by spewing, Jade. You drank my blood. I'll own you forever. Now tell me again what you want most, and I'll give it to you."

20

Unsheathe your claws, wildcat, urged Luna, but I barely heard him. The warm, male scent of cardamom filled my nostrils, so dear to me, I trembled. Cold tears spilled onto my cheeks, and my most secret words dragged over my lips, compelled. "Love Rajah. Want him to stay with me."

Dante smiled softly, shaking his head. "Even I can't make that happen. He's already forgotten you."

"No." My wits glugged like paste, cold and thick. "Won't forget."

"Trust me. How do you think I stole you away? He let me. The soultrap for the girl. He didn't even blink. Do you think he'd give up his freedom for a whore like you?" He bent closer, caressing my temple with his, mingling our hair together. His cheek brushed mine, warm, and that horrid, wonderful flavor flooded my mouth, erasing everything else, seductive as he whispered in my ear. "That's what you are, sweetie. A whore. Don't you feel that sometimes?"

The taste of his hot, vibrant blood tingled on my tongue, intoxicating and fresh. He'd fed me again. While I slept. Horror crawled up my throat like vomit, burning, but I couldn't stop the truth from spilling out. "Yes."

"Do you really believe he gives a damn about you?"

Yes. I wanted to scream it out, banish my fear with reckless, unfounded confidence, but my tongue froze when I tried to speak. The syllable wouldn't form, and my muscles contorted themselves into the vile truth. "Want to. Said he did. Took me home."

"You don't say. After watching you fuck his oldest enemy to death? Why do you think he'd do that?"

My throat clogged, and I couldn't speak. Maybe, just because he felt like it. Because rapture made his cock hard and I was the closest thing. So he'd humored me, let me think he was washing me clean, lied to make me feel special. All so I'd let him put it wherever he wanted.

So fucking pathetic. A few orgasms and I'm in love.

With a man who makes a living screwing girls he doesn't give a shit about.

Tears burned, soaking my lashes, trailing hot rivers down my cheeks. My chest swelled, swift and agonizing, the scarred skin of my heart ripping once more to shreds. I'd never wanted so badly to lie. But Dante's gaze immobilized me, remorseless, the blood allowing nothing but cold, undeniable truth.

He traced my tears with warm lips, sucking the moisture away. "It's okay, darlin'. You don't have to answer that one. Just tell me how much it hurts."

I choked on a sob. "Like the worst thing ever."

"Do you want it to stop hurting?" His lips drifted to the corner of my mouth, warm and insistent.

I didn't care. It didn't matter. Nothing mattered. I let him kiss me, drag his tongue over my bottom lip, that tempting iron taste invading my mouth. "Yes."

"And do you think it will? Ever?" His breath slid to my throat, hot razor teeth whispering over the dent where my pulse beat, thick and sore and weary. My sluggish nerves sparked in alarm, but before I could react, he slid his thigh over mine, trapping me beneath him. His body heat soaked over me, welcome in the chill, and my skin reacted with a slow flush. He inhaled my scent through parted lips, tasting me.

Luna struggled inside me, thrashing like a skewered reptile, and part of me wanted to struggle, too, but misery swamped me, smothering any desire to fight Dante off. He was right. I'd let Rajah break my heart, and it might never heal. After a thousand years, when my thrall bangles finally broke and Kane dragged me off to hell, I'd be thinking of Rajah, his cheeky laugh, the way I didn't feel alone and useless anymore when he looked at me, and I'd curse myself for being so sad and hopeless and empty that I hadn't interested him for more than a few hours. A few hours of bliss in a millennium.

Dante yanked my head back by the hair, snarling softly, spit running on curved fangs. His blue eyes shone bright, glazed, intoxicated. His body quivered, tight and coiled like a serpent about to strike, and his skin glowed with arousal. God, he was beautiful, this creature of death.

I'd thought that the night I met him, before I'd ever seen the primal animal inside. But the way he surrendered to his beast made me stare, transfixed. Envy coursed through me, hot and tempting. I wanted to touch, learn, take. Was that how I looked when the rapture stole my reason? In perfect submission, unfettered, free?

No. It wasn't. Dante loved his compulsion. I hated mine.

"Answer me, Jade. Will the pain ever stop?" He scraped his mouth over my collarbone and down to my breast, flicking his sinuous tongue over my nipple. My flesh responded, hardening, and he bit me, playful like a kitten, teasing out pleasure that swelled in my breast and slithered through my veins to heat my sex.

I shivered, helplessness welling inside me. Maybe I could have hit him, pushed him off me, jammed my knee into his swollen groin. But I didn't want to fight. I didn't want to be strong anymore. I just wanted it to end. "No. The pain won't ever stop."

He sucked me, pulling my nipple taut in his hot mouth, stinging teeth scraping my breast. Breathlessly he slid to the floor in front of me and dragged his lips over my ribs. He chewed lightly on my hipbone, his tight dark curls teasing my belly. "So what do you want from me?"

I let my head fall back, squeezing my swollen eyes shut. The words he wanted clogged my mouth, and my tongue jerked, longing to spit them out. *Don't,* Luna warned, sharp claws of caution slashing inside my abdomen, but I ignored him.

I thought of Rajah, how we'd loved, the beautiful friction between us, the way my heart swelled when he held me, kissed me, slid into me like he belonged there. For a few precious hours, I didn't hate what I was. And now only a few hours later, here I was naked under another man.

It didn't matter that I was a prisoner, that Dante would never let me go until he was satisfied. I was still here, conscious, letting it all happen while some other guy took possession of me. Got off on my body like I was a sex doll. Smeared me with lust and spit and blood, touched me in places and ways I only ever wanted Rajah to touch me again.

The reality of my thrall crashed in on me like a stinking mudslide. Kane whistled me up, and I fucked. It was as simple as that. Without the Luna soultrap, there was no escaping it. Even if I gambled on the wafer-thin chance that Rajah would even speak to me again, how could I ever look him in those beautiful golden eyes and tell him I loved him and only him, when every other week I was prostituting myself for some lustful stranger?

My horrid bangles stung, and caustic tears forced into my eyes. I tried to blink them away, in case Dante thought they were because of him, but my sorrow swelled like a cancer, strangling me. It was no good. There was no hope for us, and now I'd tasted love, breathed heavenly air in that magical place where I thought Rajah cared for me, the next eight hundred years without him stretched ahead even longer and more unbearable. Even if he did harbor some residue of sympathy for me, it was better I died now than watch his affection dissolve while I whored. Every interminable day, I'd think of him, imagine his lost smile, the missing twinkle in his eyes. Every night when I went to bed alone I'd miss him, every careless body I touched would make me long for his caress. Every guy I fucked, I'd weep for Rajah.

Dante's fangs sliced my belly, delicate, a fierce sting zipping across my skin. He scraped his tongue slowly across the cut, excruciating, and in a blood-drenched flash of memory I remembered him going down on me with just that movement, a slow, deliberate lick that left me breathless. I didn't want sex with him now. Not with anyone, if I couldn't have Rajah. But I did crave the other thing Dante offered.

His lips curled against my skin in a smile. "Say it, Jade. Tell me what you want me to do."

My hellbound soul yearned for it, my weary body ached for

it, my tortured heart bled for it. The words clamored inside, desperate to be free. I swallowed, dry with desire. I let my muscles relax, my limbs slacken. I opened my mouth, and out it spilled. "Kill me."

Rajah stirs, and cramp seizes his shoulder, excruciating.

He gurgles through a locked jaw, wanting to scream, tiles cold and wet under his jerking muscles. Gradually the unbearable tension subsides, and the agony fades to a dull ache. He forces sticky eyes open, light glaring. Glass. Earthy ceramic squares, polished metal, the smell of water and blood.

His pulse thuds. The bathroom. Dante. Jade.

Shock slams into his lungs, forcing his breath away. He scrambles up, his feet slipping in the clotted red stain, and skids out into the bedroom. Drips slide cold on his skin. "Jade?"

Cool pre-dawn moonlight creeps through the venetians, striping the room with light. The sheets lie rumpled; her smell is everywhere. But she's not there. He ducks his head out into the living room. Empty.

Rajah curses, trying to still his racing heart. Maybe she's all right. Maybe she just left, just didn't want to see him anymore.

Maybe she figured out he was leaving her, and did it before he could.

Bright guilt slashes like a blade at his heart, but he remembers the cold stab of Dante's fangs, his faint as blood rushed away, the cold curse on Dante's lips. *You'll wish I'd killed you once I'm finished with her.*

He scrabbles on the bedside table for his phone and dials with shaking, bloody fingers.

A glassy ringtone peals from the floor beside his bed, and he kicks the sheets away, stumbling. Her bag, the twisted golden strap pooling on the carpet beside Luna's shimmering silk coat. Swiftly he scoops the bag up, fumbling the magnetic clasp open. Purse, keys, phone, lipstick, soultrap. His mouth dries, crusty, his fingers clenching around crisp black satin. She'd never leave without Luna. Or without clothes. He shoves his wardrobe door aside, careless of the crash. Nothing's missing.

The soultrap hums angrily in the bag, and for a moment he stares at it. He could take it, and forget her.

He sees her in his mind, her sweet hair brushing his face, her flavor flooding his senses with bliss, and he curses himself for an idiot.

Forget her. Sure. Might as easily forget about breathing.

Resolve grips him, hot and indefatigable like rapture. Time to call in some favors, find where DiLuca is skulking. Jade is strong. She'll still be alive. She has to be. And if he has to surrender his freedom to save her, so be it. Screw freedom. Without her, it's not worth having.

He drops his phone into her bag and snaps it shut, and in ninety seconds he's dressed and gone.

21

ante groaned, nuzzling hard into the crease at the top of my thigh. "I love it when you talk dirty. Say it again."

"Kill me, Dante. Now."

He dived his head between my legs, nipping the soft inside of my thigh, but I didn't care. I closed my eyes, but didn't bother to shift my legs apart for him. Let him do that. Let him take me any way he wanted. Everyone else did.

He bent my knees and pushed them apart, baring more skin, and licked himself a clean place, inside my thigh where the vein pulsed, making it slick and ready. Hot razor teeth whispered on my skin, stinging, his hair tickling me. "You want it fast or slow?"

I wanted it fast, now, over with. But whatever I said, he'd choose the other. Luna wriggled, snapping, but I ignored him. "Just do it."

Dante bit slowly, delicately. A miserable ache cramped my thigh, and I cried out, willing him to get on with it. But he withdrew, fangs sliding cold from my skin. Pain seared, his tongue hotter as he lapped at the wound, teasing, not taking me until he was good and ready. Fear clawed me, but I gritted my teeth. Better I died now.

The hell you will.

My teeth grated with alien rage that boiled my blood, and without any spark from me, my rapture ignited, snarling. *Have I got your attention now?*

Energy swirled in my womb, hot and ravenous, leaking out to wet me. Dante murmured in pleasure, and slid his tongue into my slit to collect some, mixing it with the blood tricking hot down my thigh. He teased me, trailing his teeth over my folds, a sharp sting of fangs scraping my clit. A burning sensation crept up my body, and I gasped, squeezing my eyes tighter. *Let it go, Vorenus. It's over.*

You will not fucking flicker out and take me with you. Scaly muscle gripped my throat like a constrictor, choking me. *Stop drowning in self-pity and show some goddamn spirit, Jade. Send this prick to hell where he belongs.*

I spluttered, and some of the woolly inertia plastered over me by Dante's blood sloughed off. The idea kindled vicious longing in my heart. But it was impossible. Rapture couldn't trap a vampire's soul. Could it?

Then drink his fucking blood if that's what it takes. Use some imagination. What the fuck do you think Rajah sees in you, anyway?

Luna's wrath bubbled, roiling, and my rapture sucked it up with a growl, flaring brighter. I looked down, at Dante feasting on the wound he'd made. Blood smeared his lips, coated his teeth, ran on his tongue. He licked me, sucked me, slid his tongue under the broken skin to taste more—and an ethereal scarlet shimmer flowed over him, coating him like spectral blood.

My aura.

My heart skipped, jumping my pulse, and Dante rubbed his lips in welling blood, letting it run to stain the couch. *Terminus.* The line of division. Death. But not the mortal kind.

Luna's snide words came back to me with a hearty thud. *I ate him,* he'd said of Kane, *at least I tried.*

My heart skipped. It was worth a try. If I failed, I'd just die. But if I succeeded, I still had Luna's fragment. What if I didn't need the whole thing to make it work? What if I could still be free?

Resolve seeped into my veins, thick and needy with rapture. *Vorenus, you hungry?*

Now you're talking, wildcat. A rough chuckle shivered my skin. *But nothing's free. I want out. Give me back the rest of me, and I'll eat the bastard whole. Deal?*

Deal.

A lie, of course. But I'd worry about that later. I let my rapture roam, and concentrated on Dante's lips, the warmth, the pain, the slickness of my sex. Luna's confidence crept through my veins, glittering with life, giving me fresh strength and perspective. Dark, enchanted pleasure sizzled, swelling my flesh, and though my heart still ached, something glorious and deeply arousing called to me. *Yes,* I wanted to yell, *this is what I am. This is what I do. Sex and death are the same, this man will die before I'm through, and that's okay.*

I'm me, and fuck 'em all if they can't take it. Dante was right. He and I were the same. And if it meant Rajah would never love me, I'd just have to learn to live with it, no matter how much it hurt. I loved him, with every cursed fragment of my soul. I'd love him forever, and no one could take that away. I'd keep my love safe, like a diamond, hidden in a warm dark place where no one could ever touch it.

And if it makes me smile just once while I spend eternity screaming in hell, I'll have won.

Fuck. Them. All.

Luna giggled, sparkling. *That's my girl.*

Dante sank his teeth in once more, deepening the wound. Pain lanced again, constricting my veins, but it was distant, forgettable. He sucked, and I let a lustful groan well up in my chest as more life flowed out of me. "You want to get naked while you do that?"

He let go, blood sliding from his grin. "Why, you naughty girl. Are you rebelling?"

"Maybe." I still couldn't lie to him. Didn't mean I couldn't color it the way he wanted.

Dark lust ignited in his gaze. "Okay. How do you want it?"

I grabbed his hair, and he snapped playfully at my forearm, slashing a dark red welt. I swallowed a wince. "Fuck me. Maybe I'll come while I die."

He stood and stripped, his motions jerky and almost too swift to follow, revealing his tense, pale body, muscles lean and tendons twisted like a starving wild animal's. Still had a great ass. Nice hard-on, too, straight and thick. My pulse quickened, and I swallowed. He looked dangerous. *Vorenus, you ready?*

More than ready. Luna quivered happily, making my stomach ache. *He pretends he's straight, you know. I never got to fuck him. Let me have it.*

Now that was the Luna I remembered. He'd fuck anything with a heartbeat.

Well, I'm a succubus. So will I.

Dante climbed back on the couch and pulled me astride his lap. Blood and vampire spit dripped down my thigh, and he slid his fingers through it, smearing it into the hot wet mess between my legs. His fingertips grazed my entrance, merciless, and my flesh twitched. "Already on your way, I see."

I wriggled up on my knees to make him get on with it. I didn't want him touching me any more than I needed him to. "See if you can do better than last time."

His eyes glinted, malicious, and he gripped my hips and dragged me down on him. His cock pushed inside, forcing through my wetness until he could go no farther. His pupils dilated, and before I was ready he struck.

He jabbed burning fangs into my throat. My skin popped, and blood gushed. Pain clawed my neck, digging in, slashing down my back and over my chest. I couldn't move my head. I couldn't move at all. He ground his cock deeper, growling, his erection swelling as he sucked and swallowed.

My balance tumbled, dizzy, my skull swirling. My pulse skidded wildly, thrumming like a trapped bird's wings. Chill whispered over my skin, shocking next to Dante's warm body. My muscles loosened, my limbs limp and weak.

He withdrew his teeth and slowed down, sucking only gently, his tongue caressing my ripped flesh. He slid his thumb over my clit, spearing me with sensation, and blood flowed to my sex, leaving even less for my brain. He kept swallowing, sucking my life out mouthful by mouthful, and he rocked deep inside me, stroking me, bringing me on. "Die for me, sweetie. Come on. It'll feel good."

Luna sighed, quivering, and I couldn't help but groan, tilting my hips to press against Dante's clever hand. It did feel good, this light-headed bliss, like some exotic fairy high. I struggled to form whispered words. "Not yet. Give me more. Let me taste you."

Dante laughed and groaned at the same time, thrusting hard and deep. "You want me to infect you, is that it?" He lapped up more blood, his breath hot and short on my throat. "Sorry. Not this time."

He slid thumb and forefinger around my clit and squeezed, and I gasped, the stimulation too intense. "Please. I just want one proper taste." I forced a smile, my breath burning. "It'd drive Rajah bugfuck."

He pulled his mouth away, panting around a bloody grin. A flush reddened his face, his skin plump and succulent. "Damn, I love a spiteful woman. If you can take it, it's yours. But be careful. I might decide to infect you after all."

He made no move to help me, to cut himself or bite his lip. Just pressed his fingers over my sex and watched me, stained lips parted, glazed blue eyes shining with lust. He wanted to see me humiliate myself for him, but it didn't make him special. It made him common as dirt, and I was glad.

I licked dry lips with a drier tongue, and let my head fall to his shoulder. His skin felt soft on my cheek, and a glorious fleshy fragrance radiated, sweet and hot. The smell of my blood. I trailed my lips over his throat, grazing him with my teeth, salty male sweat tingling my tongue. I found a dip, where a faint hot pulse threaded, and I took a mouthful and bit.

My teeth crushed into thick skin, bruising it, and a tinge of his glorious, hypnotic taste wormed into my mouth. My rapture crackled with lust, and I shivered, my flesh clenching around his cock, preorgasmic delight rippling through me. God, I hated this.

Dante thrust into me in response, grunting. "Harder. You can't hurt me."

We'd see about that. But it was difficult. My teeth weren't made for this. I clamped down harder, and his skin broke with a sick crunch. Salty filth filled my mouth, hot and stinking. My eyes watered, my stomach churning, and Luna gripped me tight inside, stopping me from vomiting. *Swallow, wildcat. Do it.*

I gritted my teeth together through Dante's flesh, and swallowed. Blood coated my throat, disgusting, dribbling down.

Luna slurped it up, greedy. *More.*

Steeling myself, I sucked. More blood leaked out, and I swallowed it. Luna cackled in delight.

Dante pulled his hand from between my legs and grabbed my hair to yank me closer, his cock swelling tight inside me. His voice grated, his breath burning my ear. "Yes. Do it. Drink me."

I bit down and shook my head from side to side as he had, and more skin tore, blood vessels breaking. I sucked, and warmth spurted, splashing my tongue, running down my throat. I gagged, but Luna latched on to it, screeching. Reptilian claws scraped in my guts, frothing soul energy lurching up into my mouth, and the blood began to run of its own accord.

Rapture blossomed in me, flowing from my womb, wrapping Dante's cock, caressing us both with flaming pleasure. His energy leached into me from our sex, black and icy but nourishing. Dante gulped, his chest heaving. "Enough."

But Luna was pissed off and hungry, and he wasn't letting go. I stretched my jaws apart, my teeth still embedded in Dante's neck, pulling the ragged wound open. Sick vampire blood rushed down my gullet in a flood, burning, sucked away before it hit my stomach by Luna's ravenous shade. The thing drank and drank and drank, insatiable, swelling inside me, and I just held on and let the blood flow.

"Enough. Stop." Dante tried to yank my head away, his fingers curling in my hair. But I held on, my rapture sinking deadly claws into his strength and dragging him closer to the edge at the same time. His fist weakened in my hair, his essence sponging into us, and his muscles jerked beneath me as he fought it. His words slurred as he cursed me. "Bitch. You're not alone."

He plunged within me, helpless to stop his own death, and his cock rubbed over my sensitive flesh, too much, too fast. My rapture sighed and moaned, coiling tighter. My thighs tingled, my muscles juddering. I was going to come, but I didn't care. Let him feel it as he died.

I gritted my teeth and let the pleasure take me, slow and delicious, rolling through my core, creeping along my limbs, sparkling my fingers. I groaned. My pelvic walls spasmed, hugging him, and he squeezed his eyes shut and jetted into me. A hot flood splashed my eager womb, drenched and alive with what was left of his poisonous soul.

Energy spurted into me, and my rapture consumed it, sucking back the life he'd stolen from me. My skin burned, my rejuvenated blood racing.

Luna's shade clenched its teeth, whooping with delight, and a thick fleshy lump sucked into my mouth as the last of Dante's consciousness tore free. His scarlet aura bubbled in fury as it faded, dying. His fingers dug into my hips, jerking, and then fell slack.

The bastard was dead. We'd killed a vampire, the only way you could. The fucker bled to death, and now his soul was mine.

22

I tore my mouth away, my teeth squelching out of his mangled flesh. I pushed away, ripping him from me, and stumbled onto the floor, panting. My breath hurt my lungs, the horrid salty taste of blood bubbling in my guts. Hot bloodstained liquid dribbled down my thighs. Lust seethed in my womb as my rapture snarled, voracious, ready to consume what I'd stolen.

But Luna snapped sharp teeth, fighting it off. *Mine. Get your own.*

My heart had slowed, but now my pulse leapt, urgent. If he consumed Dante's soul, it was all for nothing.

I swept my gaze around the room, and lighted on a swan-necked glass vase on the coffee table. I crawled over and grasped it, cold and heavy in my burning fingers. *Give it up, Vorenus. Let me have it.*

Luna coiled tight like a snake, possessive. *No. Hungry.*

I roasted him with rapture, my flesh throbbing. *Give it up, or you can't have yourself back, and you'll stay there forever. That what you want?*

He sulked, vitriol seething, but he did uncoil, and angry soul energy burst in my stomach, frothing. *Should have known better than to bargain with you.*

I barely heard him through the sudden spear of agony in my belly. Acid rammed up my throat, choking me, and I cracked my teeth against the vase's glass lip in haste. Hot ruby spew splattered into the vase, clotted and disgusting, dribbling down the sides. Heat scorched my cheeks, my eyes pouring, but I didn't flinch until I'd choked up the last of it, spitting to clear my mouth of filth.

Dante's soul spat like boiling scarlet soup, and I jammed my hand over the vase's mouth lest it escape. Acid burned my palm, and swiftly I stuffed the neck with a handful of Dante's shirt, blood staining the black linen. It'd do for an hour or two, until I could tip it into a soultrap. I ripped off the rest of the shirt and prodded the plug in tighter.

At last, I fell on my backside on the carpet, exhausted. My rapture hissed at me, disappointed, but I had no sympathy.

I licked sore lips. *Vorenus?*

Luna sniffed, still pissed off with me. *What?*

You're a very sick man. But thanks.

At last, I felt him smile. Grudging, but the same handsome smile he'd had while he was still alive. *You're welcome, wildcat. He tasted pretty fine, eh?*

I wiped blood from my legs, rubbing my hand on the carpet to clean it. Fatigue dulled me, even though I'd just gotten a fix. I should go home, stash this soul properly next to Quinn's, go to bed so I could wake up and worry about finding *animus,* whatever the hell that meant. I should have been triumphant, full of hope and determination.

But I wasn't. I didn't feel like getting up. I didn't feel like doing anything. Without someone to share it with, all the excitement was taken out of it. And I didn't mean the vicious double-thinking shade of my murdered ex-lover.

Idly I rolled the vase between my palms, watching Dante's soul struggle and seethe. We'd have laughed together, Rajah and I. Clinked glasses over our soultraps—wine for me, lemon squash for him—and stuffed ourselves silly on chicken tikka and aloo paratha. Walked home in the dark, holding hands, wrapped in each other's scent and sweat. Fallen breathless onto his bed and made love, with the windows open to soft summer breeze and moonlight. Slept in each other's embrace, sharing warmth, skin, breath.

Stupid tears swelled my eyes, and I let them blur. I didn't want to see. I didn't want to move. What for?

Jade?

Uh-huh.

Don't you have somewhere to be?

Sure. At home, alone. For eight hundred years, with you and Kane fighting in my guts. Can't wait.

Luna sniffed again, his dissatisfaction sour on my tongue. *Bullshit. You just found a reason to live. You really going to let him get away?*

Sorrow pierced me like a hot wire, stinging. "Yeah, right," I muttered. "Give it a rest."

Oh, sure. Be like that if you want to. Could have sworn I heard him say something about love.

I laughed, and it caught on the swelling in my throat, choking me. "Like he meant it? That's just perfect, coming from you."

I meant it. He sounded distant, bruised. *For a while. How long do you need to make it worth living for, anyway?*

I opened my mouth for a cutting reply, but it shriveled and died on my tongue. Just how long was worth it, when it came to love? How much happiness did I need? A year? A day? An hour?

Cherish the small pleasures, wildcat. Only thing that makes immortality worth the effort. Luna tossed his head with a haughty shrug. *Not that you give a shit what I think, right?*

If I could have just another five minutes with Rajah before he left me, would I take it? Would I dare to ask the questions that branded my soul? Or would I rather live out my miserable thousand years and die without ever knowing what was really in his heart for those few precious hours we spent?

I scrambled up, my legs quivering. "Vorenus?"

You still here?

"Thank you."

23

Vine leaves drip dew onto the pavement from the canopy in front of Valentino's, shining in the morning sun. The smell of wet asphalt rises, puddles reflecting in the street after the rain, and Lygon Street bustles with the sounds of shoppers, clinking coffee cups, traffic.

Tony LaFaro shrugs skinny shoulders and slithers his spiked blue tongue into his latte, collecting a blob of white froth. "Don't know nothin'."

"Can I see Angelo, then? I just need to know if she—"

"Ange ain't here. Sorry." Tony's second set of eyelids flicker, mocking.

Rajah rakes frustrated fingers through damp hair. "Look, I've tried everywhere. She could be in trouble. If you've—"

"Ain't seen her." Tony unfolds a newspaper, ignoring him.

Rajah spins away before he can break his knuckles on the prick's snarky brown face. He stalks off, the damp pavement slick, fury and worry seething together in his guts like boiling oil. He's tried the clubs, the pubs, the whole of King Street and Southbank, where the DiLucas hang, but no one will admit to seeing them or knowing where Dante's hiding. DiLuca's fae just smile and murmur, their eyes glazed. He even tried the house in Richmond where old Sal used to live, but Antonia DiLuca just hissed at him and told him to mind his own fucking business, hate flashing in her indigo eyes.

He jogs across the street in front of a slow-moving car and ducks down the side alley, half-running the few blocks to her place. Unlikely she'll be home, but Dante is cunning, delighting in the unexpected.

A stray cat meows on her doorstep, its skinny gray body tense, and it darts away as he approaches. Remnants of his fingermarks still show in the rain-speckled dust on the glass, half-erased digits fading. The door's locked, unbroken, both a good and a bad sign. He jams her key in, shoves the door open, and dashes into her grimy living room, tripping in his haste.

A stuffed couch, bookshelves thick with dust, last week's TV listings creased on the table. A rust-stained fridge, dishes and plastic takeaway containers piled dirty on the sink.

"Princess?" But the smell is all wrong—stale, not fresh like she is—and he already knows she's not here.

He wipes a weary hand over his face with a sorrowful sigh. He can't think of anywhere else to look. He's got only one option left. Sunlight brightens the room, slanting in through open blinds, but it doesn't lighten his mood, and a chill crawls to his fingertips at the thought of making the call. Slowly he pulls his phone from her bag and keys through the address book, but he can't bear to dial just yet and he slouches against the table's edge, bitter anguish awash in his heart. On the table, red roses in a silver box grow crispy at the edges, and he sniffs them, the perfume soft and rich like her skin, but she doesn't smell of roses. She smells of woman, fresh and natural like sunshine.

On the table, her bag shifts, rocking. Luna's soul is restless, and Rajah wonders about her other soultrap, the one with Killian Quinn. If Dante gets his hands on that . . .

Swiftly he searches, opening drawers, lifting cushions, flipping back cupboard doors in the gritty kitchen. A row of brass bottles gleams under the dull steel sink, but they're all empty. He tries the fridge. Chocolate biscuits, yogurt, a stalk of celery. In the bedroom her sheets lie stripped in a pile on the floor, a faint blue stain marking the mattress. He wants to pick them up, slide his face into them, smell her. Instead he tries her drawers, and there's the soultrap, nestling in amongst slips and T-shirts.

He plucks it out, satin sliding over his sweat-damp hands. It teeters, whispering black curses, and he slips it carefully into her bag next to Luna. Taking it where he's going is a risk. He could lose it forever with a careless word. But he can't bear to leave it for Dante. He'd rather take his chances.

Back in the living room, he swallows, dread shredding his nerves. He clenches his hand to steady it, picks up his phone, and presses Call.

After three rings, Kane picks up, his voice light and pleasant. "Rajah. How sweet of you."

Rajah closes his eyes, warm tears leaking onto his cheek. "I need your help."

24

I stumbled from the elevator, sweating in the cool air. My hair tangled around the thick collar of the shirt I'd stolen from Dante's place, and my wet fingers clenched on the handle of the green shopping bag that held my makeshift soultrap. My bare feet stuck on the slate, leaving wet footprints, and I skidded turning the corner to his door.

It lay open. Ajar. Lights out.

I stumbled through, catching myself on the doorframe. "Rajah?"

Silence. Morning sun speared in open venetians, striping the carpet with white, flashing on stainless steel. I skipped into the bedroom, breathless. The mess we'd made was still there, the sheets rumpled, the smell of sweat and sex and cardamom, Luna's coat a splash of midnight on the pale floor. I kicked it aside, searching, but my foot slid across empty carpet.

My heart clenched. I stuck my head under the bed, desperate. Nothing.

My bag was gone. Luna's soul was gone.

The soultrap for the girl. Dante's taunt replayed in my mind, malicious. Not only that, Rajah had taken my purse. My phone. So I couldn't find him.

No. No way. He'd just taken the bag for safekeeping. I should wait for him. He'd be back.

But I couldn't wait here. Not here, where the walls screamed of him, the air stinging with his scent and mine. Even the coolness made me think of him, shivering my skin. And in my shopping bag, Dante's bloody soul writhed and spat, contorting the hot glass. I'd jammed the fabric in as tight as I could, but soon the foul thing would shatter the glass and escape. I needed a soultrap. Now.

I ran back into the kitchen and tried the cupboards, one by one. White dishes, tall glasses, a stainless milkshake maker. Nothing made of brass. The pantry, nothing but breakfast cereal and tinned fruit and spice jars by the dozen. I tried under the sink. Dishwashing powder, a spotless toaster. The world's cleanest garbage bin. I even peered into the dishwasher, just in case. No soultraps.

I slammed the door shut, unease rippling my pulse. What kind of incubus doesn't keep soultraps on hand? I scanned the bookshelves, under the TV, behind the sofa.

Fuck.

The bag jerked in my hand, Dante's soul squelching like hot jam. I couldn't wait any longer. I scrabbled through the pile of magazines on the floor for pen and paper, and it was the easiest damn letter I've ever written.

Rajah,

I love you. Don't give up on me. I'll be back in an hour. Wait for me. Please.

Yours forever,

Jade.

I plopped a glass on it on the marble bench so it wouldn't drift away in the air-conditioning, and dashed out.

The sun burned as I waited at the tram stop, my skin sizzling in the after-rain humidity. A taxi would be faster, but I had no cash and no one on the tram cares if you pay or not. I caught the city circle to Swanston Street, and people in business suits or gym clothes stared at me as I curled my feet up under me on the seat and cradled my shopping bag. My nerves twinged, ragged with worry, and I wanted to bare my teeth, tear my hair, scream, *What the fuck are you looking at?* But I was greasy and barefoot, wearing Dante's shirt and pants—far too big for me, and I hadn't found any shoes that didn't fall off my feet—and sporting a ragged red bite mark on my throat. No wonder they were a little curious. If they only knew what was in my bag.

I swapped trams by the shining gray monolith of Federation Square, watching the creeping hands on the clocks at Flinders Street Station for what seemed like an age. By the time I hopped off at Lygon Street, a piercing ache split my skull from dehydration and I felt light-headed and weak, like I hadn't eaten or drunk in days. I'd absorbed some good energy from Dante's death, but Luna had eaten most of it and it wasn't enough to make up for the blood Dante took.

I wanted to run. But I walked carefully toward home, clutching my precious bag, crossing slippery bluestone paving and stepping over rivulets of graying water in the gutters. More than once, my feet conspired to tangle and trip me up, and I reached my door with grazed knees and a bloody elbow where I'd scraped it on the ground to keep my temporary soultrap safe.

The door lay ajar, my key ring still dangling from the lock.

My heart tumbled. At least he'd been here, looking for me. I plunged inside, anxiety and hope plugging my throat like a scratchy clump of sand.

The usual mess, dirty dishes, old magazines, piles of washing I hadn't bothered to put away. Dante's roses, crisping and fragrant on the table, sweetening the fading smell of fairy. Sunlight, slanting through the blinds, gleaming on open cupboard doors, dishes knocked awry, my threadbare couch cushions tumbled on the linoleum.

My bag twitched, murmuring sadistic promises. Blindly I grabbed an empty trap from the open cupboard and yanked the cork free. The blood-soaked shirt squelched out like an overused tampon, and Dante's oozing soul spewed into the trap, filling it to the brim. I jammed the cork in as hard as I could, my muscles weak and unresponsive, and shoved the trap into the fridge to shut him the fuck up. Good riddance. I didn't have time for him now.

In the bedroom, my drawers hung open, clothes jumbled. I pawed through my shirts, sweat sliming my hands, and that beloved spicy scent drifted over me, warming my skin even as my heart thudded screaming into my guts.

The soultrap was gone. Rajah had taken Quinn.

My lungs convulsed, deflated, and I gasped for air, my diaphragm cramping. My only hope of an end to this foulness, and he'd taken it. Even if Luna's shade was enough, without Quinn, I'd never be free.

My bangles chimed smugly, victorious, and my knees buckled. I sank onto my barren bed, the rotten stink of moldy fairy blood crawling into my nose. My mind gibbered at me like a cage-mad rat, scrabbling for another explanation, any explanation that didn't mean I'd lost him. Dante. It could have been

Dante who took Quinn while I was still passed out in his god-damn box.

But I knew it wasn't true. Dante would have drunk Quinn's soul himself, or tipped it out onto the carpet before my eyes so I could watch it wither and die. He wouldn't have passed up the chance to taunt me. Besides, my keys were in the door, and the whole forsaken place smelled of Rajah. He'd broken in while I was captive and had stolen Quinn, just to make sure I'd never win. To make it pointless for me to fight with him over Luna.

So go get it back, sniffed Luna's shade dismissively. *Giving up so soon?*

I ignored him. If Rajah had screamed, *Don't come after me!* into my face, the message couldn't have been clearer.

My eyeballs ached with impossible tears. I wanted to scream, sob, crawl under the bed and rot away to dust. I wanted to curl up and die.

I dragged the stained quilt from the floor and pulled it over my head, burying myself in damp darkness. The flowery smell of Dante crept over me, soaking the quilt, and I wriggled out of his horrid clothes and flung them away. My legs hurt, like I'd run too far uphill, and sickness wormed cold fingers of misery in my guts, but the discomfort was dull and pleasant compared with the savage ache in my heart.

I couldn't die, but I sure as hell didn't have to live. Maybe I'd just stay here, and never get up. I wrapped the quilt in tight, my tears spilling out at last to soak the quilt and smother me.

A creeping tingle spidered over my skin, my bangles vibrating.

I clamped my teeth down on the quilt, groaning. *No. Fuck off. Not now. I'm wallowing in self-pity. Come back in a few hundred years.*

The metal heated, searing my wrists. My skin stung like a

rash, and I gurgled in frustration, kicking my legs in useless rebellion. But it was like a cloud of invisible wasps attacked me, piercing every inch of my skin with their feral stings, and the smell of the burning blisters on my forearms grew worse.

I thudded my fists into the mattress, wailing, but it was no use. Resisting thrall was futile. If I'd learned anything from this mess, I'd learned that.

I dragged myself up from the bed, defeated, and struggled into the first thing that came to hand, an old green sundress. My mirror showed a corpse, pale, black circles under staring eyes, hair limp and straggling, a fading yellow bruise splashing my throat. I didn't care. I forced one foot in front of the other and robot-walked into the kitchen to fetch Dante from the fridge, my skin still writhing with poison. A gift might at least cool Kane's temper. And Dante was no use to me, not anymore.

The black-suited troll already hulked under the stairs outside, gleaming white tusks curling up over his thick lip, and I got in the car without a word, gripping the cold brass bottle on my lap.

25

"Y ou want me to what?"

Kane reclines on his white sofa, calm blue flame twisting around his knuckles, his black eyes like mirrors giving away nothing. Soft downlights gleam on the glass table, the
creamy linen drapes drawn. Kane doesn't like the sun.

Rajah swallows. "Help me find her. Please. I can't . . ." The
words stick in his mouth, sour like rotten meat, and he forces
them out, humiliation and sorrow stabbing hot claws in his chest.
"I can't do it on my own."

A sweet red smile curls Kane's lips, delight crusting his golden
hair with frost like diamonds. "You know what I want."

"Damn it, Kane, there's no time—"

"You know what I want," Kane repeats steadily. His fingernails sharpen and grow an inch, their color mottling.

Rajah's hands twitch in fury. He'd hoped Kane would insist,
order him, take the responsibility away. But Kane is too particular in his pleasures for that. Guilt squeezes Rajah's bruised heart,
cold and bitter, but he's determined not to let it show. As calmly

as he can, he pops Jade's bag open and sets the two soultraps on the coffee table.

Kane's eyes blossom azure, a happy, childlike grin lighting his face. He scoots to the sofa's edge and plucks up the first trap, thumbing the cork aside to sniff the contents. His nose wrinkles in distaste, and behind him a tall black vase of lilies wilts, crisp petals falling to the floor. "Horrid. Is this hers, or yours?"

Rajah doesn't have time to waste on Kane's weirdness. Neither does Jade. Images brand his mind again, of her in Dante's foul embrace, her blood flowing out, and fear compels him more strongly than any thrall bangle. His voice comes tight, barely audible. "Jade's."

Blue static zaps in Kane's hair, his soft chin tightening. The flowers wither and turn black, and he jams the cork back in, hard enough to crumple the brass.

Rajah blinks. He knows that look. Angry, indignant. Jealous.

But before Rajah can figure more, Kane opens the second trap, and sparkling golden flame flickers along his fingers, his expression overwritten by a smile. "This one's been a long time coming. Very sweet of you, Rajah. You shouldn't have. But I'm afraid it's not enough."

He leans back on the couch, flicking imaginary dirt from his nails, and Rajah longs to leap up and throttle him with his bare hands. "Please, you have to help me find Jade before he hurts her. I'll give you anything you ask."

"Anything?" Kane's eyes light with a malicious green twinkle.

Humiliation and hate burn together like oil and acid in Rajah's lungs, but he forces the word out. "Anything."

Another smile twists Kane's lips, this one not so nice. "Done,"

he says lightly, his red tongue flicking his teeth in delicate pleasure. "But you needn't have. She's already here."

Before Rajah can curse or wonder, the entranceway lights
snap on behind him, and the front door clicks open.

I stared, and Rajah stared back.

Vaguely, I formed the idea that Kane was there, that my two
soultraps sat gleaming on the table. I bit my lip, my tongue dry
and useless.

Rajah looked like he was having the same problem, because
he had to swallow twice before he could speak. "I'm sorry."

I didn't know what to say. He was sorry for what? That he'd
stolen my souls and given them to Kane? That I'd made it back
from Dante's alive?

Frustration and helplessness stiffened my limbs, and I walked
forward and clunked Dante's soultrap onto the table next to the
others. Rajah closed his eyes, shaking his head softly, and I had
to look away. He was too beautiful, too sad. Too distant. A dull
ache spread in my chest, intensifying to agony when it pierced
my heart. I'd imagined myself numb. I was wrong.

"Oh, look. The set. How nice." Kane licked frosty lips, delight twinkling in his eyes, and held out his hand to me.

I waited for him to speak, to order me to come to him. But he
didn't. He just stood there, and when I didn't move he stared,
sparks fading from his fingers, a dark line creasing his perfect
brow. "Did you not . . . That is Dante DiLuca in that bottle, yes?"

His words made no sense. My throat hurt, and I could barely
speak. "You knew your answers all along. You killed those fae.
Why?"

He pouted, his gaze slipping like a sulky child's. "Couldn't help it. Not my fault. I just . . . you made me sad, Jade. The air tastes bad when I'm unhappy."

I remembered Nyx, shivering wet in my arms, and hot guilt burned my spine. If I'd stayed with Kane that night, Nyx would still be alive. I didn't want it to be my fault. It wasn't fair to land Kane's jealousy in my lap. But that didn't stop shame from tearing at my heart like I'd killed Nyx myself. "Then why give me to Dante? Why did you send me away?"

Kane's lips quivered. Tears swelled in his eyes, slipping free, and tiny diamonds clicked onto the floor, facets sparkling as they tumbled one by one. "Because I thought . . . if you wanted to, you might come back. To me."

I stared. I'd never seen Kane cry before. My heart stung, sorrow fresh on my tongue. He meant it. He actually imagined a world in which I could love him, regardless of thrall or rapture or the disgusting things he'd ordered me to do.

Strange, deluded demon. His tears cut me, all the more because I couldn't laugh at him or spit in his face. I didn't hate him, any more than I hated an insect who bit me or a bird who crapped on my shoulder. A lot of the time I felt sorry for him, and for years he'd been my only companion. In better moments, I felt fond of him, in a helpless codependent sort of way, and even being his thrall-bound lover had occasional shades of tenderness and affection. But love?

Speechless, I shook my head.

He stared back at me, flames licking his earlobe. Glitter crusted his lashes, and for a moment I thought he'd dissolve in tears, and guilt wrenched my heart.

Then his mouth tightened. His gaze flickered away, and his

fingernails flooded a deep and dangerous indigo. "Rajah, I think you owe me."

Fear stung me like a wasp, and I stumbled forward, compelled. "No, wait—"

Rajah retched, clutching his guts, and fell to his knees. Spasms racked him, curling his body like a peanut. Unbidden, my rapture flickered out, sensing, and I felt his energy start to leach away at Kane's behest.

No. No way. This was my five minutes. He couldn't die now. I hadn't yet worked up the courage to say *I love you*.

Rajah hunched on his side, choking. Honey-colored liquid spilled over his lips, splashing on the floor. His soul, golden and beautiful and perfect, just like he was, smearing wasted on the floorboards in the sparkle of Kane's scattered tears.

Kane watched, his black eyes gleaming with delight, his red lips shining.

"Stop it! Kane, please." I grabbed his shoulder, desperate to spin him around, distract him, anything.

He whirled, furious scarlet flames bursting to life in his hair. He bared jagged teeth, smoke hissing out to choke me with demonic compulsion. "No."

My thrall bangles screeched tight, and I staggered backwards, woolly stickiness clogging my throat. My spine cracked into the glass table's edge, tilting it as I fell. Pain flared, a sharp spear along the bones. My legs sprawled before me, numb, and into my lap rolled a warm brass soultrap.

I'd never stop Kane on my own.

I didn't wait. I didn't think. I just ripped the cork out, brought the crinkled neck to my lips, and chugged.

26

Foul black sickness like mud made me gag, and I fought to swallow on grit and slime. Quinn, already crazy and pissed off, his senses unhinged by what I'd done to him. His soul squelched down my throat, and Luna's shade latched on to it with sharp rodent teeth. Scaly mayhem exploded in my stomach, writhing creatures struggling to the death, and a mad, psychotic light ignited in my skull. Colors glared, the down-lights painfully bright. My nose tingled, icy and burning at the same time, and alien fury clenched my fingers until my palms bled.

Great. I've always wondered what it was like to be Quinn.

Beside me, Rajah's knees cramped to his chest, and he clutched his guts, his throat convulsing as he fought to keep his honey-gold soul down.

My head spinning, I scrabbled on the ground for the next one. The cork shot out into my palm under pressure, bruising. Kane screeched, but it was too late. Brass smashed into my teeth, rattling my skull, and Luna's soul sparkled in my mouth like sweet fruit juice, delicious and sinful. I gulped it down, swooning.

Heat spread in my abdomen, blood rushing to the flesh between my legs. My eardrums rattled, aching, drowned in minute
sounds I'd never heard before, my pulse, the squelch of my wet
fingers on the brass, the slide of moisture deep inside me. My
rapture stretched with a sensuous sigh, joined by the lithe new
sensation of Luna's senses, wild, grasping, euphoric.

Luna's fragment screamed in delight and ripped free of Quinn,
black acid searing my guts. He dived upon himself and melted,
froth bubbling, and an irresistible cackle surged up my throat. I
laughed out loud, mad, ecstatic, overcome with desperate, strange
joy.

Rajah dragged himself to his hands and knees, spitting, tears
leaking onto his cheeks as his stomach heaved. He swallowed,
gagging, trying to keep it in, but hot golden phlegm spattered
from his lips to sizzle on the floorboards.

I scrambled for the third and last trap, but it lay out of my
reach under the table. Kane slashed at me with suddenly razor-
sharp talons, his skin crisping to burnt black scales, his hair
streaming to his waist wrapped in cerulean flames. Yellow eyes
swirled with fury, his lashes caked with ash, and the acrid stink
of hellfire burned my nostrils.

I jerked back. I couldn't get past him. I'd burn. Frustration
seethed, igniting a crackling knot of current that exploded along
my nerves.

Under the table, the soultrap juddered under latent force and
rolled over.

My arm jerked, alive with the glowing sensation of Luna.
My fingers strained to hyperextension. Pain crabbed up my
forearm, and the soultrap tumbled into a roll, skidding across

the floor. Kane dived for it, smoke hissing from his joints, but it careered around his grasping talons and thumped into my hand.

I didn't hesitate. The cork squelched out, clotted and stinking, and I lifted the trap to my lips and tilted. Copper-tainted filth slid over my tongue, choking, burning as it went down. I gagged, scarlet mess spilling down my chin, but I forced my throat open and swallowed more. It hit my stomach, hot and sluggish, smearing my insides, ruining Luna's sweet rhapsody with Dante's sour disgust for everything human.

Rapture slashed through my veins, ravenous, and I screamed. My blood burned with hate, and Luna's hyperaware nerves screeched in my limbs, spasming my muscles until I shook. Desperately, I gulped for air, my lungs crushing. My taste buds sizzled with Dante's vampire perception, stray emotion splashing in the air like fragrant dust. Jealousy, tart like citrus. A splash of cyanide fury on a salty sea of regret, the warm fresh taste of summer rain that could only be sorrow.

Kane growled, spitting broken shards, and my thrall bangles squeezed tight, crushing my forearm bones to agony. I yelled, electricity flaring translucent under my skin, and my sight blurred and blackened for a moment. Kane struck, jaws snapping. But a thick, invisible wall of force solidified between us, and his teeth grated like flint on metallic nothing, sparks jumping.

He howled, his demon fury thwarted. Splinters flew from cracking floorboards, stabbing at my ankles, but I didn't stop to watch. I skidded to my knees and slid sparking fingers into Rajah's wet black hair, lifting his head to see his eyes.

He coughed with his mouth shut, gagging on another

mouthful. Syrupy liquid bubbled from his lips, smearing with the sweat running down his face.

Anguish sliced under my skin, flaying my nerves raw, and despair strangled my heart. I buried my face in Rajah's hair, black strands sticking in my tears. "No, don't. You can't die." I gripped his temples between shaking hands and forced my mouth onto his.

He coughed, his body jerking. I held on, trying to feed him, give him my energy, anything to stop his precious soul slipping away. But his strength leaked free, his muscles juddering, and his lips softened, surrendered, slipped apart. Sweet golden energy filled my mouth, rippling over my skin, sinking in like sunshine. My rapture moaned, greedy, orgasmic, and I ached with longing. Sanguine sweat soaked me, staining my dress, and helplessly I clenched my hands in his hair and kissed him deeper, sliding my tongue on his, drinking.

Effortlessly, his soul slipped into me, and I gasped, spasms of delight sliding along my limbs and into my core. Pleasure sizzled along my tendons, into my muscles, through my bones. I could feel him embracing me, enveloping me in endless warmth. Like we'd been as we loved, delicious, intimate, wonderful.

We weren't a lie. He'd meant every beautiful, breathless word.

My heart melted. I wanted to weep, laugh, scream my delight to the world. Rajah loved me. I'd tasted his soul. I knew it. I could prove it. I'd longed so many years for freedom, to end my desolate, empty life. Now, I wasn't empty anymore.

But his exquisite lips curled on mine in a last, sweet smile, and his whisper warmed my mouth like flame. "Love you, princess. Always." And then he sighed, soft like release, and his head grew heavy in my hands. His mouth slipped from mine, slack, and the golden flecks in his eyes faded to empty gray.

Dread slashed like poisoned knives in my guts, where already his heavenly soul essence frothed and fought with the others. My skin chilled. That wasn't what I meant to do.

I tried to talk, to say his name, but no sound emerged, and my treacherous nerves stung alive with blissful energy. My thrall bangles quivered and loosened, the metal humming, and as I watched, a tiny crack opened in the rolled edge, a rift widening in flawless gold.

Kane laughed, hollow like hellish drums, and ash fell from the air like dirty snow.

At the corner of my eye, golden radiance glimmered.

My gaze magnetized, drawn helplessly back to Rajah, and my heart somersaulted. Faint golden light shimmered over him, glowing on his brown skin, flickering weakly through his dark hair, caressing his perfect face.

My aura. Fading. Dying.

Breath rushed from my lungs, forgotten. I'd never figured out what *animus* meant. Soul. What kind of fucked-up clue was that? I'd thought it obscure, useless, infuriating. But it didn't just mean anyone's soul. It meant mine.

And there he lay.

I'd given him my heart, and now it was too late to change anything. This ritual was a malicious hellwrought trick, a game I couldn't win. I'd swallowed him, my fourth and final soul. My bangles were breaking. And Rajah would die.

I choked, and cinders stung bitter on my tongue, ruining the sweetness. Horror dripped icy filth over my ecstasy, a vicious ache chewing at my heart. No. This wasn't right.

My hard-won freedom loomed cold and worthless without him. I'd rather live my interminable years in thrall all over again than watch him die. If this was that final five minutes, I didn't want it.

I wanted forever.

At my wrist the crack widened, screeching, and with a horrid snap the other bangle cracked, too, the curled edge popping as gold ripped asunder.

No.

I dragged Rajah's forehead to mine, and the cool pallor of his skin sparked a shiver of fear in my core. I kissed his temple, his cheek, his idle lips. "Don't leave. Please. I can't bear this without you. Come back to me."

No breath tingled my tongue, no life stirred. My spit warmed his lips, and my guts bubbled, four disparate souls mingling. Despair clutched my chest. Mingling was no good. Soon his essence would die and it'd be too late. I needed the rest of them gone. I needed Rajah back, alone, alive before my rapture consumed his soul for good.

Before my bangles split off because I'd lost him forever.

Haste scrabbled along my spine like a frightened rat, and I forced myself to close my eyes and listen to my rapture, which sighed in my womb like a sated lioness. I summoned every scrap of experience I'd earned in 140 years of thrall, and dived my new quadruple senses deep into my own soul.

I summoned Quinn, black hatred searing my blood. He squirmed, spitting foul curses, but I pressed my will harder, and he snarled one final insult and let go, swirling with a scream into the depths of hell.

Kane screeched in a hail of hellish sparks. My bangles howled, and the cracks split further.

I stroked a seductive caress of promise over Luna. He snapped at me with sharp, mischievous teeth and grinned. *Told you so.*

I gave him one last, lingering kiss—he'd earned back that much—and tore him free. He struggled for a moment, spitting, and then he flicked loose with a careless shrug and dived head-first into the chasm with a crazy fuck-'em-all yell.

Dante hissed, fangs tearing my insides. I scrabbled, but he slid away, slime dragging through my clutches. I stung my rapture to shrieking fury, engulfing him, but still he resisted. And then a scaly purple tentacle writhed up from the deep and wrapped around him like a vile python, yanking him free. Dante screamed, but Luna pulled harder, constricting, and sharp fangs finally ripped away, leaving me sore and bleeding as they tumbled to hell together.

Now only Rajah's soul remained. My hot breath stung my lips, my mind swirling like leaves in a tornado. I dragged Rajah closer, plastering my lips on his, willing him to wake. His honey-thick soul writhed inside me, my rapture snapping at it with hungry teeth. I breathed in, tasting his fading scent, filling my lungs with him, tempting his soul back from the brink.

He didn't stir. Urgency chewed my nerves raw, and cold desperation flooded my veins. I tried to reach out my senses, dull and colorless now without Luna. I didn't know if Rajah could hear me, if anything was left. I pressed my lips on his, my fingers aching in his hair, frantic for a sign of life. *Come back to me, my prince. Don't give up. I love you.*

Sweet soul essence erupted onto my tongue, spilling over my lips and back into his mouth. His spine jerked, shaking his limp limbs and cracking his teeth against mine. A sugary ache tormented my throat, and my rapture screeched in fury, ravenous claws slashing for its lost prey, but I didn't care. I tightened my stomach, closing my gullet so the energy couldn't slip back down.

Rajah choked, liquid sloshing between us, and burning relief clawed at my heart, so desperate, it hurt. I held on, my eyes squeezed shut, and at last he gulped, sucking it down. My mouth emptied, but I didn't let go. I never wanted to let go.

He gasped, dragging air into his lungs, his face pale and slick with sweat and honeyed stains. My half-broken bangles sizzled with malice and clamped tight around my wrists, and with a blinding scarlet flash, the metal reformed.

Smoke hissed from my stinging wrists, and my nose seared in the hellish stink of ash and flesh. My rapture wailed and thrashed, bereft. I burned to lick the golden remnants off Rajah's skin, swallow, steal him again, not only to sate my rapture but also to savor his rich soul energy and crack those hell-cursed bangles off forever.

But I wanted him alive more. So much, much more.

I wiped a shaking finger across his cheek, saving the spill, and touched it to his lips. My fingertip tingled. "Welcome back."

He forced his eyes open, wet dark lashes fluttering as he squinted, and stood shakily.

I stared at the ash-strewn floor, my nerves shredded. I'd felt his precious soul caressing mine, knew his love wasn't a lie. He'd offered up his life for me. But doubt still chilled my blood. I'd cursed us both so we could be together. He'd found death. I'd found freedom. We could both have escaped. Now neither of us ever would.

Could he ever forgive me?

Rajah slid careful hands around my ribs and lifted me to my feet. Hardly daring, I looked up.

He licked his acid-burned lip, tears shimmering in warm golden eyes splintered with grief. "Why, Jade? You could have had everything you ever wanted."

Raw emotion flooded my heart, so new and precious, my throat swelled. No care for himself. Only for me. My eyes burned, but I didn't let my gaze drop, and my voice came out stronger than I'd expected. "You're everything I want."

He swallowed, and drew me closer, his hands warm and reverent on my shoulders. "But—"

"I love you, Rajahni Seth." I silenced him with my fingertip on his swollen lips. I'd already told him, when I held his soul inside me. But the words still spread warm shivers over me, sparking my skin alive under his touch.

He closed his eyes, and brushed his cheek on mine with a soft incredulous sigh. "Thank you, Jade. I won't ever make you regret it."

The warm cardamom scent of his hair intoxicated me. I flushed all over, glorious, and tilted my face up for his kiss. His lips caressed mine, tender, sparkling my mouth with a trace of his honey-sweet soul. My aching limbs weakened in the delicious warmth of his embrace, and for once my thousand long years beckoned shiny and bright, like the twinkling delight in my heart.

Air crackled, shifting, and I dragged myself away. Kane stared at us, white flame flickering in his soft golden hair, his smooth white face flawless once more. His lip trembled, as if he wanted to say something, and then he sat himself elegantly on the couch, plucked up the remote, and flicked on the TV.

I stared at my shining thrall bangles, clean, polished, not a hint of dent or damage. Fresh tears stung my eyes, but hope warmed my blood like sunshine. Together, Rajah and I would make this bitter thrall worth enduring. He gave me strength. I hoped I did the same for him.

Rajah slipped his hand into mine and squeezed. His bangle clinked against mine, and I looked up at him, his beautiful face a blur. My heart shone with love. His lips brushed my hair, gentle as a raindrop, and together we walked out.

Alone in the dark, Kane stares at the television, colored images flickering meaninglessly before his eyes. The leather sofa feels cold under his limbs. Beside him, tiny flames hiss over the splintered wooden floor, curls of black lacquer-sharp smoke drifting. Splashes of Rajah's essence still shine wet on the floor, tiny diamonds scattering like stars.

Kane flips a dozen channels, two dozen, through soap operas, cricket, garish advertisements. Now his favorite cartoon is on, the one with the purple ostrich and the coyote, and he manages a faint smile. The coyote never catches the beeping bird, but he never gives up, either.

The crack of sunlight beneath the curtains reddens, shifts, fades. The cartoons give way to news bulletins, sports wraps, cop shows, more news. Still Kane sits, squeezing a cushion in his lap, his nails pale and still. He doesn't want to go out. He doesn't want to be alone. But he can't think of anything else to do.

He wonders where she is, what she's doing. He lets his gaze lose focus, and his senses burst like an invisible shock wave, climbing, spreading, searching for those elusive cosmic eddies that mean something curious is afoot.

His invisible shade swoops batlike over the city, riding the wind above the wild scatter of lights, cars zooming below along glowing ribbons. He inhales, and distant thunder rumbles, bringing the iron smell of rain. Dive closer, a rush of summer air, golden trails like shooting stars. The warm cloud of his breath on a window, peering inside an Albert Park mansion, where an ancient mother screams ragged over the pale bloodless body of her vampire son, and in the corner a vile-smelling snakeshifter bursts glossy black fins from his skin and plots chilly revenge.

Swish, flap, focus. A vine-draped restaurant across the river, where a grinning fae-born murderer with crazy-bright lizard eyes clinks glasses in celebration with his vampire master.

Dive, along a black stone street to a tiny heat-drenched flat, dark and empty in the smell of dying roses. She's not there. Skid over bluestone cobbles and concrete tram lines to a row of bright steel apartments, where beyond shining glass his beautiful Jade sighs words of love with shimmering wet lips, her fragrant body breathless in her lover's strong embrace.

In front of his television, Kane crunches icy lashes tight, and his shade snaps cruel teeth and swoops away.

Across the river, gaslights flaring, the crawling anthill twinkle of the casino, a glittering revue where a skinny blond ex-waitress named Claire dances the show of her life. Upward on a warm jasmine-scented draft, where the wind blows fresher and moonlight slants in the broad glass window on the eighty-seventh floor of Eureka Tower. Right-angled shadows carve the pale carpet in Luna's bedroom, falling on the unmade bed, the striped blue crime scene tape, a lone sleepy boy in blue police uniform and latex gloves who seals an ancient brass oil lamp into a cellophane bag. Spectral female laughter echoes, and the policeman glances this way and that in the empty room.

Down in free fall, wind whipping, the street rushing upward, the bright blue spike atop the state theater stabbing like a blade. Vintage orange streetlamps bathe the wide tarmac lanes of Princes Bridge, where a bright silver tram clatters by and two slender white figures tumble from nowhere onto the pavement in a dense shaft of light.

Kane cocks his head, curiosity and foreboding twinging his spine.

The pale twins climb to their feet in unison, street dirt smearing their white suits. Identical white haircuts, bleached skin, sharp faces that seek each other and smile. Hand in hand, the intruders turn away from the rippling blue spire and stroll in step toward the city.

Back in Toorak, Kane's hair singes, smoke twisting to the ceiling. He ghosts his shade closer, stealthy, sniffing for honey and flowers, the telltale stink of a centuries-fled enemy.

The twins halt in midstride, and inhale.

Kane darts upward, and jerks back into his cool lounge to a black-and-white movie on television and the church-organ ripple of his telephone.

He swipes up the handset and devours the number, greedy.

It isn't Jade. Bitter charcoal stings his tongue, the taste of loss. The burning floor smokes one last time, and hisses out. He picks up slowly, his damp thumb smearing the button. "Yes."

"I have the item we discussed." Cold voice, grating and metallic with a glint of dark fae attitude. His fairy thief.

Weariness aches Kane's bones, but a tiny flood of warmth tints his nails green. Jade might still call. In the meantime, a shiny stolen bauble might make him feel better.

"The club, one hour." He hangs up and slips the phone into his pocket. Quietly, he presses Off on the remote control, and the television blinks to black. He puts the remote aside, scrapes a wet crust of diamonds from his lashes, and walks out.

Epilogue

I climb off the bed, licking slick fluid from my lips, and straighten my damp dress. The corpse sprawls naked, limbs contorted, damp with sweat and my saliva. My rapture sizzles like a frypan, sated, the soul energy already consumed, but my thighs ache, my sex still twitching. I sigh. After 140 years, I still haven't learned rule number one.

I tidy my hair and fix my smeared lipstick in the hotel room mirror before I slip my shoes back on and ease the door open.

It flies toward me, knocking me back, and Rajah pins me against the wall, his thigh pressing between mine.

My heart swells with love. He always waits for me. He's never jealous. It just makes him want me more.

His beautiful lips form a smile, inches away from a kiss. "You cheating on me again?"

God, after all this time, I still can't stop staring at his mouth. I slip my arms around him, sliding my hands over his ass. His body fits against mine like it was made to be there. Hell, maybe it was. "You bet."

"Was he good?" He teases loose hair from my neck, shivering my skin with need.

I grin, and pull him closer, harder against me. "He was okay. Had a few tricks."

"Yeah?" He's already lifting my skirt, spreading my legs, sliding hot fingers into my wet flesh. Sometimes I'm not in the mood after I've swallowed a soul. But he never has to ask me. He just knows.

I sigh, blissful, and shift to accept him. Truly, I'm the luckiest woman in the world. "Yeah. Wanna see?"

He drops to his knees, his laugh soft and warm on my thigh. "Later."

READ ON FOR A PREVIEW OF
ERICA HAYES'S UPCOMING NOVEL

SHADOWGLASS

Available from St. Martin's Griffin in April 2010
Copyright © 2009 by Erica Hayes

S tolen diamond bracelets glittered on my wrists in the colored nightclub lights, and I laughed, my wings swelling damp in the warm crush of bodies. Midnight at Unseelie Court, dark and fragrant with smoke and sweat, music ripping my ears like sweet razors, so loud the air thudded in my lungs and my hair shook to the beat. Strobe lights sliced me, snapshots in time as I danced, here, there, gone.

Blaze wrapped his long white arm around my waist, spilling flames on my shoulders from soft crimson hair. I grinned and wriggled closer, his hot firefae flesh a sweet glory on my skin. Dancing, drinking, diamonds I don't own. Doesn't get sweeter than this.

The floor's packed tonight, a mash of bright fairy wings and rainbow limbs and slick vampire smiles, the air steamy with breath and lust and chemical euphoria. Humans here, too, a few sly ones who can see, but mostly glassy-eyed and drunk on poison glamour, here for the oblivion. A sweet bubble of unreality this club, no thought, no consequences. Kiss, embrace, dance, love, drown your cares in glorious sensory nectar. A fairy kind of place, no rules, no guilt, the air so glassy with glamour it might shatter.

Even the name is a fairy joke: Unseelie Court. We fae have no court, no queen or princes or justice. We leave that to demons, gangsters, people who matter.

The smell alone warmed my insides. I'm waterfae, which makes me attuned to moisture, and the wet scent of all that pleasure pressed a sweet ache deep inside me. I shimmied on the crowded dance floor, my silky skirt sticking to my thighs, and lifted my arms in the sweet white smoke. My new diamonds sparkled over my wrists, painted blue and green and scarlet by glassy lights. We'd filched them tonight from a shiny apartment in South Yarra, along with a pile of cash and other trinkets.

My skin glowed blue with desire. Shiny things get me all warm and wriggly. I won't get to keep them. We owe the Valenti gang too much protection money. But just for tonight, they're mine. And what harm ever came from something shiny?

Behind me, Blaze rubbed his cheek against my wing, sparks showering from his pretty red hair. Ooh, tingles, all down my side like sugar. I wriggled my shoulders, fluttering golden dust that danced in manic spotlights and rippled in the glassy static of glamour. Blaze is my best friend, a dazzling firefae boy with cute muscles and a naughty sharp-toothed smile, and his glamour is good. I mean, it's really good. Humans won't see the fine crimson wings like a dragonfly's, the cheeky flame dripping from his fingers, his narrow fae-muscled body. They just see a cute redhead with naughty black eyes.

Me? Well, I do my best, but glamour isn't my forte. My nose looks a bit less pointy, my hair more blond than orange, my garish yellow skin fades to human tones. That's about it. Glamour or not, I'm still the same geeky old me.

Blaze slid his arm over my shoulder to offer his fingertip, wet and adorned with a shimmering purple pill.

Naughty boy. I giggled, licked off the pill and swallowed. It had a bitter sting, but his finger tasted of sherbet, sparkly and sweet.

He rubbed his sharp nose in my hair, and I laughed, my blood hot and urgent, my head awhirl with fizzy-sweet vodka and the thrill of our night's work. Forget the Valentis. Forget the world. Just me and my diamonds; jumping, twirling, dancing until I dropped. Yes.

Next to me, a blue-haired vampire kid in leather and his girl were kissing, bloody spit trickling on her chin as she swayed to the music, his fingers sliding beneath her skirt. A pair of shirtless trolls scoped for girls, sweat glistening on bulging green muscles and bell-pierced nipples. One winked at me, flicking ragged black hair from shiny eyes, and I pretended not to see him.

"Spice for Ice," Blaze yelled, sparks showering. He's allowed to make fun of my unfortunate name. He sizzled my pointed ear with his tongue. Shivers. Mmm. More tongue, slower and wetter than strictly necessary. Bet he's got a hard-on.

I arched my butt backwards and giggled again. Oh, yeah. He's wearing suction-tight leather pants—how he gets those on, I'll never know—and they don't leave much to the imagination.

I grinned, chemical warmth already glowing in my guts. Blaze feels as good as he looks, and when he's sparkled to the eyeballs and high from housebreaking and too much broken glass, he always tries something. But we're just friends. We've got rules, and they don't include dragging each other out back for a hot dirty shag.

Blaze is my lucky charm. Other guys will laugh at me or hit me or play tricks on me just to watch me cry. Fairy girls get that. It's a harsh fae-taunting world out there. Every week you hear about a new fairyslasher, a sadist, a murderer on the loose. Fairies aren't people, see. We're whispers, shadows, irrelevancies sheathed in desperate glamour so we won't stand out or offend anyone or make anyone feel uneasy. We're just flotsam, bobbing on the surface of real people's lives. We just hang out and party. It's what we're here for. No one cares if we die or hurt or bleed.

But I know I'm safe with Blaze, even if he is a horny little rat.

That hunky troll bumped my hip, his beady black gaze slithering down over my ass, and Blaze snarled wet sparks at him and spun me away.

I giggled, and wriggled to face him, static shifting. He tossed blood-red hair and threw me that dazzling Blaze grin. He cuts his hair short in the back and scrunches it wildly too long at the front, so he can shake it back like that and skewer you with his dirty come-taste-me stare.

But I know he doesn't mean it, not with me. He's just having fun. I tickled his pointy red teeth with my claw. "Go rub that thing on someone else, ya dirty whore."

He slid bony fingers over my hip, keeping me just an inch or two away. His scent zinged my nose, fresh like a newly-struck match. Rakish golden rings glinted in his pointy ears, and his studded, black velvet jacket was cropped at his smooth hip, with nothing underneath. Sweat caressed his narrow muscles in all the right places. He flicked his smoldering gaze to the bar for a second, ruby sparks jumping from his lips. "I can taste green. Azure's watching us. Wanna tease her a bit?"

Azure's our other best friend; as pretty and awesome as Blaze. I looked. She was, indeed, watching him, with that shiny glaze over her eyes that meant trouble. "You're cruel," I said.

"You're scared," he shot back. He edged closer, sweat-slick skin sliding on my bare midriff. My breasts pressed against his chest, burning.

Already the purple pill flowered deep and hot inside me. It can't be desire. I'm far too sensible to want Blaze. Indignation lifted my eyebrows. "Am not. I'm sensible."

"To hell with sensible. Let's be reckless. I'm good at reckless." He wetted his plum-red lips, and the smell of that moisture tripped warm, dizzy waves in my skull. Hot fae boy. Lips. Diamonds.

I couldn't keep the giggles in any longer, and I shoved him in the chest, tipping him backward. "What you are is a naughty boy with a hard-on. Get a girlfriend." And I turned and pushed my way through the fragrant crowd, laughter floating from me like starlight on the swelling currents of my high.

Colors tumbled and prismed. My diamonds dazzled me, and I stumbled over my own ankles a few times as I approached the blue neon bar. Azure pointed at me and giggled, pearlescent wings jittering as she swayed on her stool. She wore a jagged-hemmed white dress that left her back bare, and she'd piled her green hair above her head in a wild nest of knots and stolen pearls, a pair of broken chopsticks, and a cocktail fork sticking out.

My purple-drugged heart swelled with love and awe. Azure's the pretty one. Her glamour shows some weirdly beautiful supermodel, tall and willowy, with wide-spaced almond eyes. Her real appearance is the same, only with shimmering oval wings, and her skin is a dozen perfect shades of pale airfae blue.

Whereas my hair looks kinda like mango peel, half green and half moldy orange, and my wings are burnt yellow, ragged and droopy, like a sick butterfly's.

Some girls have all the luck.

Azure poked my chin with a sharp claw. "You're drunk, diamond girl."

"Not true. I'm high. You're the one who's drunk." I jumped up and down, unsteady on my heels, until the bar boy noticed me and served me two pink vodka lemonades without my asking. Maybe I was drunker than I thought. Still plenty of stolen cash left, though. I tossed him a crumpled twenty, waving my diamonded wrist grandly. "Keep it, peaches. Stop looking at him like that."

Azure said nothing, and I lurched onto a stool and tickled her slender ribs. "I said, stop staring at him."

"Who?" She tossed her pretty blue head, her wings aflutter, and concentrated too hard on stirring her drink.

"Oh, I dunno, the woolly mammoth in the corner? Who d'ya think?"

She thumped her chin into her hand and her elbow onto the bar, sea-green moisture staining her eyes. "But he's so pretty."

Guilt twinged my happy guts, and I patted her shoulder clumsily. "Yeah, I know. But it's an orchid farm in here, okay? Look around. There's other pretty ones."

"Not like him." She hiccupped and burst into proper tears, her wings flooding verdant.

I sighed. Last month she had the hots for some sweet blond vampire babe. This week it was Blaze. She'd get over it. But my heart still ached for her. Just because she falls quick doesn't mean she doesn't fall hard. And Blaze is the Court's biggest boy-whore. He'll only break her heart.

I slipped my arm around her bony shoulder and pointed to the dance floor, where Blaze was trickling orange flame down some laughing banshee's spine, singeing the ends of her long silver hair. "Look at him. See that girl he's dancing with? In the shiny silver dress? Oh, now he's tongue-kissing her, he's putting his hand up her . . . yeah. You really want that to be you?"

Az just looked at me.

I flushed, vodka-tainted water heating my muscles. Maybe I wasn't quite making my point. "Okay, let's not look at that anymore." Firmly, I spun her back around to the bar.

She glared, wet-eyed. "You're a real big help, Ice."

I gulped my vodka, pink fizz shooting fireworks up my nose. "So he's boy candy, everyone knows that. You also know what a bitch he can be. Whaddaya want me to say?"

"Promise you'll never go with him."

I flushed again, and this time the water burned my cheeks. "What?"

"Butterflies in the sun. I've seen him flirt with you. Promise me you'll never."

"Never flirt with him?" Discomfort twisted, ruining my high. Why dissemble? We were best friends. That's all. Even if I'd wanted to, I didn't have the courage to pursue it further. Believe it or not, I'm not too smooth with the boys, and courage is *not* my middle name.

Azure swatted my shoulder. "You know what I mean."

"Hide-and-seek, catch-me-if-you-can. It's just games—"

"Promise, Ice. I couldn't bear it."

She stared, so earnest and brimful with tears that I couldn't take it. "Okay, I promise. Call me a pincushion and shove safety pins up my nose if I'm wrong. It's the rules anyway, right?"

"Yeah, I guess." Azure gave a sad half-smile.

I hugged her, my hand slipping beneath her delicate wings. "You'll get over him, Az."

She hugged me back, and I felt better. I had nothing to hide. She sniffed, wiping snot on my shoulder. "I wish I was like you, Ice. You're the sensible one."

I thought of Blaze's tongue in my ear and giggled. "Yeah, that's me. Sense, dense, intense. Dripping out my ears, it is. Of course, you wanna be me. Why wouldn't you? You're only the prettiest, cleverest girl in the whole world."

She kissed me, a sweet taste of sky-blue lips, and gamely wiped her tears away in green streaks. "You're nice. Let's get drunk and find some boys."

Meaning, I'd get smashed, she'd get prettily tipsy, she'd find more boys than she had hands for, and I'd get the leftovers who were too plain to interest her and too shitfaced to care that she was a hundred times more beautiful than me. But what are best friends for?

"Yes, yes, yes." I paid for two more drinks and we clinked glasses. Sugar and alcohol burst into my brain like flares, and my nose fizzed.

Azure gasped. "Raspberries and ice cream. More."

"Careful, there's a fairyslasher on the loose."

She snorted. "S'always a fairyslasher. More."

I ordered more, and we chugged again. This time the froth did come out of my nose, laced with plummy drug-charmed mirth. I laughed, splurting pink bubbles onto the guy next to me. "Whoa. Sorry, dude." I yanked up my skirt hem to wipe his arm clean, but the frills were too short. My heels skidded out from under me and I landed in his lap in a giggling, spluttering heap.

Oops. I craned my neck up to apologize, and my laughter strangled.

Not again.

Dark blue skin, dusted with copper, so smooth and perfect it's unreal. Black hair so crisp it curled jagged. Eyes the velvety gray of softened steel. Long narrow wings like silver-shot glass.

My senses tumbled, intoxicated with hot metal scent. Warm midnight-blue hands steadied me, and my belly melted inside me like chocolate fudge sauce on ice cream, running everywhere. I inhaled molten iron and hot fairy skin. . . .

Fluid scorched into my wing veins, swelling them tight. I held my breath. Calm, Ice. He's touching you. You've practically got your face in his lap. Say something really cool and seductive.

"Oh. Um. Hi, Indigo. It's me."

Yeah. That *so* wasn't it.

Effortlessly, Indigo lifted me to my feet. Rusty wing-glitter shimmered warm on my shoulders. His coppery claws grazed my wrist, and tiny electric shocks crackled up my arms, sparking my diamonds blue.

I stared, my fingerpads itching. He wore black, as usual, jeans and a sleeveless shirt that showed off lean blue arms.

I wanted to rub my cheek against them, tickle my tongue along his biceps. Metalfae are usually twisted hunchbacked little monsters with razor-sharp metal teeth and an attitude. Indigo, well, he's tall and sculpted and moves lightly, like a cat burglar, but he's still got razor-sharp metal teeth and an attitude. Licking is strictly off limits, especially for a no-account geek girl like me.

He surveyed me, steely eyes cool. "Nice diamonds."